The Dead Travel Fast

DEANNA RAYBOURN

The Dead Travel Fast

MIRA®

MIRA®

Recycling programs for this product may not exist in your area.

ISBN-13: 978-0-7783-2765-3

THE DEAD TRAVEL FAST

For questions and comments about the quality of this book please contact us at Customer_eCare@Harlequin.ca.

www.MIRABooks.com

Printed in U.S.A.

First Printing: March 2010
10 9 8 7 6 5 4 3 2 1

For my husband. For everything. For always.

I

As he spoke, he smiled, and the lamplight fell
on a hard-looking mouth, with very red lips
and sharp-looking teeth, as white as ivory. One
of my companions whispered to the other...
"Denn die Todten reiten schnell." ("For the dead
travel fast.")

—Bram Stoker, *Dracula*

It is with true love as it is with ghosts, which
everyone talks about and few have seen.

—François de la Rochefoucauld

II

All proper stories begin with the words *Once upon a time....* But this is not a proper story— it is mine. You will not believe it. You will say such things are not possible. But you believed once, long ago. You believed in witches and goblins and things that walked abroad in the dark of the night. And you believed in happily ever after and that love can mend all. For children believe in impossible things. So read my tale with a child's eyes and believe once more in the impossible....

1

Edinburgh, 1858

"I am afraid we must settle the problem of what to do with Theodora," my brother-in-law said with a weary sigh. He looked past me to where my sister sat stitching placidly on a tiny gown. It had been worn four times already and wanted a bit of freshening.

Anna glanced up from her work to give me a fond look. "I rather think Theodora ought to have a say in that, William."

To his credit, he coloured slightly. "Of course she must." He sketched a tiny bow in my direction. "She is a woman grown, after all. But now that Professor Lestrange has been properly laid to rest, there is no one here to care for her. Something must be decided."

At the mention of my grandfather, I turned back to the bookshelf whose contents I had been sorting. His library had been an extensive one, and, to my anguish, his debts demanded it be sold along with anything else of value in the house. Indeed, the house itself would have to be sold, although William had hopes that the pretty little property in Picardy Place would fetch enough to settle the debts and leave me a tiny sum for my keep. I wiped the books carefully with a cloth sprinkled with neat's-foot oil and placed them aside, bidding farewell to old friends.

Just then the housekeeper, Mrs. Muldoon, bustled in. "The post, Miss Lestrange."

I sorted through the letters swiftly, passing the business correspondence to William. I kept only three for myself, two formal notes of condolence and the last, an odd, old-fashioned-looking letter written on thick, heavy paper and embellished with such exotic stamps and weighty wax seals that I knew at once who must have sent it. I hesitated to open it, savouring the pleasure of anticipation.

William showed no such restraint. He dashed a paper knife through the others, casting a quick eye over the contents.

"More debts," he said with a sigh. He reached for the ledger, entering the numbers with a careful hand. It was good of him to settle my grandfather's affairs so diligently, but at the moment I wanted nothing more than to be rid of him with his ledgers and his close questions about how best to dispose of a spinster sister-in-law of twenty-three.

Catching my mood, Anna smiled at her husband. "I find I am a little unwell. Perhaps some of Mrs. Muldoon's excellent ginger tea might help."

To his credit, William sprang up, all thoughts of me forgotten. "Of course." Naturally, neither of them alluded to the happy source of her sickness, and I wondered wickedly how happy the news had been. A fifth little mouth to feed on his modest living in a small parish. Anna for her part looked tired, her mouth drawn.

"Thank you," I told her when he had gone. I thrust my duster into my pocket and took up the paper knife. It seemed an act of sacrilege to destroy the seal, but I was wildly curious as to the contents.

Anna continued to stitch. "You must not be too impatient with William," she advised me as I began to read. "He does care for you, and he means well. He only wants to see you properly settled."

I mumbled a reply as I skimmed the letter, phrases catching my eye. *My dearest friend, how I have missed you…at last he is coming to take up his inheritance…so much to be decided…*

Anna chattered on for a few moments, trying to convince me of her husband's better qualities, I think. I scarce listened. Instead I began to read the letter a second time, more slowly, turning each word of the hasty scrawl over in my head.

"Deliverance," I breathed, sinking onto a hassock as my eyes lingered upon the last sentence. *You must come to me.*

"Theodora, what is it? Your colour has risen. Is it distressing news?"

After a moment, I found my voice. "Quite the opposite. Do you remember my school friend, Cosmina?"

Anna furrowed her brow. "Was she the girl who stayed behind during holidays with you?"

I had forgot that. After Anna had met and promptly married William at sixteen, I had been bereft. She had left us for his living in Derbyshire, and our little household never entirely recovered from the loss. She was but two years my senior, and we had been orphaned together in childhood. We had been each other's bulwark against the loneliness of growing up in an elderly scholar's household, and I had felt the loss of her keenly.

I had pined so deeply in fact, that my grandfather had feared for my health. Thinking it a cure, he sent me to a school for young ladies in Bavaria, and there I had met Cosmina. Like me, she did not make friends easily, and so we had clung to each other, both of us strangers in that land. We were serious, or so we thought ourselves, scorning the silliness of the other girls who talked only of beaux and debut balls. We had formed a fast friendship, forged stronger by the holidays spent at school when the other pupils who had fewer miles to travel had been collected by their families. Only a few of the mistresses remained to keep charge of us and a lively atmosphere always prevailed. We were taken on picnics and permitted to sit with them in the teachers' sitting room. We feasted on pastries and fat, crisp sausages, and were allowed to put aside our inter-minable needlework for once. No, we had not minded our exile, and many an evening we whiled away the hours telling tales of our homelands, for the mistresses had travelled little and were curious. They teased me fondly about hairy-kneed High-landers and oat porridge while Cosmina made them shiver with stories of the vampires and werewolves that stalked her native Transylvania.

I collected myself from my reverie. "Yes, she was. She always spoke so bewitchingly of her home. She lives in a castle in the Carpathians, you know. She is kin to a noble family there." I brandished the letter. "She is to be married, and she begs me to come and stay through Christmas."

"Christmas! That is months away. What will you do with yourself for so long in…goodness, I do not even know what country it is!"

I shrugged. "It is its own country, a principality or some such. Part of the Austrian Empire, if I remember rightly."

"But what will you do?" Anna persisted.

I folded the letter carefully and slipped it into my pocket. I could feel it through my petticoats and crinoline, a talisman against the worries that had assailed me since my grandfather had fallen ill.

"I shall write," I said stoutly.

Anna primmed her lips and returned to her needlework.

I went and knelt before her, taking her hands in mine, heedless of the prick of the needle. "I know you do not approve, but I have had some success. It wants only a proper novel for me to be established in a career where I can make my own way. I need be dependent upon no one."

She shook her head. "My darling girl, you must know this is not necessary. You will always have a home with us."

I opened my mouth to retort, then bit the words off sharply. I might have wounded her with them. How could I express to her the horror such a prospect raised within me? The thought of living in her small house with four—now five!—children underfoot, too little money to speak to the expenses, and always William, kindly but disapproving. He had already made his feelings towards women writers quite clear. They were unyielding as stone; he would permit no flexibility upon the point. Writing aroused the passions and was not a suitable occupation for a lady. He would not even allow my sister to read any novel he had not vetted first, reading it carefully and marking out offending passages. The Brontës were forbidden entirely on the grounds that they were "unfettered." Was this to be my future then? Quiet domesticity with a man who would deny me the intellectual freedoms I had nurtured for so long in favour of sewing sheets and wiping moist noses?

No, it was not to be borne. There was no possibility of earning my own keep if I lived with them, and the little money I should have from my grandfather's estate would not sustain me long. I needed only a bit of time and some quiet place to write a full-length novel and build upon the modest success I had already enjoyed as a writer of suspenseful stories.

I drew in a calming breath. "I am grateful to you and to William for your generous offer," I began, "but it cannot be. We are different creatures, Anna, as different as chalk and cheese, and what suits you should stifle me just as my dreams would shock and frighten you."

To my surprise, she merely smiled. "I am not so easily shocked as all that. I know you better than you credit me. I know you long to have adventures, to explore, to meet interesting people and tell thrilling tales. You were always so, even from an infant. I remember you well, walking up to people and thrusting out your hand by way of introduction. You never knew a stranger, and you spent all your time quizzing everyone. Why did Mama give away her cherry frock after wearing it only twice? Why could we not have a monkey to call for tea?" She shook her head, her expression one of sweet indulgence. "You only stopped chattering when you were asleep. It was quite exhausting."

"I do not remember, but I am glad you told me." It had been a long time since Anna and I had shared sisterly confidences. I had seen her so seldom since her marriage. But sometimes, very occasionally, it felt like old times again and I could forget William and the children and the little vicarage that all had better claims upon my sister.

"You would not remember. You were very small. But then you changed after Papa died, became so quiet and close. You lost the trick of making friends. But I still recall the child you were, your clever antics. Papa used to laugh and say he ought to have called you Theodore, for you were fearless as any boy."

"Did he? I scarce remember him anymore. Or Mama. It's been just us for so long."

"And Grandfather," she said with a smile of gentle affection. "Tell me about the funeral. I was very sorry to have been left behind."

William had not thought it fit for a lady in her interesting condition to appear at the funeral, although her stays had not even been loosened. But as ever, she was obedient to his wishes, and I had gone as the last remaining Lestrange to bid farewell to the kindly old gentleman who had taken us in, two tiny children left friendless in a cold world.

Keeping my hands entwined with hers, I told her about the funeral, recounting the eulogium and the remarks of the clergyman on Grandfather's excellent temper, his scholarly reputation, his liberality.

Anna smothered a soft laugh. "Poor Grandfather. His liberality is why your prospects are so diminished," she said ruefully.

I could not dispute it. Had he been a little less willing to lend money to an impecunious friend or purchase a book from a scholar fallen upon hard times, there would have been a great deal left in his own coffers. But there was not a man in Edinburgh who did not know to apply to Professor Mungo Lestrange if he was a man of both letters and privation.

"Was Mr. Beecroft there?" she asked carefully. She withdrew her hands from mine and took up her needlework again.

I looked for something to do with my own hands and found the fire wanted poking up. I busied myself with poker and shovel while I replied.

"He was."

"It was very kind of him to come."

"He is my publisher, and his firm published Grandfather's work. It was a professional courtesy," I replied coolly.

"Rather more a personal one, I should think," she said, her voice perfectly even. But we had not been sisters so long for nothing. I detected the tiny note of hope in her tone, and I determined to squash it.

"He has asked me to marry him," I told her. "I have refused him."

She jumped and gave a little exclamation as she pricked herself. She thrust a finger into her mouth and sucked at it, then wrapped it in a handkerchief.

"Theodora, why? He is a kind man, an excellent match. And if any husband ought to be sympathetic to a wifely pen it is a publisher!"

I stirred up the coals slowly, watching the warm pink embers glow hotly red under my ministrations. "He is indeed a kind man, and an excellent publisher. He is prosperous and well-read, and with a liberal bent of mind that I should scarce find once in a thousand men."

"Then why refuse him?"

I replaced the poker and turned to face her. "Because I do not love him. I like him. I am fond of him. I esteem him greatly. But I do not love him, and that is an argument you cannot rise to, for you did not marry without love and you can hardly expect it of me."

Her expression softened. "Of course I understand. But is it not possible that with a man of such temperament, of such possibility, that love may grow? It has all it needs to flourish—soil, seed and water. It requires only time and a more intimate acquaintance."

"And if it does not grow?" I demanded. "Would you have me hazard my future happiness on 'might'? No, it is not sound. I admit that with time a closer attachment might form, but what if it does not? I have never craved domesticity, Anna. I have never longed for home and hearth and children of my own, and yet that must be my lot if I marry. Why then would I take up those burdens unless I had the compensation of love? Of passion?"

She raised a warning finger. "Do not collect passion into the equation. It is a dangerous foe, Theodora, like keeping a lion in the garden. It might seem safe enough, but it might well destroy you. No, do not yearn for passion. Ask instead for contentment, happiness. Those are to be wished for."

"They are your wishes," I reminded her. "I want very different things. And if I am to find them, I cannot tread your path."

We exchanged glances for a long moment, both of us conscious that though we were sisters, born of the same blood and bone, it was as if we spoke different dialects of the same language, hardly able to take each other's meaning properly. There was no perfect understanding between us, and I think it grieved her as deeply as it did me.

At length she smiled, tears blurring the edges of her lashes. She gave a sharp sniff and assumed a purposeful air. "Then I suppose you ought to tell me about Transylvania."

The rest of that day was not a peaceful one. William was firmly opposed to the notion of my sojourn in the Carpathians and it took all of Anna's considerable powers of persuasion even to bring the matter into the realm of possibility. I did not require William's permission—he had no legal claim upon me—but I wanted peace between us. At length I withdrew from my labours in the library, leaving them to speak alone and therefore more freely. I had little doubt Anna could convince him of the merits of my plan. She had only to stress the cramped condition of the vicarage and the noble status of my hosts, for William had a touch of the toady about him.

But it reflected very poorly upon me as a woman of independence that I even cared for his opinion, I told myself with some annoyance. I took up my things and informed Mrs. Muldoon I meant to walk before dinner—no unusual thing, for strenuous walking had always been my preferred method for banishing either gloom or anger. I set my steps for Holyrood-house and the looming bulk of Arthur's Seat. A scramble to the top of the hill would banish the fractiousness that had settled on me with my grandfather's passing. Physical exertion and a brisk wind were just the trick to freshen my perspective, and as I climbed I felt the weight of the previous dark days rolling from me. The view was spectacular, ranging from the grey fringes of the firth to the crouching mass of the castle at the end of the Royal Mile. I could see the dark buildings of the old town, huddled together in whispered conversation over the narrow, thief-riddled closes, the atmosphere thick with secrets and disease. To the west rose the elegant white squares of New Town, orderly and sedate. And I perched above it all, breathing in the fresh air that smelled of grass and sea and possibility.

"I thought I would find you here." I turned to see Charles Beecroft just hoving into sight, breathing rather heavily, his face quite pink. "I called in at the house, and Mrs. Muldoon was kind enough to direct me here."

He climbed the last few steps, relying upon the kind offices of his walking stick to support him. He was not elderly, although he acknowledged himself to be some fifteen years my senior. But his had been a sedentary life with little occupation outside either the opera or the offices and no country pursuits to speak of. He was a creature of the city, more accustomed to the drawing room than the meadow.

"You needn't have come all this way, Charles," I said, smiling a little to take the sting from my words. "I know how much you dislike fresh air."

He laughed, knowing I meant him no insult. "But I like you, and that compels me."

It was unlike Charles to be gallant. I steeled myself, knowing what must come next. He stood beside me, both of us intent upon the view for a long moment. He reached into his pocket and withdrew a few sweets. He offered one to me, but I refused it. Charles always carried a supply of sweets in his pockets. It was an endearing habit, for it made a boy of this serious, solid man. One would look him over carefully, from the hair so tidily combed with lime cream to the tips of his beautifully polished shoes, and one would expect him to smell of money and books. Instead he smelled of honey and barley sugar. It was one of the things I liked best about him.

"So," he said at last, "Transylvania." It was not a question. He has accepted it, I thought. I was conscious of a sudden unbending, a feeling of relief. I had expected Charles to be difficult, to throw obstacles in my path. But he had, very occasionally, demonstrated a rather shrewd understanding of my character. He knew I could be bridled only so tightly before I would snap the reins altogether.

"You have met my sister," I said.

"Your brother-in-law was kind enough to introduce me. A lovely woman, your sister."

"Yes, Anna always was the beauty."

He sucked at the sweet. "You underestimate your charms, Theodora. Now, I know you mean to go and I have no authority to stop you. But I will ask you again to consider my proposal."

I opened my mouth, but to my astonishment, he grasped my arms and turned me to face him. Charles had never taken such physical liberties with me, and I confess I felt rather exhilarated by the change in him. "Charles," I murmured.

His eyes, a soft spaniel brown, were intent as I had seldom seen them, and his grip upon my arms was firm, almost painfully so. "I know you have refused me, but I do not mean to give up the idea so easily. I want you to think again, and not for a moment. I want you to think for the months you will be away. Think of me, think of the ways I could make you happy. Think of what our life together could be. And then, when you have had that time, only then will I accept your answer. Will you do that for me?"

I looked into his face, that pleasant, kindly face, and I searched for something—I did not know what, but I knew that when he grasped me in his arms, I had felt a glimmer of it, something less than civilised, something that clamoured in the blood. But it was gone, as quickly as it had come, and I wondered if I had been mad to look for real passion in him. Was he capable of such emotion?

"Kiss me, Charles," I said suddenly.

He hesitated only a moment, then settled his lips over mine. His kiss was a polite, respectful thing. His mouth was warm and pleasant, but just when I would have put my arms about his neck in invitation, he stepped back, dropping his hands from my arms. His complexion was flushed, his gaze averted. He had tasted of honey, and I was surprised at how much I had been stirred by his kiss. Or would any man's kiss have done?

"I am sorry," I said, straightening my bonnet. "I ought not to have asked that of you."

"Not at all," he said lightly. He cleared his throat. "You give me reason to hope. You will consider my proposal?" he urged.

I nodded. I could do that much for him at least.

"Excellent. Now tell me about Transylvania. I do not like the scheme at all, you understand, but your sister tells me you mean to write a novel. I cannot dislike that."

He offered his arm and we began to descend the hill, walking slowly as we talked. I told him about Cosmina and her wonderful tales of vampires and werewolves and how she had terrified the mistresses at school with her pretty torments.

"One would have expected them to be more sensible," he observed.

"But that is the crux. They *were* sensible, very much so. German teachers have no imagination, I assure you. And yet these stories were so vivid, so full of horrific detail, they would chill the blood of the bravest man. These things exist there."

He stopped, amusement writ in his face. "You cannot be serious."

"Entirely. The folk in those mountains believe that vampires and werewolves walk abroad in the night. Cosmina was quite definite upon the point."

"They must be quite mad. I begin to dislike your little scheme even more," he said as we started downward again. He guided me around a narrow outcropping of rock as I endeavoured to explain.

"They are no different from the Highlander who leaves milk out for the faeries or plants rowan to guard against witches," I maintained. "And can you imagine what a kindle that would be to the imagination? Knowing that such things are not only spoken of in legends but are believed to be real, even now? The novel will write itself," I said, relishing the thought of endless happy hours spent dashing my pen across the pages, spinning out some great adventure. "It will be the making of me."

"You mean the making of T. Lestrange," he corrected.

As yet I had published in that name only, shielding my sex from those who would criticize the sensational fruits of my pen solely on the grounds they were a woman's work. It had been my grandfather's wish as well, for he had lived a retiring life and though he enjoyed a wide acquaintance, he preferred to keep abreast of his friends through correspondence. He had seldom ventured abroad, and even less frequently had he entertained his friends to our house. Mine had been a quiet life of necessity, but at Charles's words I began to wonder. What would it be like to publish under my own name? To go to London? To be introduced to the good and great? To be a literary personage in my own right? It was a seductive notion, and one I should no doubt think on a great deal while I was in Transylvania, I reflected.

"How do you mean to travel?" Charles asked, recalling me to our conversation.

"Cosmina says the railway is complete as far as someplace called Hermannstadt. After that I must go by private carriage for some distance."

"You do not mean to go alone?"

"I do not see an alternative," I replied, looking to blunt his disapproval.

He said nothing, but I knew him well enough to know the furrowing of his brow meant he was knitting together a plan of some sort.

"Tell me of the family you mean to stay with," he instructed.

"Cosmina is a poor relation of the family, a sort of niece I think, to the Countess Dragulescu. The countess paid for her education and there was an expectation that Cosmina would marry her son. He was always from home when we were in school—in Paris, I think. Now his father is dead and he is coming home. The marriage will be settled, and Cosmina wishes me to be there as I am her oldest friend."

"Why have I never heard you speak of her?"

I shrugged. "We have not seen one another since we left school. I have had only Christmas letters from her. She was never one to correspond."

"Why has she never come to visit you?"

I made an effort to smother my rising exasperation. Charles would have made an admirable Inquisitor.

"Because she is a poor relation," I reminded him. "She has not had the money to travel, nor has she had the liberty. She has been caring for her aunt. The countess is something of an invalid, and they lead a very quiet existence at the castle. Cosmina has had little enough pleasure in her life. But she wants me and I mean to be there," I finished firmly.

Charles paused again and took both of my hands in his. "I know. And I know I cannot stop you, although I would give all the world to keep you here. But you must promise me this, should you have need of me, for any reason, you have only to send for me. I will come."

I gave his hands a friendly squeeze. "That is kind, Charles. And I promise to send word if I need you. But what could possibly happen to me in Transylvania?"

2

And so it was settled that I was to travel into Transylvania as soon as arrangements could be made. I wrote hastily to Cosmina to accept her invitation and acknowledge the instructions she had provided me for reaching the castle. William concluded the business of disposing of my grandfather's estate, proudly presenting me with a slightly healthier sum than either of us had expected. It was not an independence, but it was enough to see me through my trip and for some months beyond, so long as I was frugal. Anna helped me to pack, choosing only those few garments and books which would be most suitable for my journey. It was a simple enough task, for I had no finery. My mourning must suffice, augmented with a single black evening gown and a travelling costume of serviceable tweed.

Mindful of the quiet life I must lead in Transylvania, I packed sturdy walking boots and warm tartan shawls, as well as a good supply of paper, pens and ink. Charles managed to find an excellent, if slender, guidebook to the region I must travel into and a neatly penned letter of introduction with a list of his acquaintances in Buda-Pesth and Vienna.

"It is the only service I can offer you," he told me upon presenting it. "You will have friends, even if they are at some distance removed."

I thanked him warmly, but in my mind I had already flown from him. For several nights before my departure, I dreamt of Transylvania, dreamt of thick birch forests and mountains echoing to the howling of wolves. It was anticipation of the most delicious sort, and when the morning of my departure came, I did not look back. The train pulled out of the Edinburgh station and I set my face to the east and all of its enchantments.

We passed first through France, and I could not but stare from the window, my book unread upon my lap, mesmerised as the French countryside gave way to the high mountains of Switzerland. We journeyed still further, into Austria, and at last I began to feel Scotland dropping right away, as distant as a memory.

At length we reached Buda-Pesth where the Danube separated the old Turkish houses of Buda from the modern and sparkling Pesth. I longed to explore, but I was awakened early to catch the first train the following morning. At Klausenberg I alighted, now properly in Transylvania, and I heard my first snatches of Roumanian, as well as various German dialects, and Hungarian. Eagerly, I turned to my guidebook.

All Transylvanians are polyglots, it instructed. *Roumanians speak their own tongue—to the unfamiliar, it bears a strong resemblance to the Genoese dialect of Italian—and it is a mark of distinction to speak English, for it means one has had the advantage of an English nursemaid in childhood. Most of the natives of this region speak Hungarian and German as well, although a peculiar dialect of each not to be* confused with the mother tongues. However, travellers fluent in either language will find it a simple enough matter to converse with natives and, likewise, to make themselves understood.

I leafed through the brief entry on Klausenberg to find a more unsettling passage.

Travellers are advised not to drink the water in Klausenberg as it is unwholesome. The water flows from springs through the graveyards and into the town, its purity contaminated by the dead.

I shivered and closed the book firmly and made my way to the small and serviceable hotel Cosmina had directed me to find. It was the nicest in the whole of Klausenberg, my guidebook assured, and yet it would have rated no better than passable in any great city. The linen was clean, the bed soft and the food perfectly acceptable, although I was careful to avoid the water. I slept deeply and well and was up once more at cockcrow to take my place on the train for the last stage of my journey, the short trip to Hermannstadt and thence by carriage into the Carpathians proper.

Almost as soon as we departed Klausenberg, we passed through the great chasm of Thorda Cleft, a gorge whose honeycombed caverns once sheltered brigands and thieves. But we passed without incident, and from thence the landscape was dull and unremarkable, and it was a long and rather commonplace journey of half a day until we reached Hermannstadt.

Here was a town I should have liked to have explored. The sharply pointed towers and red tiled roofs were so distinctive, so charming, so definably Eastern. Just beyond the town I could see the first soaring peaks of the Carpathians, rising in the distance. Here now was the real Transylvania, I thought, shivering in delight. I wanted to stand quietly upon that platform, but there was no opportunity for reflection. No sooner had I alighted from the train from Klausenberg than I was taken up by the hired coach I had been instructed to find. A driver and a postilion attended to the bags, and inside the conveyance I discovered a handful of other passengers who demonstrated a respectful curiosity, but initiated no conversation. The coach bore us rapidly out of the town of Hermannstadt and up into the Transylvanian Alps.

The countryside was idyllic. I was enchanted with the Roumanian hamlets for the houses were quite different than any I had seen before. There was no prim Scottish thrift to be found here. The eaves were embellished with colourful carvings, and gates were fashioned of iron wrought into fantastic shapes. Even the hay wagons were picturesque, groaning under the weight of the harvest and pulled by horses caparisoned with bell-tied ribbons. Everything seemed as if it had been lifted from a faery tale, and I tried desperately to memorise it all as the late-afternoon sun blazed its golden-red light across the profile of the mountains.

After a long while, the road swung upward into the high mountains, and we moved from the pretty foothills to the bold peaks of the Carpathians. Here the air grew suddenly sharp, and the snug villages disappeared, leaving only great swathes of green-black forests of fir and spruce, occasionally punctured by high shafts of grey stone where a ruined fortress or watchtower still reached to the darkening sky, and it was in this wilderness that we stopped once more, high upon a mountain pass at a small inn. A coach stood waiting, this one a private affair clearly belonging to some person of means, for it was a costly vehicle and emblazoned with an intricate coat of arms. The driver alighted at once and after a moment's brisk conversation with the driver of the hired coach, took up my boxes and secured them.

He gestured towards me, managing to be both respectful and impatient. I shivered in my thin cloak and hurried after him.

I paused at the front of the equipage, startled to find that the horses, great handsome beasts and beautifully kept, were nonetheless scarred, bearing the traces of some trauma about their noses.

"*Die Wölfe,*" he said, and I realised in horror what he meant.

I replied in German, my schoolgirl grammar faltering only a little. "The wolves attack them?"

He shrugged. "There is not a horse in the Carpathians without scars. It is the way of it here."

He said nothing more but opened the door to the coach and I climbed in.

Cosmina had mentioned wolves, and I knew they were a considerable danger in the mountains, but hearing such things amid the cosy comforts of a school dormitory was very different to hearing them on a windswept mountainside where they dwelt.

The coachman sprang to his seat, whipping up the horses almost before I had settled myself, so eager was he to be off. The rest of the journey was difficult, for the road we took was not the main one that continued through the pass, but a lesser, rockier track, and I realised we were approaching the headwaters of the river where it sprang from the earth before debouching into the somnolent valley far below.

The evening drew on into night, with only the coach lamps and a waning sliver of pale moon to light the way. It seemed we travelled an eternity, rocking and jolting our way ever upward until at last, hours after we left the little inn on the mountain pass, the driver pulled the horses to a sharp halt. I looked out of the window to the left and saw nothing save long shafts of starlight illuminating the great drop below us to the river. To the right was sheer rock, stretching hundreds of feet to the vertical. I staggered from the coach, my legs stiff with cold. I breathed deeply of the crisp mountain air and smelled juniper.

Just beyond lay a coach house and stables and what looked to be a little lodge, perhaps where the coachman lived. He had already dismounted and was unhitching the horses whilst he shouted directions to a group of men standing nearby. They looked to be of peasant stock and had clearly been chosen for their strength, for they were diminutive, as Roumanians so often are, but built like oxen with thick necks and muscle-corded arms. An old-fashioned sedan chair stood next to them.

Before I could ask, the driver pointed to a spot on the mountainside high overhead. Torches had been lit and I could see that a castle had been carved out of the living rock itself, perched impossibly high, like an eagle's aerie. "That is the home of the Dragulescus," he told me proudly.

"It is most impressive," I said. "But I do not understand. How am I to—"

He pointed again, this time towards a staircase cut into the rock. The steps were wide and shallow, switching back and forth as they rose over the face of the mountain.

"Impossible," I breathed. "There must be a thousand steps."

"One thousand, four hundred," he corrected. "The Devil's Staircase, it is called, for it is said that the Dragulescu who built this fortress could not imagine how to reach the summit of the mountain. So he promised his firstborn to the Devil if a way could be found. In the morning, his daughter was dead, and this staircase was just as you see it now."

I stared at him in astonishment. There seemed no possible reply to such a wretched story, and yet I felt a thrill of horror. I had done right to come. This was a land of legend, and I knew I should find inspiration for a dozen novels here if I wished it.

He gestured towards the sedan chair. "It is too steep for horses. This is why we must use the old ways."

I baulked at first, horrified at the idea that I must be

carried up the mountain like so much chattel. But I looked again at the great height and my legs shook with fatigue. I followed him to the sedan chair and stepped inside. The door was snapped shut behind me, entombing me in the stuffy darkness. A leather curtain had been hung at the window— for privacy, or perhaps to protect the passenger from the elements. I tried to move it aside, but it had grown stiff and unwieldy from disuse.

Suddenly, I heard a few words spoken in the soft lilting Roumanian tongue, and the sedan chair rocked hard, first to one side, then the other as it was lifted from the ground. I tried to make myself as small as possible before I realised the stupidity of the idea. The journey was not a comfortable one, for I soon discovered it was necessary to steel myself against the jostling at each step as we climbed slowly towards the castle.

At length I felt the chair being set down and the door was opened for me. I crept out, blinking hard in the flaring light of the torches. I could see the castle better now, and my first thought was here was some last outpost of Byzantium, for the castle was something out of myth. It was a hodgepodge of strange little towers capped by witches' hats, thick walls laced with parapets, and high, pointed windows. It had been fashioned of river stones and courses of bricks, and the whole of it had been whitewashed save the red tiles of the roofs. Here and there the white expanses of the walls were broken with massive great timbers, and the effect of the whole was some faery-tale edifice, perched by the hand of a giant in a place no human could have conceived of it.

In the paved courtyard, all was quiet, quiet as a tomb, and I wondered madly if everyone was asleep, slumbering under a sorcerer's spell, for the place seemed thick with enchantment. But just then the great doors swung back upon their hinges and the spell was broken. Silhouetted in the doorway was a slight figure I remembered well, and it was but a moment before she spied me and hurried forward.

"Theodora!" she cried, and her voice was high with emotion. "How good it is to see you at last."

She embraced me, but carefully, as if I were made of spun glass.

"We are old friends," I scolded. "And I can bear a sturdier affection than that." I enfolded her and she seemed to rest a moment upon my shoulder.

"Dear Theodora, I am so glad you are come." She drew back and took my hand, tucking it into my arm. The light from the torches fell upon her face then, and I saw that the pretty girl had matured into a comely woman. She had had a fondness for sweet pastries at school and had always run to plumpness, but now she was slimmer, the lost flesh revealing elegant bones that would serve her well into old age.

From the shadows behind her emerged a great dog, a wary and fearsome creature with a thick grey coat that stood nearly as tall as a calf in the field.

"Is he?" I asked, holding myself quite still as the beast sniffed at my skirts appraisingly.

"No." She paused a moment, then continued on smoothly, "The dog is his."

I knew at once that she referred to her betrothed, and I wondered why she had hesitated at the mention of his name. I darted a quick glance and discovered she was in the grip of some strong emotion, as if wrestling with herself.

She burst out suddenly, her voice pitched low and soft and for my ears alone. "Do not speak of the betrothal. I will explain later. Just say you are come for a visit."

She squeezed my hand and I gave a short, sharp nod to show that I understood. It seemed to reassure her, for she fixed a

gentle smile upon her lips and drew me into the great hall of
the castle to make the proper introductions.

The hall itself was large, the stone walls draped with moth-
eaten tapestries, the flagged floor laid here and there with
faded Turkey carpets. There was little furniture, but the
expanses of wall that had been spared the tapestries were bristling with weapons—swords and halberds, and some other
awful things I could not identify, but which I could easily
imagine dripping with gore after some fierce medieval battle.

Grouped by the immense fireplace was a selection of heavy
oaken chairs, thick with examples of the carver's art. One—a
porter's chair, I imagined, given its great wooden hood to
protect the sitter from draughts—was occupied by a woman.
Another woman and a young man stood next to it, and I pre-
sumed at once that this must be Cosmina's erstwhile fiancé.

When we reached the little group, Cosmina presented me
formally. "Aunt Eugenia, this is my friend, Theodora Lestrange.
Theodora, my aunt, the Countess Dragulescu."

I had no notion of how to render the proper courtesies to
a countess, so I merely inclined my head, more deeply than I
would have done otherwise, and hoped it would be sufficient.

To my surprise, the countess extended her hand and addressed me in lilting English. "Miss Lestrange, you are quite
welcome." Her voice was reedy and thin, and I noted she was
well-wrapped against the evening chill. As I came near to take
her hand, I saw the resemblance to Cosmina, for the bones of
the face were very like. But whereas Cosmina was a woman
whose beauty was in crescendo, the countess was fading. Her
hair and skin lacked luster, and I recalled the many times
Cosmina had confided her worries over her aunt's health.

But her grey eyes were bright as she shook my hand firmly,
then waved to the couple standing in attendance upon her.

"Miss Lestrange, you must meet my companion, Clara—Frau Amsel." To my surprise, she followed this with, "And her son, Florian. He functions as steward here at the castle." I supposed it was the countess's delicate way of informing me that Frau Amsel and Florian were not to be mistaken for the privileged. The Amsels were obliged to earn their bread as I should have to earn mine. We ought to have been equals, but perhaps my friendship with Cosmina had elevated me above my natural place in the countess's estimation. True, Cosmina was a poor relation, but the countess had seen to her education and encouraged Cosmina's prospects as a future daughter-in-law to hear Cosmina tell the tale. On thinking of the betrothal, I wondered then where the new count was and if his absence was the reason for Cosmina's distress.

Recalling myself, I turned to the Amsels. The lady was tall and upright in her posture, and wore a rather unbecoming shade of brown which gave her complexion a sallow cast. She was not precisely plump, but there was a solidity about her that put me instantly in mind of the sturdy village women who had cooked and cleaned at our school in Bavaria. Indeed, when Frau Amsel murmured some words of welcome, her English was thwarted by a thick German accent. I nodded cordially to her and she addressed her son. "Florian, Miss Lestrange is from Scotland. We must speak English to make her feel welcome. It will be good practise for you."

He inclined his head to me. "Miss Lestrange. It is with a pleasure that we welcome you to Transylvania."

His grammar was imperfect, and his accent nearly impenetrable, but I found him interesting. He was perhaps a year or two my elder—no more, I imagined. He had softly curling hair of middling brown and a broad, open brow. His would have been a pleasant countenance, if not for the expression of seriousness in his solemn brown eyes. I noticed his hands were beautifully shaped, with long, elegant fingers, and I wondered if he wrote tragic poetry.

"Thank you, Florian," I returned, twisting my tongue around the syllables of his name and giving it the same inflection his mother had.

Just at that moment I became aware of a disturbance, not from the noise, for his approach had been utterly silent. But the dog pricked up his ears, swinging his head to the great archway that framed the grand staircase. A man was standing there, his face shrouded in darkness. He was of medium height, his shoulders wide and, although I could not see him clearly, they seemed to be set with the resolve that only a man past thirty can achieve.

He moved forward slowly, graceful as an athlete, and as he came near, the light of the torches and the fire played over his face, revealing and then concealing, offering him up in pieces that I could not quite resolve into a whole until he reached my side.

I was conscious that his eyes had been fixed upon me, and I realised with a flush of embarrassment that I had returned his stare, all thoughts of modesty or propriety fled.

The group had been a pleasant one, but at his appearance a crackling tension rose, passing from one to the other, until the atmosphere was thick with unspoken things.

He paused a few feet from me, his gaze still hard upon me. I could see him clearly now and almost wished I could not. He was handsome, not in the pretty way of shepherd boys in pastoral paintings, but in the way that horses or lions are handsome. His features bore traces of his mother's ruined beauty, with a stern nose and a firmly marked brow offset by lips any satyr might have envied. They seemed fashioned for murmuring sweet seductions, but it was the eyes I found truly mesmerising. I had never seen that colour before, either in nature or in art. They were silver-grey, but darkly so, and complemented by the black hair that fell in thick locks nearly to his shoulders. He was dressed quietly, but expensively, and wore a heavy silver ring upon his forefinger, intricately worked and elegant. Yet all of these ex-cellent attributes were nothing to the expression of interest and approbation he wore. Without that, he would have been any other personable gentleman. With it, he was incomparable. I felt as if I could stare at him for a thousand years, so long as he looked at me with those fathomless eyes, and it was not until Cosmina spoke that I recalled myself.

"Andrei, this is my friend Miss Theodora Lestrange from Edinburgh. Theodora, the Count Dragulescu."

He did not take my hand or bow or offer me any of the courtesies I might have expected. Instead he merely held my gaze and said, "Welcome, Miss Lestrange. You must be tired from your journey. I will escort you to your room."

If the pronouncement struck any of the assembled company as strange, they betrayed no sign of it. The countess inclined her head to me in dismissal as Frau Amsel and Florian stood quietly by. Cosmina reached a hand to squeeze mine. "Goodnight," she murmured. "Rest well and we will speak in the morning," she added meaningfully. She darted a glance at the count, and for the briefest of moments, I thought I saw fear in her eyes.

I nodded. "Of course. Goodnight, and thank you all for such a kind welcome."

The count did not wait for me to conclude my farewells, forcing me to take up my skirts in my hands and hurry after him. At the foot of the stairs a maid darted forward with a pitcher of hot water and he gestured for her to follow. She said nothing, but gave me a curious glance. The count took up a lit candle from a sideboard and walked on, never looking back.

We walked for some distance, up staircases and down long corridors, until at length we came to what I surmised must have been one of the high towers of the castle. The door to the ground-floor room was shut. We passed it, mounting a narrow set of stairs that spiralled to the next floor, where we paused at a heavy oaken door. The count opened it, standing aside for me to enter. The room was dark and cold. The maid placed the pitcher next to a pretty basin upon the washstand. The count gave her a series of instructions in rapid Roumanian and she hurried to comply, building up a fire upon the hearth. It was soon burning brightly, but it did little to dispel the chill that had settled into the stone walls, and it seemed surprising to me that the room had not been better prepared as I had been expected. I began to wonder if the count had altered the arrangements, although I could not imagine why.

The room was circular and furnished in an old-fashioned style, doubtless because the furniture *was* old—carved wooden stuff with great clawed feet. The bed was hung with thick scarlet curtains, heavily embroidered in tarnished gold thread, and spread across it was a moulting covering of some sort of animal fur. I was afraid to ask what variety.

But even as I took inventory of my room, I was deeply conscious of him standing near the bed, observing me in perfect silence.

At length I could bear the silence no longer. "It was kind of you to show me the way." I put out my hand for the candle but he stepped around me. He went to the washstand and fixed the candle in place on an iron prick. The little maid scurried out the door, and to my astonishment, closed it firmly behind her.

"Remove your gloves," he instructed.

I hesitated, certain I had misheard him. But even as I told myself it could not be, he removed his coat and unpinned his cuffs, turning back his sleeves to reveal strong brown forearms, heavy with muscle. Still, I hesitated, and he reached for my hands.

He did not take his eyes from my face as he slowly withdrew my gloves, easing the thin leather from my skin. I opened my mouth to protest, but found I had no voice to do so. I was unsettled—as I had often been with Charles, but for an entirely different reason. With Charles I often played the schoolgirl. With the count, I felt a woman grown.

He paused a moment when my hands were bared, covering them with his larger ones, warming them between his wide palms. I caught my breath and I knew that he heard it, for he smiled a little, and I saw then that all he did was for a purpose.

Holding my hands firmly in one of his, he poured the water slowly over my fingers, directing the warm stream to the most sensitive parts. The water was scented with some fragrance I could not quite place, and bits of green leaves floated over the top.

"Basil," he told me, nodding towards the leaves. "For welcome. It is the custom of our country to welcome our visitors by washing their hands. It means you are one of the household and we are bound by duty to give you our hospitality until you leave. And it means you are here under my protection, for I am the master."

I said nothing and he took up a linen towel, cradling my hands within its softness until they were dry. He finished by stroking them gently through the cloth from wrist to fingertip and back again.

He stood half a foot from me, and my senses staggered from the nearness of him. I was aware of the scent of him, leather and male flesh commingling with something else, something that called to mind the heady, sensual odour of overripe fruit. My head was full of him and I reeled for a moment, too dizzy to keep to my feet.

His hands were firm upon my shoulders as he guided me to a chair.

"Sit by the fire," he urged. "Tereza will return soon with something to eat. Then you must rest."

"Yes, it is only that I am tired," I replied, and I believed we both knew it for a lie.

He rose, his fingers lingering for a moment longer upon my shoulders, and left me then, with only a backwards glance that seemed to be comprised of puzzlement and pleasure in equal parts. I sat, sunk into misery as I had never been before. Cosmina was my friend, my very dear friend, and this man was the one she planned to marry.

It is impossible. I said the words aloud to make them true. It *was* impossible. Whatever attraction I felt towards him must be considered an affliction, something to rid myself of, something to master. It could not be indulged, not even be dreamt of.

And yet as I sat waiting for Tereza, I could still feel his strong fingers sliding over mine in the warm, scented water, and when I slept that night, it was to dream of his eyes watching me from the shadows of my room.

3

In the morning, I rose with vigour, determined to put my fancies of the previous evening aside. Whatever my own inclinations, the count was simply not a proper subject for any attachment. I must view him solely as my host and Cosmina's potential husband, and perhaps, if I was quite circumspect, inspiration for a character. His demeanour, his looks, his very manner of carrying himself, would all serve well as the model for a dashing and heroic gentleman. But I would have to be guarded in my observations of him, I reminded myself sternly. I had already made myself foolish by failing to conceal my reactions to him. I could ill afford to repeat the performance. I risked making myself ridiculous, and far worse, wounding a devoted friend.

Rising, I drew back the heavy velvet draperies, surprised to see the sun shone brightly through the leaded windows of my tower room. It had seemed the sort of place the light would never touch, but the morning was glorious. I pushed open a window and gazed down at the dizzying drop to the river below. The river itself ran silver through the green shadows of the trees, and further down the valley I could see where autumn had brushed the forests with her brightly coloured skirts. The treetops, unlike the evergreens at our mountain fastness, blazed with orange and gold and every shade of flame, bursting with one last explosion of life before settling in to the quiet slumber of winter. I sniffed the air, and found it fresh and crisp, far cleaner than any I had smelled before. There was not the soot of Edinburgh here, nor the grime of the cities of the Continent. It was nothing but the purest breath of the clouds, and I drew in great lungfuls of it, letting it toss my hair in the breeze before I drew back and surveyed the room.

I found the bellpull by the fireplace and gave it a sharp tug. Perhaps a quarter of an hour later a scratch at the door heralded the arrival of a pair of maids, one bearing cans of hot water, the other a tray of food—an inefficient system, for one would surely grow cold by the time I had attended to the other—but the plump, pink-cheeked maids were friendly enough. One was the girl, Tereza, from the previous night, and the other looked to be her sister, with their glossy dark braids wound tightly about their heads and identical wide black eyes. The taller of the two was enchantingly pretty, with a ripe, Junoesque figure. Tereza was very nearly fat, but with a friendlier smile illuminating her plain face. It was she who carried the water and who attempted to make herself understood.

"Tereza," she said, thumping her ample chest.

"Tereza," I repeated dutifully. I smiled to show that I remembered her.

She pointed to the other girl. "Aurelia."

I repeated the name and she smiled.

"Buña dimineaţa," she said slowly.

I thought about the words and hazarded a guess. "Good morning?"

She turned the words over on her tongue. "Good morning. Good *morning*," she said, changing the inflection. She nodded at her sister. "Good morning, Aurelia."

Her sister would have none of it. She frowned and clucked her tongue as she removed the covers from my breakfast. She rattled off a series of words I did not understand, pointing at each dish as she did so. There was a bowl of porridge—not oat, I realised, but corn—bread rolls, new butter, a pot of thick Turkish coffee and a pot of scarlet cherry jam. Not so different from the breakfasts I had been accustomed to in Scotland, I decided, and I inclined my head in thanks to her. She sketched a bare curtsey and left. Tereza lingered a moment, clearly interested in conversation.

"Tereza," she said again, pointing to herself.

"Miss Lestrange," I returned.

She pondered that for a moment, then gave it a try. "Mees Lestroinge." She garbled the pronunciation, but at least it was a beginning.

"Thank you, Tereza," I said slowly.

She nodded and dropped a better curtsey than her sister had. As she turned to leave, she spied the open window and began to speak quickly in her native tongue, warning and scolding, if her tone was anything to judge. She hurried to the window and yanked it closed, making it fast against the beautiful morning. From her pocket she drew a small bunch of basil that had been tied neatly with a bit of ribbon. This she fixed to the handle, wagging her finger as she instructed me. I could only assume I was being told not to remove it, and once the basil was in place, she drew the draperies firmly closed, throwing the room into gloom.

I protested, but she held up a hand, muttering to herself, and I heard for the first time the word I would come to hear many times during my sojourn in Transylvania. *Strigoi*. She bustled about, lighting candles and building up the fire on the hearth to light the room. It was marginally more cheerful when she had done so, but I could not believe I was expected to live in this chamber with neither light nor air.

She lit the last candle and moved to me then, her tone insistent as she spoke. After a moment she raised her hand and placed it on my brow, making the swift sign of Orthodoxy, crossing from right to left. Then she kissed me briskly on both cheeks and motioned towards my breakfast, gesturing me to eat before the food grew cold.

She left me then and I sat down to my porridge and rolls, marvelling at the strangeness of the local folk.

After my tepid breakfast and even colder wash, I dressed myself carefully in a day gown of deep black and left my room to search out Cosmina. I had little idea where she might be at this time of day, but it seemed certain she would be about. I hoped to have a thorough discussion with her to settle the many little questions that had arisen since my arrival. Most importantly, I was determined to discover what mystery surrounded her betrothal.

I retraced my steps from the night before, keeping a careful eye upon the various landmarks of the castle—here a suit of armour, there a peculiar twisting stair—in order to find my way. I made but two wrong turnings before I reached the great hall, and I saw that it was quite empty, the hearth cold and black in the long gloom of the room.

And then I was not alone, for in the space of a heartbeat he appeared, the great grey dog at his heels, as suddenly as if I had conjured him myself.

"Miss Lestrange," he greeted. He was freshly shaven and dressed impeccably in severe black clothing that was doubtless all the more costly for its simplicity. Only the whiteness of his shirt struck a jarring note in the shadowy hall.

My heart had begun to race at the sight of him, and I took a calming breath.

"*Buña dimineața,* sir." I noticed then the cleft in his chin, and I thought of the proverb I had often heard at home: *Dimple in the chin, the Devil within.*

His face lit with pleasure. "Ah, you are learning the language already. I hope you have passed a pleasant night."

"Very," I told him truthfully. "It must be the air here. I slept quite deeply indeed."

"And your breakfast was to your liking?" he inquired.

"Very much so, thank you."

"And the servants, they are attentive to your desires?" It struck me then that his voice was one of the most unusual I had ever heard, not so much for the quality of the sound itself, which was low and pleasing, but for the rhythm of his speech. His accent was slight, but the liquidity of a few of his consonants, the slow pace of his words, combined to striking effect. The simplest question could sound like a philosopher's profundity from his lips.

"Quite. Although—"

"Yes?" His eyes sharpened.

"The maid seemed a little agitated this morning when she discovered my open window."

"Surely you did not sleep with it open," he said quickly.

"No, it would have been too cold for that, I think. But it was such a lovely morning—"

He gave a little sigh and the tension in his shoulders seemed to ease. "Of course. The maid doubtless thought you had slept with the window open, and such is a dangerous practise here in the mountains. There are bats—*vespertilio*—which carry foul diseases, and other creatures which might make their way into your room at night."

I grimaced. "I am afraid I do not much care for bats. Of course I shall keep my window firmly closed in future. But when Tereza closed it, she hung basil from the latch."

"To sweeten the air of the room," he said hastily. "Such is the custom here."

The word I had heard her speak trembled on my lips, but I did not repeat it. Perhaps I was afraid to know just yet what that word *strigoi* meant and why it seemed to strike fear into Tereza's heart.

"I thought to find Cosmina," I began.

"My mother is unwell and Cosmina attends her," the count replied. "I am afraid you must content yourself with me."

Just then the great dog moved forward and began to nuzzle my hand, and I saw that his eyes were yellow, like those of a wolf.

"Miss Lestrange, you must not be frightened of my Tycho! How pale you look. Are you afraid of dogs?"

"Only large ones," I admitted, trying not to pull free of the rough muzzle that tickled my palm. "I was bitten once as a child, and I do not seem to have quite got over it."

"You will with my boy. He is gentle as a lamb, at least to those whom I like," he promised. The count encouraged me to pet the dog, and I lifted a wary hand to his head.

"Underneath the neck, just there on the chest, between his forelegs," he instructed. "Over the head is challenging, and he will not like it. Under the chin is friendly, only mind the throat."

I did not dare ask what would happen if I did not mind the throat. I put my hand between the dog's forelegs, feeling the massive heart beating under my fingers. I patted him gently, and he leaned hard with his great head against my leg, nearly pushing me over.

"Oh!" I cried.

"Do not be startled," the count said quietly. "It is a measure of affection. Tycho has decided to like you."

"How kind of him," I murmured. "A curious name, Tycho."

"After the astronomer, Tycho Brahe. It was an interest of my grandfather's he was good enough to share with me." Before I could remark upon this, he hurried on. "Have you any pets, Miss Lestrange?"

"No, my grandfather had the raising of me and he did not much care for animals. He thought they would spoil his books."

The count made a noise of derision. "And are books more important than the companionship of such creatures? Were it not for my dogs and horses I should have been quite alone as a child." It was an observation; he said the words without pity for himself.

"I too found solace. Books remain my favourite companions."

The strongly marked brows shifted. "Then I have something to show you. Come, Miss Lestrange."

He led the way from the great hall, through a corridor that twisted and turned, through another lesser hall, a second corridor, and through a set of imposing double doors. The room we emerged into was tremendous in size, encompassing two floors, with a wide gallery running the perimeter of the place. Bookshelves lined both floors to the ceiling, and there were several smaller, travelling bookcases scattered about the room, all stuffed with books.

Unlike the rest of the castle, this room was floored in dark, polished wood, giving it a cosier feel, if such a thing was possible in so imposing a place. The furniture was carved and heavy and upholstered in moss green, a native pattern stitched upon it in faded gold. There were a few globes, including a rather fine celestial model, and several map tables fitted with wide, low drawers for atlases. In the centre of the room a great two-sided desk stood upon lion's paws on a vast Turkey rug. Taken as a whole, the room was vast and impressive, but upon closer inspection it was possible to see the work of insects— moth upon the furniture and rugs and bookworm in the volumes themselves. It was a room that had been beautiful once, but beyond a cursory flick of a duster, it did not seem as if anyone had cared for it for quite a long time. A fire burning on the wide hearth did something to banish the chill, and the dog settled in front of it, claiming the place.

The count stood back, awaiting my reaction.

"A very impressive room," I told him.

He seemed pleased. "It is traditionally used by the counts to conduct their business—the collecting of rents, the meting out of justice. And it is also a place of leisure. No doubt you think it odd to find such an extensive collection in such a place, but the grip of winter holds us close upon this mountain. There is little to do but hunt, and even that is sometimes not possible. It is then that we too turn to books."

He moved to one of the cases and drew out a few folios. I smiled as I recognised Whitethorne's *Illustrated Folklore and Legend of the Scottish Highlands* as well as Sir Ruthven Campbell's *Great Walks of the British Isles.*

"You see, even here we know something of your country," the count remarked, his eyes bright.

I put out a hand to touch the enormous volumes. The colour plates of the Whitethorne folio were exquisite, each more beautiful than the last. "Breathtaking," I murmured.

"Indeed," he said, and I realised how close he had come. He stood right at my shoulder, his arm grazing mine as he reached out to turn another page. There was a whisper of warm breath across my neck, just where the skin was bared between the coil of my hair and the collar of my gown. "You must come and look at them whenever you like. They are too heavy to take to your room, but the library is at your disposal."

His arm pressed mine so slightly I might have imagined the touch. I stepped back and pretended to study an ancillary sphere.

"That is very generous of you, sir."

He closed the folio but did not move closer to me. He merely folded his arms over his chest and stood watching me, a small smile playing over his lips.

"It costs me nothing to share, therefore it is not generous," he corrected. "When someone offers what he can ill afford to give, only then may he be judged generous."

I looked up from my perusal of the sphere. "Then I will say instead it is kind of you."

"You seem determined to think well of me, Miss Lestrange. But Cosmina tells me you are an authoress. What sort of host would I be if I did not provide you with a comfortable place to work should you choose?"

He smiled then, a decidedly feline smile, predatory and slow. I did not know how to reply to him. I had no experience of such people. Sophistry was not a skill I possessed. Cosmina had told me the count had lived for many years in Paris; doubtless his companions were well-versed in polished conversation, in the parry and thrust of social intercourse. I was cast of different metal. But I thought again of my book and the use I might make of him there. He was alluring and noble and decidedly mysterious, all the qualities I required for a memorable hero. I made up my mind to engage him as often as possible in conversation, to study him as a lepidopterist might study an excellent specimen of something rare and unusual.

"You surprise me," he said suddenly.

"In what manner?"

"When Cosmina told me she was expecting her friend, the writer from Edinburgh, I imagined a quite terrifying young woman, six feet tall with red hair and rough hands and an alarming vocabulary. And instead I find you."

He finished this remark with a look of such genuine approbation as quite stopped my breath.

"I must indeed have been a surprise," I said, attempting a light tone. "I like to believe I am clever, but I am no bluestocking."

"And so small as to scarcely reach my shoulder," he said softly, leaning a bit closer. He shifted his gaze to my hair. "I had not thought Scotchwomen so dark. Your hair is almost black as mine, and your eyes," he trailed off, pausing a moment, his lips parted as he drew a great deep breath, smelling me as an animal might.

"Rosewater," he murmured. "Very lovely."

I stepped backwards sharply, ashamed at my part in this latest impropriety. "I must beg your leave, sir. I ought to find Cosmina."

Amusement twitched at the corners of his mouth. "She is with the countess. My mother has spent a restless night and it soothes her to have Cosmina read to her."

"I am sorry to hear of the countess's indisposition."

"So the responsibility of entertaining you falls to me," he added with another of his enigmatic smiles.

"I would not be a burden to you. I am sure your duties must be quite demanding. If you will excuse me," I began as I moved to step past him.

"I cannot," he countered smoothly. And then a curious thing occurred. He seemed to block me with his own body, and yet he did not stir. It was simply that I knew I could not move past him and so remained where I was as he continued to speak. "It is my duty and my pleasure to introduce you to my home."

"Really, sir, that is not necessary. I might take a book to my room or write letters." But even as I spoke, I knew it was not to be. There was a peculiar force to his personality, and I understood then that whatever resistance I presented him was no more than the slenderest twig in his path. He would take no note of it as he proceeded upon his way.

"Letters—on such a fine day, when we might walk together? Oh, no, Miss Lestrange. I will begin your education upon the subject of Transylvania, and you will find I am an excellent tutor."

He offered me his arm then, and as I took it, I thought for some unaccountable reason of Eve and the very little persuasion it took for the serpent to prevail.

I spent the morning with him, and he proved an amiable and courteous host. He behaved with perfect propriety once we quit the library, introducing me to the castle with a connoisseur's eye for what was best and most beautiful, for the castle *was* beautiful, but tragically so. Everywhere I found signs of decay and neglect, and I became exceedingly puzzled as to what had caused the castle to fall to ruin. It had obviously been loved deeply at one time, with both care and money lavished upon it in equal measure, but some calamity had caused it to lapse into decline. It was not until we had finished the tour of the castle proper—the public rooms only, for he did not take me to the family wing nor to the tower where I slept—and emerged into the garden that I began to understand.

The morning was a cool one, but I had my shawl and the garden was walled, shielded from the wind by heavy stones. The garden was surprisingly large and had been planted with an eye to both purpose and pleasure. A goodly part was used as a kitchen garden, untidy but clearly productive, with serried rows of vegetables and the odd patch of herbs bordered by weedy gravel paths. But at the end of this was a door in the wall and beyond was a forgotten place, thick with overgrown rosebushes and trees heavy with unpicked fruit. A fountain stood in the middle, the pretty statue of Bacchus furred with mold, the water black and rank and covered with a foul slime.

I turned to find the count staring at the garden, his jaw set, his lips thin and cruel.

"I apologise," he said tightly. "I have not yet seen it. I did not realise it had fallen into disuse. It was once a beautiful place."

I could feel anger in him, controlled though it was, and I hurried to smooth the moment. "It is not difficult to see what lies beneath. The fountain is a copy of one at Versailles, is it not? My grandfather showed me a sketch he made during his travels as a young man. I recognise the heaps of grapes."

"Yes," he said, almost reluctantly. "My grandfather commissioned a copy when he planted his first vineyard. He was very proud of the first bottle of wine he produced."

"It is an accomplishment. He did well to be proud of it," I agreed.

To my surprise, he smiled, and it was not the casual smile he had shown before but something more heartfelt and genuine. "He needn't have been. It was truly awful. The vines were pulled out and tilled over. But he was very fond of his Bacchus," he finished, his eyes fixed upon the ruined statue.

"And you were very fond of him," I said boldly.

He did not alter his gaze. "I was. He had the raising of me. Dragulescu men have always had trouble with their sons," he said with a rueful twist of the lips. "My grandfather, Count Mircea, had neither affection nor esteem for my father. When I was born, my grandfather took it upon himself to educate me, to teach me the things that mattered to him. When he died,

life here became insupportable under my father. I left for Paris
and I have not been here since."

"How long have you been away?"

He shrugged. "Twelve years, perhaps a little more."

"Twelve years! It must seem a lifetime to you."

"I was seldom here before that. My grandfather sent me to
school in Vienna when I was eight. I returned home for holidays sometimes, but only rarely. It was so far there seemed little
merit in it."

"You must have had excellent masters in Vienna," I ventured.
"You speak English as well as any native."

He flicked me an amused glance. "I ought to. My grandfather always said any gentleman worth the title must attend
university in England. I was at Cambridge. After that, my
grandfather himself took me upon the Grand Tour. It was
shortly after that trip that he died."

"How lucky you have been!" I breathed. "To have learned
so much, travelled so much. And with a treasured companion."

"You did not travel with your own grandfather?"

"No. He was quite elderly when my sister and I came to
him. He preferred his books and his letters. But he travelled
extensively as a young man, and he spoke so beautifully
about the places he had seen, I could almost imagine I had
seen them too."

"You are growing wistful now," the count warned.

I smiled at him. "I suppose I am. The loss is still a fresh one."
I hurried on, impulsively. "And I am sorry about your father.
I understand the bereavement is recent."

He said nothing for a moment, merely drew in a deep, shuddering breath. When he turned to me, his eyes were as cold
and grey and unyielding as the castle stones.

"Your sympathy is a credit to your kindness, Miss Lestrange, but it is not necessary. I have returned home for the sole purpose of making certain he was dead."

With that extraordinary statement, he moved to the door in the garden wall. "Come, Miss Lestrange. It grows colder and I would not have you take a chill."

4

He left me in the great hall to find my way alone, and I returned to my room, followed hard upon by Tereza with a tray of food. I had not realised the hour was so late, but as soon as she lifted the covers from the dishes, the appetising smells pricked my appetite. I ate a dish of steaming soup thick with cabbage and noodles, and sampled a plate of assorted cold things, cheeses and bread and salads, with a few hot, crisp sausages.

When I had finished, I went in search of Cosmina again, but no sooner had I reached the great hall than she appeared, looking pale and a little tired, and full of abject apologies. "Theodora, what must you think of me! I am so sorry to have abandoned you. The countess needed me. She is resting now."

I waved her aside and reassured her that I had spent the morning pleasantly, careful to mention the count only in passing. But at the mention of his name, her face clouded. "I must speak with you, but not here. The countess needs her medicine from the doctor. We will walk down to the village together. Later we will talk."

It was all very mysterious, but intriguingly so, and I dutifully retrieved my stout boots and warmest shawl from my room.

"The steps are quite shallow, and the walk is a pretty one," Cosmina explained when I met her again in the great hall. She carried a little basket and had donned a bright blue cloak that very nearly matched her eyes. "There are still a few wildflowers to be found and there are rocks you may sit and rest upon." Suddenly, she smiled. "But I forget to whom I am speaking. You still take pleasure in your rambles, do you not? You were always the sturdiest walker in the school."

"I do indeed," I said roundly. "I cannot think properly unless I have had fresh air."

"Then let us be off, for you have not enjoyed Carpathian air, and it is like wine to the senses."

I almost agreed with her about the excellence of the mountain air until I realised I had not told her about my tour of the garden with the count. But I was not eager to introduce him into our conversation, so I remained silent and followed her from the hall.

We ventured out into the early afternoon, and almost as soon as we left the confines of the castle, a weight seemed to drop away from Cosmina. I had not realised how bowed down she seemed, how anxious, until I saw her pause and take a great, deep breath, raising her face to the sun. After a moment she turned and grasped my hand, and I fancied I saw the glitter of tears in her eyes.

"It is so good to see you, my friend." I had forgot how demonstrative she could be, and I withdrew my hand, but only after a moment, and gently.

"It is good to see you as well," I said warmly. "I have missed you."

"And I you. I ought to have written more," she said, her expression somewhat abashed. "But there always seemed to be something to do. The countess's health, the needs of the villagers, my duties at the castle. My aunt has given me copies of all her keys as chatelaine," she added proudly. "But it means I am often so busy between the castle and the village." Her voice trailed off. "Now things will be different, I know it."

"You mean now the old count is dead?" I ventured.

She nodded. "Count Bogdan. I must not speak unkindly of him, for it was he who permitted the countess to bring me here to live. But he was…he is not mourned," she told me.

I thought of this and of what the count had told me about his father. I thought too of the decaying castle and wondered precisely what sort of man Count Bogdan had been.

She lifted her face to the sun again, closing her eyes and smiling. "I do not want to think of him today. I do not want to talk about unpleasant things yet. You are here and the weather is glorious and all will be well, I know that it will." She opened her eyes. "It must be," she added firmly.

True to her word, we did not speak of unpleasant things, only the scenery and the history of the place as we picked our way down the mountain to the valley below. I had been so tired upon my arrival and the night so dark, I had not even realised there was a village tucked at the base of the mountain some little distance from the lodge.

We had almost reached the bottom of the climb when Cosmina ventured off the rough stairs and onto a little grassy patch thick with stalks of odd little hooded flowers that put me greatly in mind of monkshood. Cosmina drew on a pair of gloves and took a small knife from the basket to take careful cuttings from the plants.

"*Omagul*," Cosmina said happily, showing me the plant she

had found. "The proper name is *Aconitum anthora,* the healing wolfsbane. It grows only in the mountains here, and it is a true remedy for rheumatism and pain and it is said to strengthen the heartbeat. It is still in flower, but perhaps only a few days more." She brandished the tall, spiky plant with its rows of capped blooms with her gloved hands. "I have promised to bring some to the countess's doctor. He uses a number of native plants for his remedies."

We made our way into the little hamlet. It was scarcely more than a cluster of houses, bright as an artist's paintbox, gaily decorated with carving and pargeting, and each set apart from its brothers by a small patch of garden bordered by an iron fence and topped by a rose madder roof. A pair of the houses had been set aside for use as a smithy and an inn, their proprietors keeping living quarters at the back for their families. The gate of the inn was closed and over it hung the bleached white skull of a horse.

"To keep away ghosts," Cosmina explained, passing by without further comment.

Hard by was a tiny church decorated in the Eastern style, a firm reminder that I had come to a land once menaced by the Turk and ruled by Byzantium. It was exotic and strange, and yet the villagers might have been from any country, any age. They were dressed simply in long shirts of coarse woolen and linen, with high boots and wide trousers for the men and full skirts for the women. Their animals looked well enough, sleek and fat, and the people seemed cheerful and pleasant, calling greetings to us or accompanying their work with snatches of song.

But the further we moved into the village, the more signs of neglect I detected. The bright paint was weathered and in need of refreshment, and the road was dirty and rough. Even the little school was shuttered tight, the lock upon the gate rusted into place.

"The village children do not attend school then?" I asked carefully. I did not wish to seem critical, but it chafed that the children should not be educated. There were few things more precious to a Scot than a thorough education.

Cosmina kept her eyes fixed upon the road. "It was closed when Count Bogdan inherited. Perhaps it will be opened again. It is for the count to say."

To the rest of my queries—about the state of the road, the church that also proved locked and abandoned, the dry and abandoned well, the river meadow that flooded but might make excellent pasturage when drained—to all of these Cosmina made the same reply "It is for the count to say." I began to understand the power that he wielded then. He was a feudal lord in a modern world, the villagers reliant upon him as children for the proper management of their crops and livestock, the education of their children, the health of their bodies and souls. It was a weighty responsibility, but also a necessary one, and I began to wonder at the character of a man who could treat his dependents in so cavalier a fashion. Cosmina held great hope that the new count would effect change, and the villagers seemed to hold that hope as well. In any other locality such neglect would have engendered resentment and despondency, perhaps even rebellion. But here was only resignation to what had been and anticipation of what might yet be. The native temperament of the Roumanian was a complex one, I decided, and therefore interesting.

At last we walked the length of the little village and emerged into a narrow track that led into a wood. Closer and closer the trees pressed in upon us until we could scarcely walk abreast. It was shadowed and greenly gloomy in the little glade, and I was not sorry when upon reaching a little turning in the path we came to a clearing. Set within was a pretty house, old-fashioned and solid, with a steeply pitched roof dotted with gables. Ivy climbed the walls and smoke rose from the stone chimney. A little stone path led the way to the door, and I noticed it was bordered not in flowers but herbs, and each plant was marked with a sign neatly lettered in Latin.

"This is the house of Dr. Frankopan, the countess's doctor, a Hungarian," Cosmina informed me. She led the way down the path, but before she could raise her hand to knock at the door, it was thrown wide.

"Cosmina!" bellowed the bewhiskered little gentleman who stood upon the threshold. He wore a red coat fitted with bright brass buttons that gleamed almost as brightly as his eyes. "How good it is to see you, my dear. And is this your friend from Scotland? Of course it must be, for we have no strangers here. Except you, Miss Lestrange. The stranger, Miss Lestrange!" he added with a waggish smile, enjoying his little joke.

I returned his greeting, and he hurried us inside, taking our wraps and hanging them upon pegs, all the while keeping up a ceaseless patter.

"Ah, you have found my *Aconitum anthora,* very good, very good. This will be enough to see me through the winter, I think, so long as I am careful. You must go in, my dears, the fire is laid and Frau Graben was kind enough to send down a cake from the castle. You must share it with me. I hope the path was not too muddy—no, no, you mustn't worry about your shoes. The carpet is an old one and wants sweeping anyway. Go on through now and take chairs by the fire. I will come along in a moment with cake."

Cosmina and I took chairs as instructed and the doctor's absence gave me a little time to look about the room. It was comfortable, lined with books and smelling of tobacco and woodsmoke. There were cosy armchairs and a pretty bird in a cage by the window, and everywhere were draped little bits of colourful needlework, doubtless payment from the villagers for his services. I glanced at Cosmina and she smiled.

"I do hope that you like Dr. Frankopan," she murmured. "He is a very great friend to the countess, and has been so kind to me. We have worked together in the village, or rather, he has been kind enough to allow me to assist him from time to time. I would have described him to you, but there did not seem to be words," she finished, and I was forced to agree. She might have said he was elderly and bald as a baby, with bright pink cheeks and an enormous set of white whiskers, but she could never have conveyed the perfect amiability of his manner, the waggish charm. When she had spoken of the countess's physician, I had expected someone dry and serious, but Dr. Frankopan was like something out of a storybook, with his twinkling eyes and bright red frock coat.

Before I could reply, he hurried in, carrying a tray set with a plump teapot and a cake rich with spices and dried fruits. Cosmina attended to the tea things while the doctor poked up the fire until it blazed merrily upon the hearth.

"There, there, now we have every comfort!" he said, taking his chair with a sigh of satisfaction. "Now, Miss Lestrange, I do not detect the famous Scottish brogue in your speech. Tell me why that should be so."

"My grandfather was a scholar, sir, and born in England. He had the raising of me, as well as that of my sister, and while he maintained there was no finer city than Edinburgh to achieve an education, he was careful of his vowels to the end."

"Just so, just so," he replied, nodding. "And do you consider yourself a Scotswoman or an Englishwoman?" The question was an intimate one, and yet I could not feel the intrusion of it, so genial and open was his manner.

"Both and neither," I answered truthfully. "I remember no home but Edinburgh, and yet I am a person without a country at present."

"As I am!" he exclaimed, sitting up excitedly. "I have come to live here in Transylvania, but I was reared between Buda-Pesth and Vienna, one foot in Hungary, the other in Austria, and my heart in the Carpathians," he finished, sweeping his hand dramatically to his chest. "So, this we have in common. You must tell me more."

He commenced to ask a series of questions about Scotland and my travels and my perceptions of Transylvania, and so thorough was his inquisition that I was hardly able to manage a sip of my tea or a crumb of the delicious cake. But I enjoyed the conversation immensely, and in turn I learned that the doctor was the son of a noble Hungarian family, the house their hunting lodge. His elder brother was a baron and happy to leave the lodge in the doctor's hands while he lived in Vienna.

"And Vienna no longer entices you?" I asked before taking a hasty, stolen bite of my cake.

For a moment, his eyes seemed shuttered and his animation faltered, and I wondered if Vienna held a sad memory for him. But as soon as the melancholia touched him, he recovered himself. "Not at all," he said heartily. "I believe country air is necessary for good health. Country air and brisk walks, wholesome food and good friends. These are the key to excellent health, my dear Miss Lestrange. Besides, Transylvania has other attractions." He fell silent then, and although the topic of conversation wandered, he never seemed to entirely recover the high spirits of his welcome.

At length we finished our tea and cake and as we rose to

leave, he pressed a bottle upon Cosmina. "That is for the countess. Three drops in a glass of wine before retiring. I will call upon her tomorrow. Three drops, no more, no less," he said firmly to Cosmina.

"I shall remember," she told him.

He gave her hand an avuncular squeeze. "I know you will. You are a good girl."

His expression grew pensive again and we made our goodbyes.

"What a charming man," I said as we gained the little path through the trees.

"Do you think so? I have always been so fond of him. He has lived here for many years. He knew the countess as a girl, can you imagine that?"

"I wonder what she was like as a girl," I mused, thinking of the austere and remote lady I had met so briefly.

"Beautiful," Cosmina said promptly. "There is a painting in the castle of her and my mother, painted the year of their debut in Vienna. It hangs in the countess's bedchamber. I suppose she keeps it to remember Mama. I would have thought it would make her sad, but she says it is good to remember."

"Does it sadden you?" I had no such painting of my own mother and I wondered if my loss had been the easier to bear because I had no image of her face to mourn.

Cosmina thought for a moment, then shook her head. "No. It comforts me. I do not remember her, although sometimes I think she must have smelled of lilies, for she holds a lily in the painting. And it is only because of the painting that I know I have her eyes," she finished.

"And very lovely eyes they are too," I said, for Cosmina had fulfilled the promise of beauty she had carried as a girl. It was no surprise to me that the count would wish to marry her; the only surprise was that the betrothal was not announced. Was there some difficulty with the match, some opposition? But from what quarter? His mother was her aunt and guardian. Surely if she approved, others must.

As if intuiting my thoughts, Cosmina raised the subject herself. "I know you must wonder why no one talks of my marriage," she began.

"It did seem a little strange that I was invited to see you married and yet you asked me not to speak of it," I said slowly.

She said nothing for a long minute, then stopped upon the path to face me. "There will be no wedding. Andrei came home to settle his father's affairs and that is all. He has said he will not abide by his mother's wishes and marry me. It is finished."

Tears welled and spilled from those beautiful eyes and I felt suddenly, violently angry. How could he hurt so fragile and lovely and loyal a creature as Cosmina?

I put my arms about her. "He cannot do this. If there was a formal betrothal, then surely—"

"There was no formal betrothal," she admitted. "It was his mother's wish and mine. Nothing more. It was never fixed. We simply assumed he would wish to please her in this matter."

"But what reason did he give? Surely there can be no one more suitable than you," I said hotly.

She gave a shuddering sob against my shoulder. "No. It is not that. There were difficulties because we are cousins, but they are not insurmountable. It has been done before. He refuses because he did not wish to marry *me*."

I petted her hair. "Then he is a stupid, wretched man," I said by way of consolation. "He does not deserve such a wife as you would have made him, and I hope someone disappoints him as painfully as he has disappointed you."

She shuddered again, then lifted her head, and to my astonishment I saw that she was smiling. "Oh, Theodora. You think I am disappointed? I am *relieved*."

Cosmina fell to silence after her revelation, and resumed the walk back to the castle. I trailed after her, my mind working feverishly. I was grateful she had turned away, for I do not think I could have hidden the confusion that had come upon me. I had seldom in my life suffered such a rapid alteration of feeling. I had been angry with the count for his unkindness to Cosmina, and further angered with myself for favouring a man capable of such ungallant behaviour. And then those three words had changed everything. *I am relieved*. Joy, swift and savage, had coursed through me, and I had been shocked to realise that my first thought had not been for the suffering of my friend; it had been the selfish pleasure of knowing that the count was not attached.

We made our way back to the castle in comparative silence, first because the village was too close upon us to permit intimate conversation, and then because the climb was rather too arduous for us to talk with ease. But once we had gained the castle, Cosmina turned.

"I must see the countess. Come to my room in an hour and we will talk more. I am so changeable these days, I hardly know myself," she added by way of apology.

She left me then and I went to my room, unravelling the twisted threads of our conversation. Cosmina *had* been changeable, shifting between confidence and evasion during our walk. It was as if she longed to tell me everything, and yet feared to do so as well.

I washed my hands from the dusty walk and changed my boots for lighter shoes and neatened my hair. These ministrations took only quarter of an hour, and so I occupied myself with writing a letter to Anna, saying only that I had arrived safely. Any strangeness or misgivings I omitted, and I was struck by the dishonesty of my words. I told her the truth, but I concealed much besides, and I did not like it. But how could I possibly explain to Anna what I did not yet understand? And how could I describe the count when there were no words yet invented for such a man?

I ended my hasty scribble with fond notes for my nieces and nephews and took my letter in hand when I went in search of Cosmina's room. She had explained how to find it, and I had little difficulty. It was the ground floor chamber of the tower opposite my own, perhaps a little smaller than mine and furnished in a similar style, with heavy carved wooden pieces and mouldering hangings of pale blue and silver. I saw at once that the room was arranged to suit her favourite hobby and I gave a little cry of delighted recognition upon seeing the small frames upon the walls.

"Your silhouettes! I had quite forgot," I told her, moving at once to study them. She had been proficient with her scissors even as a schoolgirl, and her talents had been often in demand. Girls exchanged silhouettes with their favourites, but only if Cosmina consented to cut them. For girls she thought fondly of, she demanded little—a pocketful of candy or a length of pretty lace. But there were few enough girls she liked, and once she had made up her mind not to befriend someone, her resentment was implacable. It was one of the qualities that had attracted me to her from the first; no matter how wealthy or fashionable a girl, Cosmina could not be persuaded to friendship unless she genuinely liked her. I had taken it as a badge of honour that she had befriended me, and so we had sat apart from most of our schoolmates, I with my scribbles and Cosmina with her scissors, despising their silly ways and their irritating chatter. We had thought ourselves above such nonsense, and with the wisdom that comes with a few years and a better understanding, I wondered if we had not been frightful bores.

"Why, here is mine!" I cried, peering at the sober black image hung near the bed. "How petulant I look—surely my mouth is not so sulky as that."

Cosmina stepped close and looked from the silhouette to my face. "You have grown into yourself," she said kindly, and I followed her when she gestured towards a pair of comfortable chairs. One was a small thing, upholstered in blue and silver to match the hangings, but the other was covered in a violently clashing shade of green, a discordant note in the harmony of the room.

Cosmina gave me a shy smile. "I had only a single chair here, but when I learned you were coming I asked Florian to find me another chair so that we might sit together in privacy."

I was oddly touched by this. My life, as reclusive and quiet as it was, must be a whirlwind compared to the hermetic existence Cosmina lived. The castle with its ruined grandeur and magnificent setting offered less diversion than the small house in Picardy Place, I reflected, and I was suddenly glad I had come. In whom could she confide her truest feelings? Certainly not the countess, for if Cosmina had only meant to carry out the betrothal to please her aunt, the countess could not like any criticism of her beloved son.

I glanced above the mantel and saw a cluster of silhouettes—castle folk, for there were images of the countess and Frau Amsel and Florian, and I saw the servants there as well, Tereza and the pretty Aurelia. A little distance apart, aloof from them all, the count, rendered in black and white and no less arresting than the man himself. I longed to study the silhouette, but

I could not permit myself the indulgence, not with Cosmina sitting so near. I tore my eyes from the image and fixed them upon my friend.

"If you do not wish to speak of it, I will honour your wishes," I began.

She shook her head. "It is not that. I know I can confide in you. But I am so long out of the habit of revealing myself. I think I have only ever really been myself when I was with you at school. There I was Cosmina, nothing more. Here I am poor relation and nursemaid."

There was a note of bitterness in her voice and she looked abashed. "Oh, do not think me ungrateful. I know what would have become of me without the countess's kindness. I would have ended in an orphanage and then put out to service. There was no one in the world to care for me but her, and she has been so good to me. She always wanted me for a wife to Andrei, and I thought I must do this thing to repay her for her kindnesses to me, her generosity. I would do anything to settle a score, do you understand?" Her eyes were feverish with intensity and I hurried to assure her. I knew what it meant to be understood, to have a friend and companion to see one's truest self. I had had that with Anna and Cosmina, but none other.

"Of course. It must rest heavily upon your conscience that she has had the rearing of you. You wish to give to her in return the one thing she asked of you."

"That is it precisely," she said in some relief. "How glad I am you have come! It is bliss to be understood. Yes, I wanted to marry Andrei to make her happy. She and my mother are Dragulescus by birth, did you know that? They were of a lesser branch of the family tree, from a younger son who went to Vienna to make his fortune. They had money, but no title, and it burned within them to return to these mountains, to their home. When the countess had a chance to marry Count Bogdan and restore her family's heritage, she did so, even though she did not love him. I had heard the story so many times, I knew what she expected of me. I was to marry Andrei even if I did not love him. It would be the final link in the chain to reconnect the two branches of the family, and I was prepared to play my part. I studied hard to become accomplished. I learned languages and I learned to dance, to paint, to sing. And all the while I thought *I am doing this for him*. And it terrified me. I lay awake at night, wondering how I might be delivered, praying for God to show me a way to live here without that sacrifice." She gave a little laugh. "It never occurred to me that Andrei himself might serve up my deliverance."

"When did you discover his feelings?"

"When he returned home, shortly before your arrival. The countess expected he would come after his father's death for there was much to be settled with the estate. She hoped he would choose to make his home here. She loves him so and they have seen each other so little since Count Bogdan became the lord and master. He seldom permitted the countess to travel to Paris to visit Andrei, and Andrei refused to come here after his grandfather's death. It grieved the countess, and she has been so unwell. I had hoped Andrei would remain here for her sake, but it is not to be. He announced almost as soon as he arrived that he meant only to stay for a month or two and then return to Paris. He will take the countess if she wishes to go, but I think she will not leave her mountain. She has lost the habit of city life and would mourn this place."

"And you?" I prodded gently.

She drew in a deep breath, but she shed no fresh tears. The loss was not a painful one. "They spoke of it in the library one day. They did not realise I was in the gallery above, but I heard them. She demanded an answer as to his intentions, and he spoke plainly. He told her he would never marry me, that he thought of me as a sister, and could never think otherwise. She argued with him, but he would not be moved. He made himself perfectly clear, and there is no hope that he will be changed. And when they left the room, I sat down upon the floor and wept."

"From relief, you said," I put in, thinking of her startling revelation on the forest path.

"I have never wanted to marry, Theodora. I am not romantic, nor do I wish for children. I want only peace and quiet, my books and my music and this place. If I were religious, I should have made a good nun, I think," she added with a small smile. "I am not like you. You have always thirsted for adventure, for independence and exoticism, but I am cut of less sturdy cloth. I am a wren, and I have made my nest here, and I am content to be alone. Perhaps I might be persuaded otherwise for a different man, but not for Andrei. I can think of no man less suited to securing my happiness."

I chose my next words carefully. "Is there some flaw in him that makes him unsuitable?"

"I loved him once," she said simply. "I loved him when I came here, as an unwanted child will love anyone who is kindly, for Andrei was kind in those days. I saw him seldom. He was often far from home, but when I did see him, he was all I could admire. He taught me to ride and to shoot an arrow true enough to spear a rabbit and he gave me adventure stories to read. But then he would leave again and I was forgot, cast aside as he would put off his country tweeds or his Roumanian tongue. I was nothing to him but a pretty nuisance," she added with a rueful smile. "But as I grew older, I realised he was not as I imagined. I had thought him noble and virtuous, in spite of his neglect of me. It was only years later that I began to hear snippets of his life abroad, the seductions and scandals. I saw the countess break her heart over him a hundred times when news would come from abroad. There were duels and gambling debts and unsavoury associations. He has formed attachments to the lowest sort of people, permitted friendships with the scandalous and the insincere." She leaned closer, pitching her voice low, even though we were quite alone. "It was even said that he was cast from the court at Fontainebleau by the emperor himself for attempting to seduce the Empress Eugenie. He indulges in wickedness the like of which you and I cannot imagine. He dabbles in the dark arts and illicit acts. He is insincere and untrustworthy, the weakest vessel in which to sail one's hopes. He would dash them upon the rocks for his own amusement and call it fair. He is cruel and twisted and there is no good yet in him, save that he loves his mother and treats her with kindness. Be not mistaken, my dear, he is a monster. And would any woman not rejoice to be delivered from such hands?"

I remained silent during this litany of his evils, thinking back to his peculiar treatment of me since my arrival, his familiarity, his forwardness. It was not the attitude of a gentleman to a guest in his home, and viewed in the light of Cosmina's revelations, it sickened me that I had been so easily moved by his sophisticated little stratagems.

At length I was aware of Cosmina, watching me and waiting for me to make her a reply. "You are well and truly delivered," I told her. "And I am glad of it for your sake. One hopes he will discharge his duties by his people as their count. And when he is gone to Paris again, we will have many a quiet night to enjoy the peace of his departure."

The pretty face was wreathed in smiles. "Do you promise? You will stay, even though I am not to be married? I had not hoped my company enough would be sufficient to keep you."

"Of course I will stay," I promised. "I am quite charmed by the castle and the village, and I mean to write my novel."

"You will have all the peace and solitude you could want," she vowed. "I will leave you to your work, and when you wish society, you have only to find me and I will be your amusement."

We concluded the visit by making plans for the rest of the autumn and into the winter when the snows would blanket the mountains.

"Who knows? Perhaps the snows will be too thick and we will keep you here until spring," she added mischievously.

"Perhaps, although I think my sister might well come and take me back to England with her should I stay gone for so long." I brandished the letter I had written. "I have been here a day and already I must write her to say I am arrived."

Cosmina put out a hand. "I will see it is delivered for you. We may not have many of the modern comforts here, but we do have the post," she told me with a little giggle. I wondered then how long it had been since she had truly laughed, and I was suddenly glad I had come.

She sobered. "And do not worry about Andrei. He behaves badly, but I promise you, I will not permit him to harm you, my friend."

She looked stalwart as any soldier, and I smiled to think of her, fierce in my defense should I have need of her.

"You need have no worry on my account, Cosmina. I rather like to catch people behaving badly. It gives me something to laugh at and fodder for my stories."

She slanted me a curious look. "Then there will be much here in Transylvania to inspire you."

5

The evening meal was a more formal affair than I would have expected given the quiet and isolation of the castle. But I dressed with care in my one evening gown of deepest black, a slender ribbon of black velvet at my throat as my only adornment. I arranged my hair in the customary heavy coils at the nape of my neck, and as I did so, I thought again of the count reaching past me in the library, his warm breath skimming over the skin of my neck, his hands sliding over mine in the warm waters of the washbasin.

"Do not think of it," I warned myself severely in the looking glass. "It cannot be." Whatever my inclination towards the count, Cosmina's confidences had persuaded me he was not to be trusted, and I freshened my resolve to think upon him only as my host, as an inspiration for my work and nothing more.

The others, including the count, were assembled in the great hall when I arrived. I was pleased to see the countess among them, for her health must be improved if she could rise to dine with us. She was dressed in a beautiful gown of deep green velvet, a little old-fashioned in its style but still magnificent. Perhaps the colour did not suit her, for I thought she looked very pale, and when she rose from her chair she gave a little cough, then mastered herself to greet me.

"Good evening, Miss Lestrange. I hope you will forgive my absence today. I was unwell, but I am better now. Our cook has prepared her very best dish in your honour." I returned her greeting and nodded to the others in turn. She instructed Florian to lead me in to dinner. She took the count's arm herself, and Cosmina and Frau Amsel were left to shift for themselves.

"I shall have to acquire more gentlemen," the countess said lightly as we were seated. "Or the pair of you will have to keep a lady upon each arm, like Eastern potentates."

The count made some rejoinder in a low voice, but Florian said nothing. His expression was unaltered, and I was struck again by the aura of sadness that surrounded him. His mother seemed unaware of it, or perhaps merely reconciled, for she seated herself with a mien of pleasurable expectation as a dog will when it smells a bone. Whatever disappointments Frau Amsel had suffered in her life, she seemed to have consoled herself with food.

I glanced about the room, recalling the count's remarks from the morning's tour of the castle. I noted afresh its splendour, for it was the most luxurious and lavish room he had shown me. The walls were panelled in gilded wood and hung with enormous oil paintings in heavy gilt frames. The table itself was inlaid in an intricate pattern of birds and flowers with no cloth to hide its beauty. The chairs were of a medieval style, with lion's paws for feet and great high backs upholstered in scarlet velvet. A series of sideboards ranged along the walls, each more elaborately carved than the next with hunting scenes, and heavily laden with pewter and silver marked with the Dragulescu crest. Even the carving set was large in scale and impressive in both design and execution. It depicted a stag chased by wolves, a masterpiece of the silversmith's art. The lines of it were blurred by use, and it had clearly taken pride of place in the dining hall for many generations.

In all, it was a grand and impressive room, and for a little while it was possible to forget the decay elsewhere in the castle. The candlelit gloom concealed the tarnish and moth I had detected by daylight, and the fire burning in the tremendous hearth and the great dog lounging beside it lent an air of medieval grandeur.

The food itself was excellent, rather heavy and Germanic in flavour, but wonderfully prepared. The conversation proved less palatable. Frau Amsel did not speak, preferring instead to apply herself to the array of dishes set before us, tasting each with a resounding smack of the lips. The count seemed distracted and spoke little, and even then only to a direct question put to him by his mother. Perhaps there was an unspoken rule of etiquette, for I saw that the others did not address him, and as he did not notice them, they took no liberty to engage him. Cosmina darted a glance or two at him, her expression watchful, but when he did not speak, she seemed to give a little sigh and relax. I observed him looking at me curiously once or twice, but apart from that he seemed sunk deep in his own thoughts, drinking his wine and occasionally pushing his food about on his plate but eating little. The countess—who took only a tiny portion, refusing everything but a slice of roast pork and a warming plate of consommé—attempted to compensate for his silence by putting to me questions about my impressions of Transylvania and the castle itself. Her pride in her home was apparent, and I was careful to praise the natural beauties of the place. I remarked to her also that I had made the acquaintance of Dr. Frankopan and found him quite charming.

"Ah, Ferenc! Yes, he is quite a prop to me. I could not manage without him. He has known me from girlhood, and sometimes it is good to be with someone who knows one best," she told me. Frau Amsel frowned and studied her plate as the countess continued. "Of course, I have my devoted Clara as well. We were at school together, did I tell you, Miss Lestrange?"

She had, and I wondered anew how Frau Amsel had come to work as companion to her former school friend. Had the countess climbed so far above her raising or had Frau Amsel fallen so low? She must have married to have borne Florian, yet there was no mention of Herr Amsel, and it suddenly became clear to me that widowhood had likely reduced her circumstances and driven her to take a post in this remote and distant place.

The countess chatted on, mentioning a few diversions I might enjoy during my stay. "There is a passable inn in the village where you might take a meal. Florian could show you, some morning when he is not occupied with his duties or his lessons with Cosmina."

Florian had glanced up at the mention of his name, but upon meeting my eyes, he flushed deeply and fixed his attention upon his roast pork.

"He is a very talented musician," the countess explained. "He had just won a place in the conservatory in Vienna when Frau Amsel decided to make her home here. He was but twelve years old, and yet he had already studied for a number of years and was quite accomplished. He plays for me sometimes to

soothe my nerves and he gives lessons to Cosmina on pianoforte and harp."

"I am afraid I try his patience," Cosmina said with a graceful
drop of the head. "I am passable with the pianoforte, but the
harp makes me quite stupid."

"No, indeed," Florian put in hastily. "It is only that I am a
poor teacher."

I noticed then that the count was watching this exchange with
interest, his eyes agleam with speculation. For myself, I wondered at the capricious hand of fate in Florian's life. To have
secured a place in any conservatory in Vienna spoke to both his
talent and the habit of hard work. He might have become a great
composer or musician, playing to the crowned heads of Europe
or the crowded concert halls of the capitals. Instead he had come
to live in the distant Carpathians, put to work as a steward with
ledgers and books in place of strings and bows. I could not
imagine that his occasional performance for the countess or his
lessons with Cosmina could satisfy any artistic temperament.
Perhaps this was the source of his sadness, I mused.

With a start I recalled myself to the conversation and
Cosmina's protest that she was an indifferent student. The
countess put in matter-of-factly, "Of course you are stupid on
the harp, Cosmina. You do not practise. One must work to
improve oneself, is that not so, Miss Lestrange?"

I framed my reply carefully. "It is hardly fair to appeal to me,
madam. I am a Scot. It is a point of national pride to prize work
above all else, to our detriment at times."

The countess seemed intrigued by this, for she left off
speaking to Cosmina and focused her attention upon me. "And
do you work, Miss Lestrange?"

"I am a writer. I earn my keep by my pen."

The countess snapped her fingers and I noticed then the

jewel she wore, a great pigeon's blood ruby, shimmering in the candlelight. "Of course. Cosmina has told me of this. But I spoke of self-improvement, Miss Lestrange, not employment. Work must be undertaken by everyone according to his station for the development of proper character, but it is not fitting for the dignity of a gentleman or a gentlewoman to accept pay for his or her efforts."

"It is if the gentleman or gentlewoman wishes to eat," I countered too hastily, immediately regretting it. I was not surprised the countess believed work was vulgar; I was only caught unprepared that she should speak of such things so freely, and before so many of us who were bound by circumstance to make our own way in the world. And then I thought of her son, heir to a great estate but determined not to make a success of it, and I felt a rush of anger heat the pit of my stomach. I pushed away the plate of roasted pork, so delectable only a moment before.

But the countess, either from her own good breeding or perhaps an easy temperament, did not take offence. Rather, she smiled at me, a warm, deliberate smile, and for the first time I felt the strength of her charm. "Of course, Miss Lestrange. You speak of necessity, and I meant something quite different. Ah, here is Tereza with dessert. Miss Lestrange, you must like this. It is a rice pudding, flavoured with caraway and other spices. I would know what you think of it."

I dipped a spoon into the pudding and took a bite. It melted, creamy and luxurious against my tongue, the comfort of a nursery pudding dissolving into something quite exotic and otherworldly. What had been bland and uninspiring in Scotland here was mysterious and almost sensual. It seemed a fitting metaphor for the place itself, I decided with a flick of my gaze towards the count. I dipped my spoon again and gave myself up to the pleasures of the table.

★ ★ ★

After the meal was concluded, the countess's energy seemed to flag and Frau Amsel roused herself to overrule the countess's suggestion of an impromptu concert.

"You did not sleep an hour last night," Frau Amsel told her in a gently scolding tone. "You must be put right to bed. If you have a good night and keep to your bed tomorrow, perhaps you may stay up tomorrow evening. Florian will prepare something special for your amusement."

At this she threw a look of significance to her son, who responded promptly. "Of course, madame. It would be my pleasure. But I have nothing prepared tonight and would disappoint you, I am certain."

"You play like an angel," the countess rejoined. "But I will play the little lamb tonight and go where I am led. I confess I am just a bit tired."

She seemed nearer to exhaustion, for her eyes had sunk into shadows during our meal and her cough had worsened. She leaned heavily on Frau Amsel's arm and waved the count away when he stepped up to assist her.

"No, dearest. I have my Clara to help. And Cosmina," she added. "I think I should like to hear more of the book you began reading to me last week, Cosmina, if Miss Lestrange can bear the loss of your company." The countess turned to me. "I am longing to hear the conclusion, and unfortunately my dear Clara does not read French. You will not mind an early evening, Miss Lestrange?"

"Of course not, madame. I am quite content to retire to my room and do a little writing."

She nodded her thanks and we moved as a party into the great hall. Tereza and her sister appeared with candles for everyone to light their way to bed. I took mine up hastily, realising that the count and I should be left alone as soon as the others departed.

"Good evening, sir," I said, giving a quick nod for the sake of politeness. I scurried from the hall, but not before I caught his expression, mildly amused it seemed, but I did not stop to wonder why. I hurried to my room and closed the stout oak door behind me.

Tereza, or perhaps Aurelia, had made up the fire, and the room was warm enough, but I was too restless to retire. I sat for a little time in the embrasure of the window, watching the stars rise above the great craggy peaks of the mountains. One in particular shone with a brilliant silver light, illuminating the valley below almost as brightly as the moon might have done. I regretted that I had not thought to wish upon it, but no sooner had I thought it, than I heard a noise outside my door.

It came again, and I realised it was the sound of footsteps approaching. I moved closer to the door and pressed my ear upon it, straining to hear through the thick oaken planks. Another footstep, and this time I knew it was the sound of someone climbing the tower stair. I believed I lodged alone in the tower, for the family wing where I had later visited Cosmina was far to the opposite side of the castle. My fire had been made up, my bed turned down. There was no call for the maids to come. Who then approached, each footstep ringing closer upon the stones, striking with the same rhythm as the beating of the blood in my ears?

Seizing my courage, I grasped the handle of the door firmly and jerked hard, thinking to surprise whoever lurked upon the stairs. Instead I reeled back, startled to see the count.

He raised his brows. "Are you quite all right, Miss Lestrange? You look as if you had seen a ghost. Or rather, you look as if you *were* a ghost. You have gone quite pale."

I was conscious of my hand, flown to my throat, and I dropped it. "I am perfectly well, only startled. I thought I was quite alone in the tower, and I remembered the tales I have heard of bandits in these mountains."

He did not smile at this absurdity. "And monsters in the castle? There are no bandits here, Miss Lestrange—at least not the sort who would dare to enter my castle uninvited. And you are not alone in the tower. My chamber is directly above yours."

This piece of intelligence was both comforting and unsettling. Comforting because it was a relief to know that another human being rested within the sound of my voice should I have need of him; unsettling because it was the count. I knew not what to make of him, and as the only other inhabitant of this part of the castle, I fell even more within his power than I had realised.

Suddenly, he put out his hand. "Come with me, Miss Lestrange. I wish to show you something."

I hesitated and he reached further. "There is no call for reluctance. I was not entirely honest. I do not wish to show you something. I wish to see something, and I would rather not be alone. Your presence would be of service to me, and I think you are too gracious to refuse your host," he added with the slightest touch of imperiousness.

He waited, his hand outstretched. I thought of the revelations Cosmina had made about his character, his evil habits. I thought of them, and still I went, putting my hand willingly into his. His fingers clasped over mine and I felt a sense of completion, as if something I had not realised was lost had been restored to me. It was disturbing, for I knew my own intentions would be nothing to him or to me should he choose to ignore them. There was a powerlessness, a lassitude that came over me at his touch, and I knew it was madness to follow him.

But follow him I did, up the spiralling stairs to the upper

floor. We entered his bedchamber and I gasped aloud, for this room was handsomer than any I could have imagined. The furnishings were lighter than those elsewhere in the castle—more graceful, though still decidedly masculine. The great bed was hung with dark blue velvet spangled with starry knots of silver thread fashioned to mirror the ceiling, although nothing could compare to the scene overhead. Arching above was the whole of the night sky rendered in countless shades of blue and black and violet, shading subtly from evening through midnight and into the first light of dawn. Each of the stars was carefully picked out in silver and gold, shimmering to magnificent effect in the dim light.

"It is extraordinary," I breathed.

The count smiled. "This was my grandfather's room. He had the ceiling painted to commemorate my birth."

I must have looked quizzical, for he raised his arm and pointed. "This is the sky as it looked on the night of my birth. Each constellation, each star, precisely where it was when I first drew breath in this room."

I spun slowly in a circle, taking in the heavens arching above me. "How? A painter surely would not know the location of the stars."

"But my grandfather did. He made sketches and instructed the painters. Every detail was done to his exacting orders."

I would have marvelled at the ceiling for hours but he moved to a little door set within the panelled wall and beckoned. "Come."

I followed and we climbed another twisting stair, emerging into a workroom of sorts, fitted with a desk and bookshelves and a chest with great flat drawers for charts or maps. But the drawers were open, the contents spilling across the floor and the books had been dashed from the shelves, some of the spines broken. A variety of telescopes stood ranged in a corner, forlorn and forgotten, only the glitter of broken lenses betraying their wounded condition. The whole of the room was thickly veiled with dust and cobwebs, and the scrabbling in the walls spoke of mice.

The neglect was pitiable, for this room was far more decayed than any I had yet been shown, and the odour of mildew and mould was heavy in the air. The curtains hung rotting from their poles, the velvet shredded to ribbons.

The count muttered something under his breath, an imprecation from the sound of it. There was no light save the candle he carried, but even by that feeble flame it was possible to see both the decay of the room and his anguish.

"Was this your grandfather's room?" I asked softly. My voice seemed odd and unnatural in that place, an intrusion against an atmosphere thick with ghosts.

"Yes. He was one of the foremost amateur astronomers in Europe in his day. From this tower he studied the stars and wrote scientific papers. He corresponded with some of the greatest minds. He even discovered a comet. And this is all that remains of his work," he finished, his features twisted by anger.

His bitterness was not to be wondered at. I remembered the care with which I had treated my own grandfather's things after his death. It had been my last service to him, and it would have been a desecration to the man himself to treat his books and papers with disrespect.

"I suppose the maids did not secure the room and the elements and perhaps wild creatures have wreaked havoc."

He gave a mirthless laugh, scorning my simple explanation. "This is not the work of a forest animal, my dear Miss Lestrange. This was deliberate." His voice fell then; what he said next was barely audible, rendered in a harsh whisper and—I was quite certain—not directed to me. "You cannot be rid of him, even as I cannot be rid of you."

The remark was a cryptic one, but if I did not understand what had happened in this place, at least I knew why he had urged me to accompany him. He had feared this and not wanted to learn the worst of it alone. He had needed me, and I understood that he needed me still. It is a powerful and intoxicating thing to a woman when a man has need of her, and in that moment I put aside much of what Cosmina had revealed. His habits might have been unsavoury, but he was not so vicious as she had painted him if he still cared so deeply for a beloved grandfather's memory.

"It can be put right," I said calmly. "The books may be mended and the papers sorted. I suppose those are star charts there upon the floor. They want only to be pressed with an iron, barely heated, and they will come right. The curtains are quite beyond repair, but I daresay you can find others. As for the telescopes—" I went to them, peering closely through the gloom and picking carefully amongst the rubble "—this one seems to have escaped the damage."

I retrieved the smallest of the instruments and placed it into his hands. The lenses were unbroken, the body of the telescope damaged only by a single long scratch. He turned it over in his hands, his expression inscrutable.

"This was his gift to me when I was twelve years old. I never took it when I travelled because there was no better place to see the stars than here, he always said," the count told me, his voice low. He seemed calmer then, his anger banked but not diminished.

He glanced to the window, and the starlight I had seen from my room must have beckoned him, for he went to an iron ladder I had not noticed and pulled hard upon it. Satisfied that it was firmly fixed to the wall, he pocketed the telescope and began to climb towards a door in the ceiling above.

"When I have opened the trap, I will come back and help you up," he promised. I heard a great metallic clang, and before I could refuse he had swarmed back down, agile as a monkey, and taken my hand.

"Put your hand here and your foot upon this," he instructed. I did as he bade me—slowly for I was hampered by my heavy skirts—and soon emerged onto an open platform bound by a stone battlement that stood just higher than my waist. It was a precarious place to stand, for the tower's conical roof rose high and pointed from the centre and our perch was the narrow footing at the base of it. But it felt as if we had climbed to the top of the world, and I looked about in wonderment. As far as the eye could see, the dark shadows of the Carpathians rippled in peaks and valleys, shrouded in forest and faintly lit with starlight. Above us the vault of the cold black sky stretched to eternity, the stars scattered over it in thousands of pinpricks of light.

"I have never seen its like," I told him as he climbed up to join me.

He took a deep breath of the cold night air and expelled it slowly. His eyes were shining, his manner more animated and vital and yet more relaxed than I had yet seen him.

"You are happy here," I observed.

"As I am never happy elsewhere," he agreed. "It is my own private retreat. There is a trapdoor in each tower," he explained, nodding towards the towers punctuating battlements. "Originally they were put into place so that the watchmen could have the vantage of the highest point in the valley to keep watch against invaders. They are connected by a single walk along the battlements, and the whole of it had fallen into disuse until my grandfather. It was he who discovered the entire walk could be put to use as an observatory." He took another deep draught of the crisp air. "Exhilarating, is it not?"

He turned to smile at me, and I felt the force of his pleasure as a creeping warmth in my blood. I had never known anyone like him. He was so strange a mixture of imperiousness and informality that I could not understand him. But even if I had had the grasp of his character, still I could not have explained my own feelings towards him. He had only to stand near me and I was aware of him, keenly aware, sharp to any emotion, any shift in his mood. As for myself, his approbation, the fascinated looks he fixed upon me, the warmth of his interest, all of these effected reactions I was quite powerless to overcome in his presence. My blood ran hot or cold, I shivered and felt myself unable to move. I was restless within my own skin, tossing like a creature in heat, and it ought to have embarrassed me. Instead I was intrigued by these feelings and by the man who created them.

I should not have reflected upon such things in such a place with such a man. I ought to have stayed in my room with the door bolted against him. Instead I had followed him up to the ends of the earth and would have cast myself over the edge if he had asked it of me. I shivered in the chill of the east wind and he gave a short curse.

"I ought not to have brought you here. It is far too cold," he said, removing his coat and wrapping it about my shoulders. The warmth of it enveloped me, and the scent of it—of him—clung to the fabric, and later, I would discover, to my skin. It was a rich and sensual smell, like that of overripe fruit just before bursting.

He should have dropped his hands when he finished arranging the coat, but he did not. He stood, his body blocking the wind from mine, his hands twisted in the lapels of his own coat, drawing me closer to him.

"Better?" he asked, his lips hovering at my ear. I nodded and he stood and lingered a moment more beside me.

Suddenly a flutter of wings brushed past and I dropped my head, crying out.

"It is nothing," he assured me. "Only a bat, intent upon its nightly hunt."

I rose to discover the creature flying away, darting from tower to tower as it chased the darkness.

"Come," said the count, urging me forward. He pointed upward into the night sky. "That bright spot just there is Venus. Fix it in your mind."

I did as he instructed. Then he reached into the pocket of the coat he had placed about me to retrieve the small telescope. "Look again."

It required a few attempts to master the instrument, but when I did I was rewarded with the sight of Venus, fairly dancing in the sky above us, the brightest star in the heavens.

"Do you observe anything peculiar?" he asked. He stood behind me, still shielding me from the wind, and the air carried the scent of him to me.

"She is lopsided, as if a bite had been taken from her."

"Precisely. Even as she rises and seems to grow larger and brighter, she loses her roundness, forming eventually a crescent at her zenith. Galileo discovered this phenomenon."

I proffered the telescope. "Thank you for that. I have never observed the stars before, at least not with someone who knew them so well."

He took the instrument from my hands. "Now that you know where to look, you might even be able to determine Venus in the daylight sky. Napoleon did so once while he addressed the people from a palace balcony. He believed it was an omen of success for victory in Italy. He was quite correct."

"It is a harbinger of good things to see Venus then?" I asked lightly.

"Of course. The planet was called after the goddess of love because it was supposed to shine a kindly light upon lovers' meetings. I will show you."

He stepped closer and leaned near to me. "Close your eyes," he said, putting a hand over my face.

I complied, waiting expectantly for what would come next. My lips parted a little in delicious anticipation of the touch of his. I think I leaned forward just a bit, and even as I did so, he removed his hand.

"Open your eyes and look at me."

I did, surprised and disappointed that he had not taken the opportunity to kiss me. I was shocked at myself, for such a thing was not to be wished. It was inappropriate and unseemly and yet it was what I wanted above all things.

But if he desired it as well, he betrayed no sign of it. His expression was calm, his tone even as he explained.

"Now, keeping your eyes fixed upon me, look with the tail of your eye at the wall. What do you see?"

I strained my eyes, looking without looking as I tried to discover what he wished me to see. And suddenly, there it was.

"There are shadows but no moon," I said.

He gave me an approving look. "Very good. It took me quite a bit longer to understand when my grandfather taught me to see them. It is said that any love affair begun in the shadows of Venus will last an eternity, for it is blessed by the goddess herself."

I did not know what to make of this. He was both scientist and mystic, capable of blending fact and legend to suit him. But to what end? What did he want of me?

Before I could puzzle over him further he put out his hand.

"Come, Miss Lestrange. It grows late and the day has been a long one. You must be tired."

But as he helped me down from the observatory, through his rooms and to the door of my own bedchamber, I was not aware of being fatigued. Instead, I felt more alive than I had ever done in my life, aware of the sound of my own blood rushing in my veins. I might have tarried on the roof with him a hundred years and never slept.

And yet, when he had kissed my hand and taken his leave, I scarcely managed to wash myself and put on my nightdress before I fell into bed and dropped into a deep and dreamless sleep.

6

Through the next several days at the castle a pattern emerged, each day as like to the next as beads strung upon a rosary. Each day I breakfasted alone in my room, then passed the rest of the morning in solitude, working on my book. I wrote in the library, but the count left me strictly alone—to my disappointment and relief. Something about the atmosphere, charged as it was, gave a fresh fillip to my work. I had not thought to begin so soon after my arrival, but the setting was so evocative I could not help myself. I remembered too what Cosmina had told me of the count's plans. He meant to stay only a month or so, hardly enough time for me to take the proper measure of him. If I meant to use him as an inspiration, I had to begin, and quickly. Even with this determination, I found myself gazing often at the library door, wondering if this would be the day he provided a pleasant interruption to my labours.

But each morning ended with my collecting the sheaf of

pages into a morocco portfolio and returning them safely to my room before taking a midday meal with Cosmina. If the countess was well, we ate together with the Amsels in a pretty little room with views of the mountains. More often, the countess kept to her rooms and Cosmina and I were served trays in her bedchamber. We talked of many things, but the count was not among them. After her first outburst she was content not to speak of him, and I hesitated to introduce the subject. I could not trust my own emotions not to betray me, and I knew I could not confide in her where I spent my evenings, for they were always passed in his company. The household dined together formally each night, and if the countess was strong enough some little entertainment followed, cards or perhaps music. But even those evenings we spent together were concluded early and I went to my room with hours yet to pass before I retired. The count, whom I had come to learn was largely nocturnal in his practices, knocked each evening upon my door soon after we retreated to our rooms. We passed our evenings in his grandfather's workroom or, on clear nights, out upon the observatory walk itself watching the full moon rise over the valley. The count had cleared away the worst of the rubble in the workroom himself, refusing to permit the maids access to this most private of sanctuaries. The fact that he invited me there when no one else was granted such a privilege was not lost upon me, and as he conducted himself with propriety and restraint, I found myself increasingly at ease in his company. If his hand or gaze occasionally lingered a heartbeat too long upon me, this was countered with a seeming indifference that could only rouse my interest. Our evenings were spent in conversation that touched upon all subjects, and for the first time in my life I experienced the acute pleasure of being treated as an intellectual equal, for we sparred as often as we agreed, and I held my ground against him, frequently to his amusement, and always with his approval. I knew that he enjoyed me; I believed that he liked me, and the novelty of it was intoxicating.

I also came to enjoy the society of Dr. Frankopan, whose path crossed with mine nearly every day. He called often to see the countess and stay to a meal, and sometimes I ventured down to the village to accept one of his kindly invitations to tea. It was during one such visit, perhaps a week after I had come to the castle that I began to understand how deep the mysteries of Transylvania flowed. Cosmina had stayed behind to read to the countess, but I had grown familiar enough with the countryside and with the good doctor to call on my own. Usually we were alone, and I poured out while he sliced pieces of cake or cut bread and butter. But this day a dark, sullen lady attended us, and Dr. Frankopan introduced her as his housekeeper. As she passed me a cup, I realised her manner was brooding rather than surly, and the hostility she exhibited was not directed to me. Rather, she suffered from some calamity that worried her, for I saw that her nails were bitten cleanly to the quick and her eyes were rimmed red as though she had recently wept.

When she left us, Dr. Frankopan leaned near, his voice pitched low. "I must apologise for her, my dear. My good Madame Popa is very lowly at present. She has been at home these past days for there has been trouble in her family. Her husband, as they say in the vernacular here, has gone wolf."

"Gone wolf?"

He sighed heavily. "Yes. Poor Teodor Popa. He has done what so many of his family have done before him. He has taken to the hills to live as a wolf."

I stared at him, not even realising I had burnt my hand upon the teacup. I put it down hastily and summoned a polite smile.

"Forgive me, doctor. I must be very dull, for I do not understand. Do you mean he has gone to live in the forest, amongst the animals?"

"No, no, my dear. I mean he has *become* an animal. It is a failing of the men of his family. Some of them are perfectly normal, and some of them fall victim to this disorder or curse, I hardly know which to call it. On the main, they live as normal men, but once a month, they will take to the mountains to hunt and to howl when the moon rises."

I started to laugh. Cosmina had told her tales of peasant superstition, but surely this educated gentleman did not profess to believe in werewolves. "Now you are making sport of me."

But he leaned forward still further, his face deadly earnest. "I assure you, I am not. I am not. This is the way of these men. Many of them make good enough husbands save for the nights of the full moon when they must run with their own kind. But sometimes the lure of the moon is too strong, and they leave their wives and children forever, content to roam the mountains in the shape of wolves."

I gaped at him. "You are a man of science, Dr. Frankopan. Surely you do not really believe such things."

He shook his head sorrowfully. "Child, child, do not let your imagination fail you, for this is a place like no other. Perhaps I would not have believed in such things were I not brought up in the shadow of these mountains. The rest of my family live in Vienna, and they have all forgot the old ways, or they pretend to. They say it is nonsense and they will not speak of such things in Vienna lest they be mocked and ridiculed. But I, who have come back to this place and lived here for so long, I know the truth. The first time I was brought to this house I was five years old. My father wanted to hunt the bear and the lynx and the wolf. He gathered a great group of his friends and they went out together in a hunting party. The first night, they hunted by moonlight, knowing the great full moon would light their way. My father was the first to see the wolf, a tremendous, solid creature, high as a man's waist and with two red eyes glowing in the darkness. He fired, but the shot was a poor one, and it only took off the animal's paw. He ran off into the night, streaming blood from his wound and howling. The next day, my father saw the village blacksmith, his arm swathed in bandages, his left hand completely missing. It was no accident, my dear. My father had shot the blacksmith, for he too was a Popa, one of these men who ran wolf when the moon was full."

I strove for kindliness towards the old man and his fanciful tale. "Dr. Frankopan, I am certain your father did hunt a wolf, and that the blacksmith lost his hand. Who is more likely to lose a hand in the course of his work than a smith? But is it not possible that you imagined the link between these two events? You were a small child, such things would have impressed you. And doubtless your nursemaid told you stories of wolves to keep you safe within the house."

He smiled at me, then rose and took a box from the mantelpiece. It was a pretty thing, a fine example of the Roumanian carver's art, painted with bright colours. He opened it and withdrew something almost as large as his own hand, but covered in grey-black fur and crusted on end with what looked horribly like dried blood. The other end was spiked with nails, long and curved and black as night.

"A wolf's paw," I whispered.

He put it into my hand and I felt then the weight and the gruesomeness of this place.

"My father brought home the wolf's paw as a trophy. It has stayed in that box ever since, a reminder to us that in Transylvania, that which is impossible becomes possible," he finished in a darkling voice.

"But this might have been only a coincidence," I protested, even as I held the paw in my hand. It was heavy and real, but was it real enough to persuade?

Dr. Frankopan's expression was one of pity. "My dear child, you are a writer, a teller of tales. In this land, that is a sacred thing, for it is the storyteller who passes the legends, the storyteller who makes certain we do not forget. But to tell the tales, the storyteller must believe. Can you not believe, even a little?"

I looked down at the paw, the terrible remains of that long-ago hunting party, and I wondered. Was it possible? Could I allow that such things *could* happen? I had explained to Charles that the uneducated folk in the Carpathians held such beliefs, but could I? My grandfather had spoken of such things; I had been reared with tales of witches and selkies, mermaids and faery changelings. I knew that some people still believed in them. Even Mrs. Muldoon, with her stolid Irish sense, had put out a cake for the faeries on the garden step on Midsummer Night. How much easier would it be to believe in these wolfen men in a place such as this, where the howling carried on the wind and the forests pressed in about us, thick and black and knowing?

"I suppose," I said slowly. Suddenly, I remembered the little maid Tereza and the word she had spoken. "Dr. Frankopan, what is *strigoi*?"

He put down his cup and fixed me with a solemn look. "Where did you hear the word?"

"The maid, Tereza. She seemed to be cautioning me against sleeping with an open window, and she hung basil upon the casement latch. What am I to fear?"

The doctor gave another sigh and settled further into his

chair, looking rather older of a sudden. "I presume you know what a vampire is?"

I nodded. "Of course. Cosmina used to talk of them at school, and my grandfather was a scholar of folklore. He wrote a monograph upon the subject of vampires. I cannot recall to mind the details, but I do remember his thesis was that such creatures exist in almost every known civilization."

"This is true, this is true. And here, the word for such a monster is *strigoi*. There are two varieties, but the *strigoi morţi* are the dead who will not rest. Death has taken the *strigoi mort,* only he does not lie easy in his grave. He walks in search of blood, to take it and feed his monstrous need with a bite to the neck or above the heart." His eyes took on a faraway look, and I was not certain he even saw me as he continued to recite in a dreamy tone. "The *strigoi mort* comes at night to take the life of those left behind, of those most dear to him. He is immortal so long as he steals blood from the living. He is a monster, risen from the grave to take what does not belong to him."

"And the other form?" I asked.

"*Strigoi vii,* living men who have given up their immortal soul, either by choice or happenstance. One might be the seventh child of a seventh child, or perhaps have suffered the bite of a *strigoi mort*. These living vampires draw sustenance not from blood, but from the life force of those around them. A *strigoi viu* is doomed to become a *strigoi mort* after his death."

It seemed an impossible thing to accept. The stories I had read about these creatures had been unreal to me, no different than any other bit of dark folklore. Somehow even as I had lectured Charles on the subject, I had failed to grasp that these creatures were very real to the folk who believed in them.

"But vampires, Dr. Frankopan," I told him. "Surely they do not exist." And even as I said the words I heard the shiver of doubt.

To my astonishment, the doctor leaned forward and covered my hands with his own. "My dear, you are a friend to the Dragulescus, and for this reason, you are dear to me as well. I must care for you as they would in their absence, and you must be warned."

"Warned against what?" I demanded. I felt a little impatient with him now, and I struggled against it. It was not his fault that he had been brought up with such superstitions; indeed most folk had. Even in Edinburgh, a city that prided itself upon learning and sound common sense, I had heard of the ways of the peculiarities of the country folk and their odd beliefs about unseen things. How much more easily could they thrive here, in this fertile land of myth and magic?

He did not loose his hold upon my hands. "You cannot guard yourself against what you will not believe. There have been troubles here, long ago, but the memory of them is fresh. Should trouble come again, whilst you are here, you must be prepared. The *strigoi mort* is a creature of revenge, created out of the evil misdeeds of a once-living man. He will repay the slights suffered in life at the hands of his family by attacking them after his death. It is said the *strigoi mort* first works his evil in small ways, bringing bad dreams and rendering men incapable with their women. Then he begins to feed, first upon cattle, then upon children and youths, draining them of their blood. There is no mistaking the work of the *strigoi,* either living or dead."

In spite of myself, I felt chilled at his words.

"But surely there are rational explanations for such things," I reminded him gently.

"The explanation is evil!" he replied, dropping my hands abruptly. I noticed then that he had gone quite pale and sweat had begun to bead upon his brow. He wore his usual red coat with the brass buttons, and I wondered if he ought to remove it.

"Dr. Frankopan, you are unwell. Let me call for Madame Popa," I began.

He waved me away and drew a green silk handkerchief from his pocket. "No, no. It is only that I become too excited sometimes. Because I am afraid," he finished in a whisper.

I caught my breath on a sudden inspiration. "You believe it has already begun," I said.

He flinched. "Absolutely not, absolutely not. Do not even suggest such a thing."

"But it has happened before," I prodded.

He nodded, still wiping at his brow. "Yes, yes, it has. It was a dark time for us. It happened when the old count, Mircea, died."

"The present count's grandfather? When Count Bogdan became the reigning count?"

"Yes. I see you are well-versed in our history," he said with a ghost of a smile. "There was trouble then. Dark deeds were done, but in time all was made right again. The people began to forget. But I am afraid, now that Count Bogdan is dead…" He trailed off, too distressed to continue.

But I was too engrossed in the conversation to leave off. "What do you fear?" I asked softly.

He pressed the handkerchief to his lips for a long moment, then burst out, as if a dam had broken. "The *strigoi mort* is a creature of evil, of misdeeds in life brought to horrible fruition after death. No good man has ever become a *strigoi*. It requires a special sort of viciousness to cheat death," he said bitterly. "And Bogdan was the most vicious man I ever knew."

"You are afraid he will become a *strigoi mort,*" I concluded. "Oh, I see."

Dr. Frankopan replaced the handkerchief in his pocket. "I know you must think me a silly old man, a silly old man indeed.

But I have seen much in my long life, and some of these things I do not wish to see again."

I pressed his hand. "I understand."

"I fear most for the family," he said earnestly. "If Bogdan walks, he will destroy them. Just the possibility could send them into madness. The Dragulescus are, in the end, people of the mountain. They pretend to be worldly and educated, they want to be sophisticated, but the truth is they are no different from the woodcutter in his cottage. They will work themselves into a frenzy over this. Madness is no stranger to this family. It is a weakness that runs in the blood. If they must sit, waiting for this dreadful thing to walk among them, they will make themselves mad."

"So it is for Count Andrei and the countess you fear most?"

"I fear for all of them. Hysteria is a contagious thing, my dear. It can settle into a house like a disease and it will poison the atmosphere until none are left who can resist it. But you can."

He grasped my hands again, this time in supplication. His palms were cool and smooth, like new paper.

"You are not of this place. You are from the cold grey north, where common sense and order prevail."

"I am not so sensible as all that," I protested.

"You are a great deal more sensible than any of the Dragulescus," he said with a rueful smile. "I love them dearly. They are family to me as much as my own kin. But I cannot be there at all times to keep watch over them. You are the only one who can do that now."

I made to pull my hands away but he held them fast. "I am not asking for extraordinary heroics, child. All you need do is keep your wits about you, and if something seems not quite right, send for me. I have my duties in the village, and sometimes I am called far from home for my patients. I cannot keep as close as I would like."

I did not like the notion of spying upon my hosts for this man, no matter how kindly his manner. He must have sensed my hesitation, for he released my hands, and gentled his tone.

"I do not ask you to break any confidence or to meddle. I only ask that you be watchful, and that if you see something peculiar, you will tell me. Is that so much to ask of you?"

"Of course not," I said. "The Dragulescus are very lucky to have someone who cares so deeply for their happiness."

His plump face was wreathed in smiles. "How happy you have made me! Come, we will have another cup of tea and talk of pleasanter things."

I left the good doctor some time later, wrapping myself warmly against the late-afternoon chill. The sun had sunk low and I realised I must hurry if I meant to make the castle before dusk. I told myself I hastened because the dangers in the mountains were manifestly greater after dark—rockfalls, a treacherous staircase to ascend, the threat of wolf or lynx or bear. But the truth was that I had taken Dr. Frankopan's conversation very much to heart. Speaking of such things before a cosy fire in a snug cottage was spine-shivering enough. To dwell upon them on a dark forest path was quite another.

I hurried along, noting the scudding clouds lowering above the castle towers. A storm was gathering and I hastened still faster, chiding myself for tarrying so long at Dr. Frankopan's comfortable hearth. And with each step I noted the rising wind speaking in the trees. The villagers had fled for the safety of their houses, and though I could see the warm glow of candlelight in their windows and smell the sharp comforts of woodsmoke from their chimneys, I knew I had a cold and lonely climb ahead of me.

Just as I put a foot to the Devil's Staircase, I heard my name called, the voice carried upon the wind.

"Miss Theodora!" I saw Florian, scrambling quickly down the last steps of the staircase, relief writ in his features. I was happy to see him as well. Florian interested me deeply, both for his little kindnesses and his air of sadness. If Cosmina and I wanted to walk in the garden, Florian was quick to ensure that a bench was scrubbed and the path swept. If we wanted music, he obliged us, sometimes working late into the night upon his ledgers to compensate for these indulgences. He was a gifted musician, and whatever instrument he put his hand to, something quite astonishing issued forth. I had wondered how deeply he mourned the life he had not finished, but I had sensed in him no regret. He seemed to take a solid pride in his work as steward; more than once had we seen him buoyed in spirits because Count Andrei had waved a hand in assent when he had requested some trifle for the villagers that would ease their troubles. No, his sadness seemed to well up from within, as if his very core was fashioned of lamentation, and I had often wished for a chance to speak with him alone, the better to gauge his character.

He put out a hand to me. "We have not much long before the storm come down," he explained in his quaint English. "We will hurry. You are welcome to my arm."

I smiled in my relief and availed myself of his kindly offer. "I am very happy to see you," I told him. "I enjoy a good brisk walk, but I think this will be quite strenuous indeed."

He said nothing more, and neither did I, for the climb was indeed a strenuous one. Florian proved the perfect companion, stalwartly lending his strength when the pace proved too quick for me, and matching his steps to my own so that I should not be left behind. The sky had blackened alarmingly and the clouds were tinged with a strange, luteous light.

"It is raining hard soon, but we have been fast," Florian advised me as we gained the last turning towards the top. He looked up and nodded. "We may here rest a moment." He gestured towards a boulder set just off of the staircase path and gallantly placed his handkerchief upon it for me to sit.

"Thank you," I said, resting myself gratefully. "I do not think I have yet made that climb so quickly. It was very kind of you to come for me."

He shrugged. "Miss Cosmina worries. She says you are in village and I am to go."

And he had seized the opportunity to come alone for me, I reflected, wondering uncomfortably if Florian had developed a *tendresse* for me. He was always attentive to our needs, Cosmina's and mine, always within calling distance if we had need of him. That he might have formed an attachment to me was faintly troubling. He was a servant, albeit an upper one, and it would take dexterous handling to make certain he was neither embarrassed nor angered by my reaction to his attentions.

Deliberately, I diverted the conversation. "I spent the afternoon with Dr. Frankopan. He was talking of Teodor Popa."

To my surprise Florian responded with a grave nod. "Yes. He has gone wolf," he said soberly, as if commenting upon a spell of bad weather or the loss of a cow. It was nothing extraordinary to him, nothing beyond the pale of possibility.

"Madame Popa seems quite distressed."

He shrugged again. "She have many children. They have no father now."

"A difficult thing for a woman," I agreed. "Still she is lucky to have employment with Dr. Frankopan. I cannot imagine he will let any evil befall Madame Popa or her children."

Florian fell silent then, and I realised we had exhausted his conversation upon the subject of Teodor Popa. Were such things really so commonplace as to require no further discussion?

I chose my next words carefully. "And then we spoke of *strigoi*. He explained the difference to me. It was very unsettling. We do not have vampires in Scotland," I finished with a little smile of invitation. But he did not wish to converse upon this matter either, for his expression became flinty.

"There are greater evils in these mountains than werewolves or *strigoi,*" he said flatly, and it did not escape my attention that the sentence had been rendered in perfectly composed English.

I longed to urge him to elaborate, but he put out his hand. "We will go now. The storm comes."

I looked up just in time to see a jagged bolt of lightning shred the black veil of clouds shrouding the castle towers, and the rain began to fall. I put my hand in Florian's and we set our steps for the castle.

7

When we arrived in the great hall, soaked and shivering, Cosmina was waiting.

"Theodora! You are wet through. Come at once and change into dry things," she ordered. She led me out of the room and I looked back at Florian. He was even wetter than I, for he had tried to shield me from the worst of the storm, and I regretted stopping to rest upon the staircase. He stared after us, his face a study in misery. I called my thanks to him, and for a brief moment, a faint smile warmed his face before he turned away, sunk again into his sadness.

Cosmina hurried me on, pausing at the foot of the tower. She nodded towards the little wooden door I had passed so many times.

"We will hang your wet things here," she instructed, leading the way.

I stepped inside, catching my breath at the sudden gust of cold air. The room was unfurnished, the cold stone walls and floors unrelieved by tapestry or carpets. The only light came from the arrow slits in the walls, for there were no proper windows. A curious stone bench was set into one wall.

"This was the castle garderobe in medieval times," Cosmina explained.

She did not elaborate, but I knew that this room would have served two purposes when the castle was first built. A garderobe was a privy, but sometime in the mists of the past some enterprising soul had discovered that the resulting odours discouraged moth and the most valuable clothes would have been hung there as well. The iron hooks for the garments were still in place, albeit crumbling to rust. And the stone bench that ran along one wall was still partially open to the valley below, fashioned so that it would be easily sluiced clean from time to time, as could the floor itself through a wide square drain in the wall. I peered down the disgusting flue to see the same river view I enjoyed from my window. The garderobe was vastly colder than the rest of the castle, and I shivered as Cosmina pulled off my sodden shawls.

She draped them over the stoutest of the hooks and turned to me. "I will bring your dress to dry here as well. Your things would dry faster in your room, but here they will not spoil the carpet or be in your way. Your shoes we will stuff with paper and place upon the hearth."

I agreed, too cold and woebegone to care. She guided me to my room and waited for my gown before she helped me into bed and drew the heavy coverlets over me. The fire had already been built up, and Cosmina promised to send Tereza with a fresh pot of tea to warm me.

"You needn't come downstairs to dine if you feel too poorly," she told me, putting an anxious hand to my brow. "You are not starting a fever, at least not yet."

I smiled at her from my comfortable downy nest. "I have been caught in more rainstorms than I care to remember. Once I am warm again, I will be quite well."

Her brow was still furrowed. "I hope so. I would feel very responsible if you were to fall ill."

"Why? The fault would be my own for tarrying too long at Dr. Frankopan's," I said, feeling warmer and rather drowsy.

Her worry seemed to ease a little. "You enjoy his company, do you not? Such a kindly old man."

"Very," I agreed. "He was telling me of poor Madame Popa and her troubles with her husband and then we talked of *strigoi.*"

Cosmina's brows lifted slightly. "*Strigoi?* That is hardly a topic for pleasant teatime conversation. I hope he did not frighten you."

"No more than you did when we were girls at school together," I teased.

She looked a little abashed and began to fidget with my coverlet, tucking it more securely. "I do not remember what I said." She hesitated, biting at her lip, before bursting out, "I would not have you afraid here, Theodora. Whatever this place is, whatever walks here, I could not bear for you to leave. Not yet."

She seized my hand and gave it a quick kiss, pressing it to her cheek before she rose abruptly. "I will leave you to rest now. Forget what you have been told this day, and dream of pleasant things."

I longed to ask her what she meant, but before I could do so, she left me, taking away my wet gown, and I felt a delicious, creeping lassitude overtake me and I surrendered to the arms of Morpheus.

Dinner that night seemed a tense affair—most likely from the storm, which howled and thrashed about the castle—and I was not sorry to retire. As had become his custom, the count collected me after a little while and we retreated to his grand-father's workroom. A clammy chill had settled upon the castle, but he had built a fire upon the hearth, burning tree roots instead of logs. They were twisted, monstrous things, and I sat upon a cushion near the hearth to watch them burn. The roots looked like claws, reaching out in supplication, wicked and un-earthly, beckoning. Tycho had followed us and the great dog stretched out next to me, his head upon my lap. I petted him slowly, from the coarse fur of his neck to the silken ears that twitched at my touch.

The count lounged upon a sofa he had unearthed, a com-fortable affair in green velvet. He smoked a pipe as we sat in silence, and I sniffed at the air, taking in the sweetly pungent odour of ripe fruit. It was unlike any pipe I had seen before, and I noticed the ritual for lighting it was quite intricate.

After a long while, he saw that I watched him. "It is opium. Would you care to smoke?"

I shook my head regretfully. I would have liked to have smoked the opium, to have taken that sweet smoke into my mouth and held it on my tongue. But I knew opium dulled the senses, and it had become my practise to memorise every moment spent in his company. He meant to leave in another month's time and I wanted to commit every feeling, every sen-sation, every cell of him to memory.

He shrugged and tamped out the pipe. "You do not approve of my pleasures?"

"It is not my place to judge such things."

He gave a low rumble of laughter. "So primly she replies, all prickles like a pretty Scottish hedgehog. And yet you are not so conventional as all that, are you? There is more to you than meets the eye, or I do not know women."

"I am not conventional in all of my attitudes," I allowed.

"Propriety dictates I ought not to spend my evenings in your company, and yet I do."

"And to what do you owe such freethinking? Did your grandfather encourage you?"

I felt Tycho give a low snore under my palm. "He did, after a fashion. Mine was a unique education. I was left to my own devices for many years before I went to school, and he gave me free rein to read anything I fancied in his library. I educated myself from whatever books he brought into the house. I read philosophy, comparative religion, history, languages. And from all of these I formed the foundation of my philosophy as a writer, that man is a universal creature."

"In what way?"

I warmed to my theme. "All men, no matter their station or situation, desire to be fed and sheltered. Beyond that, there is a need for self-determination, to work according to one's interests and talents and to shape one's own destiny."

"Ah, the good American pursuit of happiness," he said.

"You think me naïve."

"No, I think the Americans naïve. You presume that all men are happier for being permitted to decide their own fate. I have seen differently. The average peasant in this valley is happy enough to have his roof and his bed and his full belly, you are right. But beyond that, if each was permitted to please himself according to his own desires rather than what was best for the community, what would happen? Suppose the blacksmith's son decides to become a poet. Shall we shoe our horses with sonnets?"

"I should not expect a man born to feudalism to see the merit in another system," I replied evenly.

"Indeed you should not. I am a feudalist—if there is indeed such a word—because I was born to be, just as the peasant in the field is born to be."

"And a man may not better himself, ought not to change his station with hard work and education?"

"God forbid!" he said roundly. "Miss Lestrange, it is perfectly well for the Americans to have embraced such ideals. They had a new country to build. Without an aristocracy of birth, they had to establish one of merit. But we Europeans have an older way—a better way—that has served us for two millennia. Would you stage a revolution to make us other than we are?"

"No, but neither would I wish to be what I am told I ought to be, a proper wife and mother," I said slowly. "It was the notion that I could decide what my own life should be that prompted me to leave Edinburgh, to make my own way in the world upon the strength of my pen."

He gave me a slow, warm smile. "You claim not to be a bluestocking, and yet I have discussed far weightier subjects with you than I have ever discussed with any other woman. I find I can speak to you as easily as I do a man, a singular thing in my world, Miss Lestrange."

"Are there no ladies of your acquaintance with whom you may converse about such things? No educated women from your own circle? I understood Parisiennes to be most highly opinionated and articulate."

"Not the ones who dance at the Paris Opera," he said, his eyes bright with mischief. "Serious women have always given me dyspepsia, but you are different. Somehow you say the most appalling things and I am intrigued rather than horrified."

"Do you not cultivate the friendship of thinking women?"

"What need have I for a woman who thinks? Ah, the hedgehog bristles are out again. I have insulted your sex and you will take up cudgels on behalf of your sisters! And yet, you must reflect, I keep low company. The women of my acquaintance are giddy, silly creatures, but not bad ones. They talk only of clothes and jewels, and it is enough to drive a thinking man quite mad, and yet I have come to expect that when I marry, it will be just such a creature, a woman who cares only for the next pleasure."

"I thought your betrothal was already decided," I remarked carefully. We had not spoken of Cosmina, I had not dared. But I longed to know the depth of his regard for her, whether he held her in esteem or affection.

He stared at me, his grey eyes wide and guileless. "Do you refer to Cosmina? Ah, schoolgirl gossip, of course. Let me guess, the two of you whispered into your pillows about me after the schoolmistresses doused the lamps. Yes, it is my mother's fondest wish that I marry Cosmina. But it will not happen," he said decisively. "There is no power in Heaven or on earth that could move me upon this point."

"Then you are not to be married," I said slowly.

"No, Miss Lestrange. I am as free and unattached as you."

There was something in his voice, some subtle shade of meaning I could not quite interpret.

"But how do you know I am unattached?" I asked, slanting him a mischievous glance. He need not know that I had refused Charles absolutely. Even Charles expected me to capitulate eventually.

He looked suddenly more alert and not at all pleased.

"You have a connection? Ah, I can see by the pretty way you preen yourself that you do. You are a woman of great personal attraction and a remarkable mind. It was stupid of me to assume you were not attached. Tell me about the man. Is he dull and predictable? Of course he is. I expect he wears brown suits and always eats his peas before his mutton and will not take port after dinner because it upsets his digestion," he finished nastily.

I struggled against the rising mirth. "Do not be so hard upon

Charles. He is a good man, and unlike most gentlemen, he would not object to keeping a novelist for a wife."

"Oh, Charles! Its name is Charles, how utterly predictable," the count rejoined. "But you do not deny my description of him, so I will take it as accurate. No, do not attempt to defend him. It will only make me more determined to dislike him. Come, Miss Lestrange, what are you thinking? Surely you would not be happy with such a man."

"I could be as happy with him as you could be with such a wife as you have described. It would be a very long life with nothing to discuss between you but the colour of the new drawing room curtains," I countered.

He shrugged casually, but his expression was one of pleasure. He was enjoying sparring with me, and for my part, I had seldom felt so exhilarated as I did in that small room with the cosy fire and the storm raging without.

The count parried my last thrust. "Any pleasures a wife does not bring to the marriage can—and perhaps ought to—be found elsewhere. A wife is necessary only to provide an heir."

"I begin to think that you despise my sex," I told him.

He sat up straight, his hand to his heart, the heavy silver ring upon his forefinger gleaming in the firelight. Tycho raised his head, then gave a snuff and dropped it to my lap again. "You wound me, Miss Lestrange! Nothing could be further from the truth. I adore women. I have studied them as deeply as old Dr. Frankopan has studied his little pills and potions. And like a true scholar and proper scientist I have even developed a Linnaean taxonomy for my seductions."

"I tremble to ask."

"It is quite simple," he said, warming to his theme. His eyes were alight with enthusiasm, his lips turned upward in amusement. "I have sampled women the world over, from courtesans to countesses, and I can tell you there are only three types of women who matter in a man's life—those he marries, those he seduces and those he takes. I have only to tailor my behaviour to become whatever the lady in question wants me to be and I am assured of success."

The air felt heavy within my lungs and something inexplicable began to rush in my blood. The conversation had turned inappropriate, wildly so, and yet I could not, *would not* put an end to it.

"And how do you determine which women are which?"

"Birth and breeding, of course. One marries a woman whose blood is impeccable because one needs her only for the creation of an heir. Nothing matters except that her blood is sound and her pedigree is good. If she has beauty and money, all to the better, but I have money enough of my own and beauty can be found elsewhere. Nothing but blood matters in a wife."

"And those you take?"

"The least diverting of the lot. Serving wenches, maids, village maidens, chorus girls. Any commerce with them is a simple matter of business, an exchange of services for coin. They may want it in the form of a carriage or a new gown, but make no mistake, the courtesan is no different than the innkeeper's comely daughter who tumbles any traveller in the barn for a piece of copper. Their commodity is pleasure and they are in trade, as surely as if they hung a shingle above the door. They may interest one for a night, perhaps longer if they are clever and well-trained. But in the end, they are tradesmen, and one cannot love a butcher for the way he cleaves the meat, can one?"

He stretched his legs out in front of him, crossing them at the ankle and folding his arms behind his head in a posture of ease. He was indeed enjoying himself, and for the first time I wondered if it was at my expense.

"The third class of women, those one seduces, these are by far the most interesting. Unlike the wives and the whores, these cannot be bought. They can only be persuaded, and that is the test of any gentleman's skill. They are ladies, but barely so. The governess, the poor relation, the novice nun."

"Surely not!" I interjected, but he held up a hand.

"I am merely quoting from the memoirs of Casanova, not personal experience," he said seriously. "But make no mistake, when one is not certain of the outcome, victory is much the sweeter. A man values what he has worked for, Miss Lestrange. Consider the hunt. When I ride out, do I aim for the cow chewing placidly in the field? I do not, and yet why not? It would provide good meat for my table. It would be fat and tender and keep me well fed. But I despise it because there is no sport."

He drew back his legs and sat forward, resting his elbows on his knees, fixing me with the intensity of his gaze. "But when I have been in the saddle all day, legs astride a fast horse, riding hard, sweating and cursing with the wind in my face, jumping hurdles and risking my very neck, I never know until the very last moment if I am going to be successful, if I will achieve my aim and bring home my trophy. I have pursued something wild and beautiful that will sustain and feed me and I am more a man for having taken it on its own ground."

My mouth felt suddenly dry and I swallowed hard. "You have indeed given this a great deal of thought."

"I take my pleasures very seriously," he said, leaning closer still. I caught the scent of him then. The smell of opium clung to him, not unpleasant, but primeval, like windfallen fruit on freshly turned earth. He studied my face, his gaze moving slowly from eyes to lips, lingering there as if to memorise every contour. It was a challenge of sorts or perhaps an invitation.

"Indeed," I murmured. "And if you assume a facade of manners calculated to please the lady, I wonder you are not unmasked and seen for what you truly are."

He shrugged, the wide shoulders moving easily beneath the excellent tailoring of his coat. "I am never with a woman long enough for her to penetrate my pretty deceits. She sees what she wants to see, and if she glimpses something underneath, she persuades herself she was mistaken. By the time she has come to realise her error, I have withdrawn from the field to meditate upon the pleasure of my spoils and embark upon a new siege."

He leaned nearer still. I wondered if he meant to kiss me then, but even as I parted my lips, he rose and lifted a finger in command, whether to Tycho or to me, I could not say.

"Stay there. I have something for you."

He disappeared down the little staircase and returned a moment later bearing a slender volume.

"Have you read this?" he asked, proffering the book.

I took it from him, admiring the beautiful gilt tooling on the soft scarlet morocco cover. I traced the title. *Les Fleurs du mal.* "Baudelaire!" I exclaimed. "I wanted to read this, but Charles said it was not available in Edinburgh."

A small, knowing smile twitched at the corners of his mouth. "I suspect your gentleman was trying to protect you. I believe he would say it is not suitable for ladies."

"That is precisely what he said," I admitted, thinking of the row Charles and I had had over the poems. The book had been published the previous year to both acclaim and outrage. "However did you find a copy? I heard they were seized by the French government."

He shrugged. "I know the poet."

I stared at him, openmouthed. "You know Baudelaire? What is he like?"

"Read the poems," he urged. "They will tell you all you wish to know about the man."

"I will." I pressed the book to my chest. "Thank you for the loan of it. I will be most careful."

"What a prim schoolgirl you are!" he exclaimed, but he smiled to take the sting from his words. "Besides, it is a gift."

"I could not possibly," I began, but he waved my words away.

"We have discussed my guiding philosophy, Miss Lestrange. I do nothing which does not give me pleasure. It pleases me to give you the book more than it would please me to keep it. It is a trifle."

"Still, it was kind of you. Thank you."

He nodded slowly, a peculiarly Eastern gesture of acknowledgement that seemed unique to the Carpathians. For all his Parisian sophistication, there was still much of the Transylvanian about him.

I rose then and he walked me to my door, Tycho following quietly behind.

"I will begin it tonight," I told him, brandishing the slender volume.

"I shall be eager to hear your thoughts," he said, touching my hand briefly to his lips.

"Do you mean to educate me?" I asked *en badinage.*

"No," he said seriously, "to corrupt you."

And with that he turned on his heel and left me.

Tereza had come in my absence to prepare the room for the night. A hot brick wrapped in flannel had been tucked at the foot of my bed, and a mug of warmed milk, laced with honey and spices, had been placed upon my bed table. I drank it off, feeling pleasantly drowsy and content and reflecting that there is nothing quite like a warm bed in a cold room to make one feel all is right with the world.

Burrowed far down into the soft mattress, I opened the book at random and my eyes fell upon "The Revenant."

Like angels with wild beast's eyes
I shall return to your bedroom
And silently glide toward you
With the shadows of the night;

And, dark beauty, I shall give you
Kisses cold as the moon
And the caresses of a snake
That crawls around a grave.

When the livid morning comes,
You'll find my place empty,
And it will be cold there till night.

I wish to hold sway over
Your life and youth by fear,
As others do by tenderness.

I longed to read more, but as I reached the last line, I slid regretfully into sleep. I dreamt, for hours it seemed, and in my dreams I walked the corridors of the castle, searching for something. But all of the doors were locked, and though I pushed hard against them and beat the door with my fists, none of them would yield. I began to weep and felt something soft against my cheek, taking up my tears. Hot breath rolled across my skin, and I bolted awake, suddenly aware that I was not alone in my room.

All that remained of the fire was cold grey ash; the candle had long since burned to nothing. But something was there, breathing in the darkness. It had touched me, and as I put out my hand, I felt rough fur.

I scrambled backwards across the bed. I groped on the bed table for a lucifer match and struck it. The light flared, illuminating two great yellow, lamplike eyes glowing in the shadows. I gasped and dropped the match, nearly setting the bed alight. I beat the single flame with my hand, and once more the room was black as pitch. I heard a snuffling sort of sound, and suddenly cursed myself for a fool. It was Tycho, doubtless accustomed to roaming about the castle at night.

I reached for another match and struck it, intending to scold the miscreant for frightening me so and show him to the door. But when the flame flared up, I saw that I was quite alone. The dog had gone, shown himself out, I thought with a smile.

But the smile faded when I realised that the door was still firmly bolted. The dog had disappeared into the shadows without a trace.

8

The rest of that night I slept but poorly. I banked up the fire and dozed in a chair before it, rousing myself whenever the flame burned too low to feed more wood into it. By the time the grey light of dawn began to lighten the chamber, I was numb with fatigue. Only then did I return to my bed and surrender to sleep. Some time later there was a sharp rapping upon the door. I stumbled to it, drawing back the bolt to admit a scolding Tereza.

She bore in my tray, and it was not until she left and returned with my washing water that I realised she was more annoyed at having to do her sister's work than at being locked from my room.

"Where is Aurelia?" I asked. I knew she would understand only her sister's name, but I shrugged my shoulders and made a show of looking about the room to convey the rest of my question. I had learned that Tereza had a few words of German, but not enough to permit proper conversation, and I rather enjoyed our attempts at pantomime.

She made a comprehensive gesture that left no doubt. Aurelia was ill, messily so, from Tereza's little pantomime. I made a face of concern, but Tereza flapped her hands as if the ailment were nothing to worry over. She uncovered my dishes and I fell upon them, suddenly too ravenous to attempt further conversation. The food was the same as it had been for the last fortnight, but the cooler weather had brought the addition of a bowl of porridge, called *mămăligă* by the local folk. It was tasty and well-prepared and I scraped the bowl clean and ate two of the bread rolls. A few cups of strong, dark Turkish coffee helped to clear my head, and washing myself attended to the rest.

The day passed quietly, for the storm held, and no one dared the Devil's Staircase in the heavy rain. I made excellent progress on my book, larding the tale with the superstitions I had discussed with Dr. Frankopan. I crafted a character based upon Frau Amsel, with a fondness for strong drink and hearty food, whose husband—like poor Madame Popa's—abandoned his family to roam the mountains as a lycanthrope. It was a horrifying tale, and I was enthralled with it as I had never been with my writing before. I had written pretty little horror stories to frighten ladies, I thought with some satisfaction. But now I was writing a book to chill the very marrow of the stoutest man.

I returned to my labours in the afternoon, and that evening, though the household retired early, the count did not come for me. Piqued, I took to my bed with the poems of Baudelaire, hesitating only a moment, for it had occurred to me to wonder if perhaps such sensational reading before bed had caused my unsettling experience the previous night. I read for only a little while before snuffing my candle. As soon as I blew it out, the room was softened by a silver glow from the moon falling through the casement, sometimes shining brightly through the broken storm clouds, sometimes covering her face with the stormy veil. It was the night of the full moon, the time for superstitions of the great and the mundane, the hour when werewolves are said to roam the shadows to feed, and an expectant mother must not go abroad lest the babe in her womb be born harelipped and dull of wit.

I slept fitfully because of the moonlight, dreaming of things I could not later remember. I heard a chorus of wolves, first a plaintive cry and then a response from far away, not the tricksters of faery tales, but the simple, slavering beasts that would devour the unwary traveller. I turned towards the wall and stopped up my ears with my hands, falling into a restless sleep even as I thought of poor Madame Popa and wondered if she heard them too.

The wolves began to howl again, just before dawn, and above them a high, keening wail from somewhere quite close. I came awake slowly, stupidly, surfacing from a dream. I lay still for some minutes until I heard the cry again and a commotion in the corridor. I rose and flung a coverlet about my shoulders.

Outside my door the noise was louder now, a terrible banshee cry I knew would echo in my ears so long as I lived. It came from the garderobe at the foot of the tower. I hurried down the small flight of stone stairs, stopping short when I reached the open door of the garderobe.

The small, icily cold room was full of people, all in varying states of undress. The count, pale and unshaven, wore his evening clothes of the previous night, his collar and neckcloth abandoned. Florian had drawn trousers over his nightshirt, and Frau Amsel and Cosmina supported the countess, all of them wearing nightdresses and wrapped in shawls or furs. They crowded around something huddled on the floor, and as I approached, they shifted enough that I could see Tereza, crouched like an animal over a bundle of clothes. A single candle trembled in her hands, the flame guttering as she swung it wildly in her panic.

The count took it from her and held it steady and only then could I see the pale form of Aurelia lying on the stone floor, her head twisted, her unbound hair covering her face.

The count reached out to touch the girl and her head rolled to the side, exposing the pale marble flesh of her shoulder and neck. Her nightdress had been torn, baring much of her smooth, plump bosom, unblemished save for two punctures rimmed by the dark, rusty red of crusted blood.

Pandemonium broke out. Florian groaned and Cosmina fell to her knees, crossing herself. The countess cried out to Heaven and Frau Amsel began to chant her prayers. Only the count remained silent, his fathomless expression unchanged in the pale pewter light of morning.

Tereza crawled forward to gather her sister's body into her arms. She keened over her, lifting up her sorrow in lamentation, until the count murmured something, urging her to come away. She raised her hand and pointed at the count, uttering a single word, pronouncing it as both a judgement and a condemnation. *"Teufel,"* she spat.

He took a handkerchief from his pocket and wiped at the spittle on his cheek. Tereza crouched, holding her dead sister and trembling as his cold grey gaze held hers. Then, with infinite calm, he replaced the handkerchief to his pocket and turned away. For a long moment the only sound was the rhythmic click of his retreating footsteps and the muttering of Frau Amsel's prayers.

"Miss Lestrange, come away," Florian said softly. "The countess will be having care of her."

Like a coward, I permitted him to lead me away. Tereza's grief was too palpable, a thing living apart in that tiny room, squeezing out the air until there was nothing left to breathe.

He walked me to the door of my room. "I will go back. Aurelia is dead," he said by way of explanation, and I realised the servant girl was now simply a body, a burden to which attendance must be rendered.

"Florian," I said finally, calling him back. His eyes were full of pain, and I felt a surge of pity for him, for all of them. I opened my mouth, but he shook his head to quiet me.

"It is not the time to make questions. Dress yourself. Someone will be bringing food."

Food! The very thought of it turned my stomach to water. I closed the door, shooting the bolt behind him. I had seen the marks upon the girl's breast, two distinct punctures, perhaps three inches apart. I had seen the bloodless, drained look of her. And I had heard the word Tereza had hurled at the count. *Devil,* she had called him.

I reached under the bed and extracted my boxes and began to pack.

Within a very short time I was ready to leave, neatly dressed in my plain travelling costume of dark tweed, travelling boxes at my feet. Frau Graben, the castle cook, brought a pot of thick Turkish coffee and some rolls from the previous day. She was a German woman of stout form and sober mien, and she did not tarry to gossip about the tragedy in the castle. She merely instructed me to dip the rolls into the coffee to soften them and apologised for the paucity of the meal. She looked for a long moment at the boxes I had packed, then left without a word, dipping me a sad-eyed curtsey as she withdrew.

I ate nothing, but fortified with two cups of the strong black brew, I made my way to the library, intending to speak with the count about making immediate arrangements for my departure. As I approached, I heard voices through the door, his and the higher one of the countess.

They were speaking in Roumanian, but the tones were impassioned and unmistakable, hers pleading, his implacable. I lifted my hand and knocked.

The countess called out sharply, and I entered. The count was standing at the fireplace, his hands braced upon the mantel, his head bowed. The countess was standing near him, her posture one of supplication.

When she turned to me, I saw that her eyes were glittering with emotion. "Miss Lestrange."

"I apologise, madame, I believe I have come at an inopportune moment," I began.

"No, I am glad to see you. Perhaps you will be my ally." She put out a withered hand and I went to her, suddenly sorry for what I was about to do. It seemed a terrible and cowardly thing to abandon my hosts when their household had suffered such a calamity, but neither did it seem polite to linger.

"Madame, I—"

"You wish to leave us," she said. The count's head came up sharply, but he said nothing.

"Yes, madame."

"Oh, Miss Lestrange. I must beg of you to reconsider. Selfishly, for I know these things must be strange and frightening to you. But I know what is afoot, and I would have you here with me for the battle we have yet to fight."

I flicked an uneasy glance to the count, but he made no move to respond to her extraordinary statement. He was pale, unnaturally so, perhaps not an unusual thing given the ghastly circumstances. But I was too wary to spare him much pity. As much as I fought against the notion of vampires and monsters stalking the Carpathians, there was still the body of that girl, punctured horribly and drained lifeless. And there was this man, whom the dead girl's sister had pointed to in accusation and called "devil."

As if intuiting my thoughts, he dropped his head again, giving a little groan of anguish, and it was this sound, this small animal sound of desperation that roused my doubts. Was it possible that there had been some horrible, tragic misunderstanding?

The countess gestured towards a chair. "Please sit, Miss Lestrange. What I have to say to you will be very difficult for you to understand. But I must ask you to remember that we are in Transylvania, and things happen here that happen nowhere else in the world."

"Do not tell her," the count put in. "She will think you mad. She will think all of us mad, and who would fault her, for we are."

"Andrei," the countess said sharply, "be peaceful. Miss Lestrange has a right to know what is afoot in this place. She has seen the girl and she ought to know what you are."

My eyes darted to his face. "I am no vampire," he said bitterly, his cold grey eyes locked to mine.

I dropped my gaze. There was no response to be made, not even an apology for thinking such a monstrous thing.

"No, Andrei is no vampire. But there is a *strigoi* who stalks this castle. He must be destroyed before he kills again."

I struggled to understand. "Madame, these things are impossible. They are faery stories, meant to frighten children and peasants."

"Was that girl frightened to death then?" she asked softly. "Because I do not think even Aurelia's vivid imagination could have punctured her neck and drained her of her life's blood."

"Don't, madame," I begged her. "It is too horrible."

"It is horrible," she agreed. "And it must be stopped before it happens to another." She turned to the count. "Andrei, you know what you are and you know you are the only one who can possibly put a stop to him."

He groaned again, something inhuman and protesting rising from his lips. So must Prometheus have sounded when the gods bound him to his rock.

"I cannot," he said in sudden anger, raising a fist to smash it into the mantel. A pretty little Dresden shepherdess went flying, shattering against the hearth. There were splinters of porcelain on the hem of my skirt, but I did not move to collect them. The statue was broken beyond repair.

The countess appealed to him again. "I know what this will cost you, my boy. I know the price to your soul to destroy him. But you have no choice. It is the call of your own blood, your own destiny. This is what you were born for. You are the *dhampir!*" she said fiercely, fisting her hands at her sides. "Even as a child your father knew what you were. From the moment of your birth, when he saw the caul over your face, he knew you would destroy him. Why do you think he tried so hard to destroy you? Beating you? Starving you? He would have killed you with his bare hands were it not for your grandfather's protection. And Bogdan knew the old man had kept you safe in order to ensure his destruction. Why else would he have desecrated his memory? Despoiled his very corpse?" She moved closer to him with each question, pressing her urgency upon him whilst I watched in horrified fascination.

She remained at his side for a moment, letting her words penetrate as salt into a wound, bleeding it afresh until it ran clean.

She turned to me. "Miss Lestrange, you see now why I need you. I have not strength enough to convince my son of his duty to this place, to his family. He is the *dhampir,* the only one who can send the *strigoi* back to the grave. He was born to this role, as his father was born to destroy us."

"You think it is Count Bogdan who has done this, who has risen from the dead and has murdered this girl?" I asked.

"Impossible," the count said, his voice strangely tight. His knuckles had turned white as he gripped the mantel. One of his hands was bleeding from the shards of the shepherdess and I was half surprised to see the normal crimson flow seeping from his flesh. He was mortal then, as human as I was. I sagged against my chair in relief.

"Then how can you explain this thing?" the countess demanded. "It is the curse of the *strigoi* to destroy his family. Bogdan was steeped in viciousness. He nursed every grievance, caused every evil to flower in his heart. He knew what he could become, and he welcomed it. He wanted to be revenged upon us all."

"Even if this is true," the count began, "and it cannot be, it is madness—why would my father wish to attack that girl?"

The countess's beautiful eyes took on a sorrowful cast. "You know why. A *strigoi* begins by feeding upon his own kin, his own child. No one who is linked to him by blood is safe."

"His own child," the count echoed.

"Yes, a bastard, but still his child. Aurelia carried his seed within her womb. Your father and I quarrelled about this before his death and he threw the fact of it in my face. He had got the girl with child, and she carried his son beneath her heart. Now Bogdan has begun his reign of evil by destroying it. He must strengthen himself before he can attack you. He will take others to feed his monstrous needs. Who will be next, Andrei? In this house, no one is safe. He will begin with his blood kin, but who shall be next? The servants? Miss Lestrange?"

I gave a start, but the countess made a gesture to soothe me. "Forgive me, Miss Lestrange. I did not wish to frighten you. But I know that Andrei thinks well of you, and he must be made to do his duty. Upon him falls the protection of us all."

I was startled that the countess knew of our erstwhile friendship, but I ought not to have been. They had always been close, Cosmina had told me, with only Count Bogdan's cruel machinations to part them. But he had not interfered with their letters, and although the count refused to take his mother's choice for a bride, he had to my observation always been kindly and even deferential to her.

I looked at the count to find his eyes upon me, no longer cold, but somehow pleading. He was trapped and something within him beseeched me.

"What is his duty?" I asked through stiff lips. "If this monstrous thing is true—and I do not say I believe it—what is it you are asking him to do?"

"You will be sorry you asked," he put in bitterly. "It is medieval—grotesque."

"It is the only way," the countess rebutted calmly. "There is a ritual for banishing the *strigoi* back into the grave, putting him to rest once and for all. It is best if the head of the family does it, and if it is done by a *dhampir,* then all the better. The *dhampir* is the chosen one, blessed by God with the strength to vanquish the evil that walks among us. Such men are rare, but they are marked at birth with a caul, the symbol of their destiny. Andrei is such a man," she finished with a look of pride at her son.

The count continued to look at me, his gaze penetrating. After a long moment, I spoke, slowly, cautiously.

"I think, if this thing will bring peace to the castle, if it will convince folk that you have done all that you can to lay your father's ghost and fulfill your own destiny as *dhampir,* you ought to do it."

"You do not know what you are asking," he returned, colour rising harshly in his cheeks.

I thought of what Dr. Frankopan had told me of the mental

weaknesses of the Dragulescus, of the superstitions of the peasants, and I knew for everyone's sake the sooner this evil was banished, the better for all concerned. "I know that you do not believe it, but what of the others? They do believe, and to them you are the only salvation. If you do this thing, you will have saved them from their poisonous fears. What harm can there be in giving them what they need?"

I stopped to give him time to consider my words. The countess was wise enough not to speak. At length he spoke, his voice cold and clipped.

"Very well. Tonight. The second night of the full moon. I suppose that is a good enough time to work this magic of yours, *Maman*. I will do it. Assemble the household and tell them my intentions." He turned to me, and his gaze was that of a stranger. "As for you, since you are so determined to see me do this thing, you *will* see me. You will stand at my side, and when the time comes, you will hand me my father's heart when I have cut open his chest. And then you will know what you have asked of me," he finished.

I had read of such things, but the fact that folk still practised such barbarity astonished me. I stared at him in horror, but the countess had folded herself onto her knees, tears streaming down her cheeks. She lifted her hands to heaven.

"May God and all His Angels bless and keep the last of the Dragulescu *dhampirs*," she intoned. She rose and lifted me into her embrace, her tears damp against my shoulder.

"There is no reward great enough for what you have done," she murmured.

The countess left then, leaning heavily upon her stick as she retired. I sank back into the chair, looking at the shattered shepherdess as the door closed softly behind her.

"I am sorry," I whispered. "I did not realise——"

He gave a short, mirthless laugh. "No one does. It seems mad that people can still believe such things, but they do. And the worst of it is they can make you believe it as well."

I said nothing for a long moment, thinking on what Dr. Frankopan had told me of the two varieties of *strigoi,* the living and the dead. I looked at the smear of the count's blood upon the mantel and thought of my first, impulsive rush of relief and wondered if a *strigoi viu* could still bleed like a mortal man.

"Do you really mean to leave?" he asked suddenly.

"Not before tonight," I temporised. "I have given my word and I will honour it."

"But still you mean to go," he said, his voice harsh in the quiet room.

"There are things here I do not understand," I began evenly.

He surged forward and took hold of me, his hands tight upon my shoulders. He lifted me from the chair and pressed me to the length of him. I felt the hardness of him, muscle and bone, through the layers of burdensome cloth, and a sob rose within me.

"You cannot leave me," he said, and then he began to kiss me, my eyelids and my temples, raining kisses upon me as though I were the most precious and sacred of things.

I put my arms about his neck and twisted my fingers into his hair, opening my mouth to his.

He moved from lips to neck to brow and back again, feverish and rough, his fingers bruising my waist. "You cannot leave me," he said over and again. "I will protect you. But do not leave me. Promise me."

He traced my lip with his finger and I tasted blood, his or mine, I did not know.

"Swear to me," he groaned, his lips to my ear.

"I swear."

9

The rest of that day passed in the same quiet disorder that always follows unexpected death. Meals must be got, floors must be swept, messages must be sent. A semblance of normality must prevail, and yet there is always a moment when one is brought up sharply, caught fast between the pull of death and the mundane demands of life. It seems gruesome to carry on as though nothing at all has happened, but perhaps it is that very act of carrying on that sees one through.

Such were my feelings, and doubtless those of others, during that long and dismal day after Aurelia's death. There was a sense that something had intruded upon this household, something dark and unnatural, and we moved through its shadows like sleepwalkers, barely speaking, making only a pretense at eating. Cosmina and I spent the day polishing silver in the dining hall, saying little, but glad of something to keep our hands busy. We had known one another long enough to sit companionably and not speak of the horrors we felt. But our silence was not entirely a comfortable one, for Cosmina roused herself from time to time to fret about the housekeeping—one of the spoons had been spoilt by Tereza and another piece had gone missing entirely—while I could not banish the image of that poor girl, lying white and bloodless upon the stone floor of the garderobe.

Both of us were sunk in dismal thoughts, and nature herself took some part in our deepening gloom. The sky had darkened as a fresh storm swept through the valley, raising the river to a tumbling sheet of grey silk over the jagged rocks. I watched it for a long while, thinking of the strange land I had come to. I thought too of Aurelia, carrying the old master's child, and I wondered how it had happened. His son was a handsome and personable man. Had Bogdan possessed charms of his own? Had he, like his son, practised the seductive arts? Or had he taken her, roughly and without kindness, the price she must pay for being a servant girl in a noble household? How had she felt when she learned she had conceived? Surely she had been afraid. But I had seen for myself the self-possession, the annoyance with her tasks as a servant. Had she felt herself exalted then by his attentions? Had she nursed the hope that within her she carried the last child of Count Bogdan and a possible heir?

There was much to ponder that long, dreary day, not the least of which was my own part in persuading the count to rise to his duty in banishing the *strigoi,* a decision I was deeply afraid I should regret before the night's work was done.

At the countess's insistence, Dr. Frankopan had been sent for, and Florian seemed relieved to be given the task of delivering the message from the countess. He wrapped himself in a long coat of oiled leather and took up a wide-brimmed hat, promising to return with the doctor before we dined.

In fact, it was long after the meal had been served and cleared that they arrived. They had been delayed by an *accouchement,* then later a rockfall upon the Devil's Staircase. We had not been a merry party at table in any event. We had picked at our plates, stirring listlessly the bowls of *mămăligă* and the cold meats Frau Graben had prepared. The count had looked at the food and shuddered, taking only a glass of wine. The countess had pressed her lips together and pushed her plate away, even as she encouraged Cosmina to try a few morsels. I managed a bite or two of cold roasted pork and an apple, nothing more. We moved into the library when Florian arrived with Dr. Frankopan, dripping with rain and bowed with the heaviness of the occasion.

Hushed greetings were exchanged, and almost immediately a discussion arose regarding what was to be done with the body of the girl.

"She has been put for now in the crypt with the family," the countess told Dr. Frankopan. "We did not like to act without speaking to you."

He nodded, his jovial smile absent for once. "You would do well to leave her there. If she is buried in the village, the gossip will only fester, and we do not want these stories spread abroad. One must stay out of the range of Vienna," he said firmly. "One must give them no cause to come looking. The *obergespan* from Hermannstadt would never understand such things. In his capacity as sheriff, he would launch an investigation, poking and prodding for every evil he could find. He is far enough away that if we can manage matters ourselves, quietly, tales of this may not reach his ears. Bury her with the Dragulescus, give her sister enough gold to stop her mouth, and let the dead bury the dead," he finished, almost angrily.

The count said nothing, but the countess cast an anxious eye upon the clock. "You speak wisely, Ferenc. It shall be as you say. It is nearly midnight. That is the hour this thing must be done."

The doctor spoke again. "I must ask you if you are certain that this is the only way. This ritual could cause tongues to wag should anyone from the castle speak of it." He looked from the count, who would not meet his gaze, to the countess. "I am the first to believe in the old ways, Eugenia, but this...to give in to the superstition of the peasants—"

"Our people," she corrected sharply. "The Frankopans have been here for two hundred years. The Dragulescus have been here for a thousand years longer. Who are you to say to me this is what must or must not be done? I, too, know the old ways, Ferenc, and they are the ways of these people, *my* people. I ask you here not as a judge but as a friend, because I am weak and old and I am afraid of this thing we must do."

She ended on a little cry—of rage or frustration or sorrow, I could not tell. The doctor bowed his head. "I am sorry, Eugenia. I only thought to speak sense and I have blundered. These are not times for friends to quarrel. Let us move forward as one and banish this evil from the castle together."

I said nothing, but I studied him, surprised that a gentleman so entrenched in the rectitude of the Austrian empire would take part in this medieval rite. He might claim to believe in werewolves and vampires in the snuggery of his little cottage in the woods, but if word reached Vienna that he had been present for the dark things we were about to do he would become a laughingstock, a figure of fun for the sophisticated Viennese, acquiescing to the ways of mountain peasants instead of dismissing it as nonsense and sending for the proper authorities.

But the more I considered it, the better sense it made for the doctor to participate in the ritual of banishment. It was a small village; it was entirely possible the peasants would begin to speculate about what had happened to Aurelia. I had learned from Frau Graben that the girls had no kin in the little hamlet, but these villagers were like those in any small town anywhere in the world. They gossiped, and clacking tongues could raise unrest. Dr. Frankopan was doubtless right to worry that the story of a *strigoi* at the castle would spread and fear would infect the peasants. But the deeds of this night could well assuage those fears and put the stories of a revenant to rest. There were few educated folk in the district from what I had gleaned. Once word passed among them that the doctor had sanctified the ceremony with his presence and that the count had cast out the murderous vampire, the valley-dwellers would be calmed and there would be very few to question whether a vampire had actually killed Aurelia. The castle folk seemed to take it as fact that old Count Bogdan had destroyed his paramour, and I realised that, surrounded by such conviction, it would not be long before I, too, was swayed into believing that some supernatural agency had committed this murder. It seemed so impossible that anyone else would have a cause to kill her, I reasoned, but the alternative—that a vampire had attacked her—seemed too fantastical to be believed.

And yet. People did believe it, I saw, looking about the room. Fear hung there, sour as old sweat, thickening the air. They were afraid, each of them—Florian, his hair still damp from the journey, his cheeks pale and hollow with black crescents shadowing his eyes; Cosmina, her hands twisting a handkerchief until it fell to bits in her fingers, her thumbs bitten and bleeding; the countess, on the verge of collapse, her face a mask of grim determination to do what duty demanded of her even as she worried her rosary beads. And Clara, stoic and dry-eyed next to her mistress, but her knuckles white with strain as she gripped her skirts. Then the good Dr. Frankopan, quietly sorrowful, wishing not to believe and yet conceding as we exchanged silent glances that it was just possible. And the count, his jaw set as he caught his cheek between his teeth, biting it, perhaps so he would not speak out even now.

Yes, fear was present in that room, and as my gaze fell to the rosary clutched in the countess's hands, I understood why. The Christian faith, Roman and Orthodox alike, teaches that there are unseen worlds, that good and evil must exist together. If there is heaven and all its joys, must there not also be hell and all its torments? For every angel borne aloft on feathered wings, there must be something else, dark and loathsome, feeding upon fear and gorging itself upon destruction. Light and dark, good and evil, angel and demon. Two halves of a darkling moon. If we believed in the comforts of the one, we must believe in the terrors of the other. Perhaps the only thing that saved me from madness that night was that I did not believe in anything. I carried no faith in my heart, only questions, and in the end, it was the questions that saved me.

When the three-quarter hour chimed, the countess led the way to the great hall where Frau Graben was waiting. I was not surprised to see that Tereza kept to her room. There was no place for her here. The cook lit candles for each of us, thick church tapers smelling sweetly of beeswax. Gravely, Cosmina gave them out, keeping back one for herself. We stood in a circle, resembling nothing so much as some unholy coven as the candlelight played off our faces, throwing them into sinister half shadows.

The countess looked around the circle. "My friends, what we do this night is done to save the lives of those present and those not yet in danger. We do not do this lightly or easily, for it is a very old magic and it is a dangerous thing to force a *strigoi* back into the grave. If any of your hearts are not strong enough for this battle, you must stay behind, for I will not risk the lives of those who are so dear to me."

She paused to look around the circle again, lingering on each of our faces, her expression one of sorrowful benediction. "Very well. Then I will pray to the good God who protects us all to lend us His strength and that of His Angels and saints and to help us do this thing that we must. Come now, my friends, and let us hope we will live to see the dawn."

The words chilled me and the others too, I think, for I saw Cosmina shudder, and Florian crossed himself quickly. The countess led the way to a tapestry hanging upon the wall, a scene of the seductions of Jupiter stitched in silks. Florian stepped forward to wrestle the great panel aside. Behind the tapestry was a stout wooden door, and beyond that descended a stone staircase, wide enough to admit four men walking abreast. As we descended, the air grew quite dank and chill, and I shivered, as much from foreboding as the cold.

After several turnings, the staircase led us into an antechamber that opened into a wide room. It was fashioned of plain, heavy slabs of grey stone and looked as if it had stood for a thousand years—which it might well have, I thought, remembering the countess's words to Dr. Frankopan. The ceiling over our heads was vaulted, the ribs ending in stout columns that punctuated the space. At one end was a high stone altar, the family chapel, I realised.

I stepped towards the altar, marveling at the detail. It was carved into intricate scenes and behind it was hung a triptych of Orthodox icons, heavily gilded and looking mournfully down from thick gilt frames.

To my surprise, the countess did not stop at the altar but proceeded to an iron door set behind it. In the stone lintel was carved a motto, so faint I could scarcely make it out: *Non omnis moriar.* I shall not wholly die. A horribly apt sentiment, given what we meant to do.

The countess paused at the iron door, stepping aside and bowing her head to her son—son no longer, for it was apparent that she honoured him in his role of *dhampir.* The count moved forward, steeling himself visibly. He opened the iron door, and it swung back silently upon its hinges. I would have expected a groan of protest, but the silence was more unsettling, as if the crypt itself beckoned in mute invitation. The rest of us followed in turn, passing through the door and descending a wide, shallow stone stair.

Unbidden, the lines of Byron's poem "The Giaour" sprang to mind, each syllable marking another step as we ventured deeper into the crypt:

> *But first, on earth as vampire sent*
> *Thy corse shall from its tomb be rent;*
> *Then ghastly haunt thy native place,*
> *And suck the blood from all thy race.*

The air was thicker here, smelling of mould and wet stone and incense. This chamber had clearly been cut into the heart of the mountain, and at the very back of the room the wall was composed of the living rock of the Carpathians. Into the other walls were recesses of stone shelves, and upon each of these rested a stone coffin, some with elaborately carved effigies, some with simple entablatures. In one discreet spot a body had been placed, wrapped in linen and crowned with a coronet of basil. Aurelia, resting forever amongst the bones of the long-dead Dragulescus.

I shuddered and turned my attention to the centre of the

chamber. There, on a bier of intricately carved stone stood a newer coffin of polished black wood. The lid had been removed, and inside I could see a shroud of white linen, a mouldering wreath of lilies resting atop. Candles had been fixed into iron holders in the walls, and a small table had been laid with a snowy white cloth and a collection of oddments including a sharp-bladed knife and a long wooden stake. A small brazier stood in the corner, sending up puffs of sweet, heady smoke, making the atmosphere close.

Without design, we circled around the coffin, the count at the head, I at his right hand. The count bowed his head and stood silently for a long moment. I felt the chill of the stone creeping through the thin soles of my shoes, reaching upward along my flesh with cold fingers. At length he lifted his head and said, his voice low and resolute, "We begin with a chant, to force the *strigoi* back to eternity."

He began to chant then and we, one by one, took it up, intoning the words in Roumanian. I did not understand them, but it was simple enough to guess their meaning. It was a charm of banishing, a spell chanted to cast Count Bogdan from this place. We began to chant faster and faster and at a gesture from the count, we moved widdershins, walking three times anticlockwise around the corpse of his father—still lying immobile under its veil of purest white.

After we had circled the third time, we halted, warmer now and flushed from the movement, our clothes untidy and our hair disheveled. We looked like pagan revelers, and I was struck by the knowledge that we were performing a ceremony that had been unchanged for centuries, conjuring some benign magic to aid our purpose.

Just then the count reached out and dashed the wreath of lilies from his father's body. It fell at Cosmina's hem but she did not look down. Then, pausing only a moment, the count took up the corners of the linen shroud. I half expected him to whisk it aside like a conjurer's cape, but he did not. He drew it back slowly, the linen folds retreating from the body like some pale sea leaving the shore. Slowly, inch by inch, the body was revealed to us. He was unveiled like a bride, but what lay underneath was no blooming virgin, and neither was it a proper corpse.

The count pulled the last fold of linen free and someone gasped. Someone else cried out, and at least one person invoked the mercy of God upon us.

Old Count Bogdan, twelve weeks dead and lying in a damp coffin, who ought to have been reduced to scraps of flesh clinging to ivory bone, was fully intact. His cheeks were plump and rosy, his belly round. And at his mouth were the fresh ruddy drops of blood just like those I had seen at the wounds upon Aurelia's pale breast.

Cosmina had closed her eyes tightly, clutching at Florian's hand, but I looked over the corpse carefully, taking in the gruesome details. His features were not unlike his son's, strongly marked and with a certain symmetry that even Praxiteles would have admired. Even in death he was not entirely uncomely, although his condition was clearly degraded from the handsomeness he must have enjoyed in life. His cheeks, at one time apparently clean-shaven, were roughened with a fresh growth of whiskers, and his nails were long and sharp. The mouth was pulled into a horrible rictus of amusement.

Just then, the countess gave a wheezing gasp and I looked to where her glance fell, just below the count's waist.

"Impossible," I heard Clara Amsel whisper in horror. But the sign of arousal was unmistakable. The dead count bore all the traces of a man not only alive in some fashion, but subject to the baser passions.

Count Andrei's complexion was flushed, the blood beating in his cheeks, and I realised he was deeply angry. "Let us proceed," he commanded harshly.

Frau Graben stepped forward and gathered up an armful of basil, handing the branches round as Frau Amsel followed with a bowl of holy water. One by one we dipped our branches in the water, holding them for a sign from the count.

When Frau Graben and Frau Amsel had resumed their places, he raised his own branch high and we did the same, as if he were a priest presiding over his congregants. We shook the holy water onto the corpse, sacred rain to banish the evil.

Cosmina was weeping openly now, and Florian stood at her side, murmuring words of comfort as we continued to sprinkle the corpse with our makeshift aspergilla. Some of the water fell upon the brazier, and the room filled with hissing as if from a hundred snakes.

When the blessing was concluded, we each put our basil upon the little fire on the brazier, piling them up until the sweet-smelling smoke filled the chamber.

The count hesitated then, looking sharply at his mother. She gave him a slow, sober nod of assent and he took up a knife from the little table. I realised with a quickening of my pulses that the terrible thing he had alluded to in the library was upon us.

With a swift motion of the sharp blade he flicked aside his father's clothes, cutting easily through waistcoat, shirt and undershirt. The belly of the revenant was taut and round as if he had just fed, the flesh pale but seemingly flushed with life.

The count put the tip of his knife to his father's breastbone and began to cut. As soon as the blade pierced the flesh, Cosmina, overcome by the horror, crumpled to the floor.

At once, the solemnity of the ceremony was broken as she was attended to. Frau Amsel loosened her bodice, Florian fanned her with a handkerchief, and the doctor retrieved a flask of brandy from his coat pocket to revive her.

I looked to the count, his hand still poised atop his blade, his father's flesh gaping in the small wound he had made.

"No more," he said in disgust, flinging the knife down into the coffin. He retrieved the linen shroud and covered his father's body. Cosmina had regained her senses and was sitting upon the floor, resting her head against Frau Amsel's breast.

The countess started forward towards the count, brandishing her walking stick. "You cannot stop now. You must finish. The ceremony is not complete."

The count put up a hand in a gesture as commanding as any warlord in battle. "I am done with this. It is barbaric and medieval and I will not do it."

Her eyes were wide and piercing in the gloom of the crypt, her skin ghostly pale in the shifting shadows. "You must. If you do not finish it, he will kill us all. Is that what you want?"

The count fixed her with an anguished stare, imploring, and when he spoke it was as her son and not the *dhampir*. "I will not do it."

She took up the great wooden stake that had been prepared. "If you will not remove his heart, at least ensure he cannot rise again," she begged. "It may save us yet, my son."

The count hesitated, his reason clearly warring with his sense of obligation. His eyes dropped to the shrouded figure in the coffin. Perhaps the thought of the fresh blood at the lips convinced him. Perhaps it was nothing more than a desire to keep the peace. Whatever moved him, he said nothing.

He took the stake from her and the mallet from the table. Standing over his father's corpse, he drew back the veil once more. He poised the point of the stake just where the knife had opened the flesh of the chest. With one great stroke, he penetrated the ribs, spreading them apart and puncturing the heart. As he did so, a deep, rattling groan sounded from the body, echoing through the crypt.

Cosmina screamed and Frau Graben averted her face. Clara crossed herself and began to chant the rosary. The countess gave a deep sigh of pained satisfaction, and Florian looked as if he were about to be sick. Only the doctor, who had doubtless seen worse in his labours, remained unmoved.

As the count struck again, forcing the stake further into the heart, a great well of dark blood bubbled forth, spewing from the wound and from the lips and nose of the corpse, bracketing his teeth in gore. The blood spilled down his chin, staining his collar and the pillow beneath him. After a moment, the flow was staunched and the corpse seemed to settle with one last shudder.

"It is done," the count said with an air of terrible finality. He dropped the mallet upon the floor, and for a moment, the ringing of it against the stone was the only sound.

The count motioned for his candle and I passed it back to him. He blew it out and dropped it to the floor. The rest of us did likewise. We moved slowly out of the crypt.

I heard the countess murmur to Clara, "I only hope it is enough."

And behind her, Florian supported Cosmina, helping her from the chamber. In her hands, she clutched one of the broken lilies from the coffin, pleating the withered petals in her fingers as she wept.

I followed behind, thinking of all I had seen and wondering if I could ever possibly understand it.

10

Upon quitting the crypt, the somber company parted ways in silence. Cosmina clung to me, moving from Florian's ministrations to mine, and I saw her to her bedchamber, clucking under my breath when I realised the room had not been readied.

"Never mind," I said brightly. "I will play the maidservant tonight. Let me just poke up the fire a little. There, is that not lovely? It's blazing very high now. And here is a brick to warm your bed." I bustled about the room, keeping up a continuous flow of chatter, as much to distract her as myself. I could not yet bear to think on what we had done that night.

Cosmina sat shivering in one of the low armchairs by the fire. I hung her nightdress by the hearth to warm it, and when the brick was hot, I wrapped it carefully in flannel and slid it between the sheets of her bed.

"Come," I said gently. "It is time to change into your night-dress."

She obeyed, quiescent as a child. She said nothing, but as I slipped the nightdress over her head, I saw tears falling to her cheeks. I took a handkerchief from my pocket.

"There now, it is all over, and you mustn't weep. You will spot your nightdress," I said in a teasing voice.

She did not smile, but she did blink away her tears with a great, shuddering breath.

Just then Frau Graben appeared with a mug of hot, spiced milk and her apologies.

"There has been much to do," she said, flapping about like a farmyard goose.

"Do not trouble yourself, Frau Graben," I replied. "I am happy to attend to Cosmina."

"I will leave your milk in your room, Fraulein," she said, bobbing both of us a swift ungainly curtsey.

I brushed Cosmina's hair and began to plait it. "Drink your milk," I urged. "You will feel better. Perhaps Frau Graben has been thoughtful enough to add a little something to help you sleep."

"Brandy," she said, wrinkling her nose a little after the first sip.

"Then you must finish it all," I instructed.

Cosmina leaned her head against my arm. "You are so good to take care of me. I am your hostess. It is I who should be attending you."

I took up a bit of pretty ribbon and tied a bow at the bottom of the plait. "You suffered a great shock."

"I never swoon," she said, almost angrily. "Why were you able to keep your composure? You looked so very cool and unruffled."

"Did I? I was trembling like a leaf," I confessed. "I suppose it is easier for me because I am an outsider. I did not know Count Bogdan."

"Perhaps it is because I remember the last time only too

well," she said. She took another sip of her milk, but this time she did not pull a face.

"The last time?"

She nodded. "After Count Mircea, the present count's grandfather, died. Stories of *strigoi* spread through the valley, and Count Bogdan insisted it was his father, roaming the countryside as one undead. He demanded we perform the same ceremony upon Count Mircea."

I slipped to my knees beside her. "You were there? Cosmina, you must have been a child."

"Thirteen," she said soberly. "I had nightmares for more than a year after. That was the night Andrei left this place, vowing never to return. To watch his father despoil his beloved grandfather was too much for him. For all his sins, Andrei is not so vicious as his father," she added with an odd, blank look. "Count Bogdan finished the ceremony."

"And you watched it all?" I was outraged, appalled. Cosmina had always been a sensitive soul. I could not imagine the cruelty of a man who would force a child to witness such a thing.

"Watch it? No, I was part of it. We all were." Her eyes took on a faraway look and she began to tell the tale in a flat, emotionless voice. "We began at midnight, just as we did tonight. Dr. Frankopan was there, and the Amsels. Even Frau Graben. Count Bogdan presided, and you could see from the gleam in his eye that he relished every moment of it. We did not circle widdershins thrice as we did tonight. Count Bogdan made us circle for hours, chanting all the while. I thought I should collapse from the exhaustion of it, but he prodded me to keep going. The countess and I clung to each other to stay on our feet. At last he ordered us to stop and gave us basil to dip into holy water. When we had shaken it over the corpse of poor Count Mircea, Count Bogdan stripped him to the waist and took up his knife. And then he cut out his father's heart. He lifted it into the air, watching as it splashed crimson drops onto the body. Then he dropped it into the fire. When it was burned to ash, he mixed the ash with what was left of the holy water. And one by one we drank of it."

I covered my face with my hands.

"Only Andrei refused. He threw the glass to the floor and cursed his father. He left, and it was only afterwards, when we had washed the taste of ashes from our mouths, that we realised he had gone from the castle forever."

I dropped my hands and Cosmina seemed to recollect herself to the present. "It is a terrible thing that Count Bogdan made us do. But it is more terrible that Andrei did not finish it. Bogdan will kill us all if he is not stopped."

I took her hands in mine, not surprised to find that hers were cold as death. "He was a cruel and vicious man, but you must know he is dead and gone and cannot harm you now."

She smiled then, a pitying smile, as a mother might give a child. "You do not understand such things, Theodora. We are not like other folk. There are terrors here you cannot imagine."

She bent to embrace me. "I will not let harm come to you. You must believe me."

I returned her embrace, then rose to help her into bed. She settled into the pillows, sighing at the warmth of the brick at her feet.

"You have been so kind to me. The sister I never had," she murmured drowsily.

I thought of the terrible deeds she had witnessed in the crypt, of the odd upbringing she must have had at the hands of such a monstrous man, and I felt a rush of affection and pity for her.

Impulsively, I pressed a kiss to her cool white brow.

"I do not think I can sleep just yet. Would you read to me, Theodora?"

"Of course," I told her. I moved to the little bookshelf that stood against the wall and paused, studying the titles. Charles would have approved, I thought wryly. The shelf was neatly organised and stocked with appropriate volumes, including the entire canon of Jane Austen. I started to reach for *Northanger Abbey,* but in the end I decided against it on the grounds it was too atmospheric and chose *Emma* instead. Something about the silly heroine and her meddlesome ways appealed to me, and I thought the tone just right for banishing the gloomy atmosphere of the castle and helping Cosmina to sleep.

But as I approached the bed, Cosmina drew a slender volume from beneath her pillow. "This one, I think," she told me, her voice a whisper. She looked like a guilty child caught conspiring to steal a sweet, and I turned the book over in my hand.

"But this is a translation of Gautier's *La morte amoureuse,*" I protested. It was a bloodthirsty tale, both seductive and ghoulish.

"You know it?"

"Of course. Vampires were a pet theme of my grandfather's researches."

She darted me a furtive look. "I know I should not read such things. They are sensational and unfeminine. But I find it comforting to know that others believe."

I started to remonstrate with her, then fell silent. I could not imagine the horrors she had suffered at growing up in such a place, nor could I appreciate where comfort might be found for a person who had. If she wanted to read sensational stories, it was no affair of mine.

Reluctantly, I opened the book.

"'Brother, you ask me if I have ever loved,'" I began. I had not passed three lines when Cosmina gave a sigh and settled deeper into the pillows.

I read on, detailing the misadventures of the poor priest Romauld and his tragic love for the revenant courtesan Clarimonda. The room grew darker as the candles began to gutter, extinguishing themselves one by one. At length, only the fire and a single candle remained. Cosmina closed her eyes and began to sink deeper still. I dropped my voice and read more slowly, pausing at the words of the priest Serapion as he counsels the doomed Romauld.

"'I am bound to warn you that you have one foot over the abyss. Beware lest you fall in. Satan has a long arm, and tombs are not always faithful.'"

I paused, and realised Cosmina was slumbering deeply. I used a bit of ribbon to mark the page and left the book beside her bed. I had no desire to read it on my own. The last candle was burning low as I took it up to light my way to my room. I crept from her chamber, cupping a hand over the feeble light. The passage was dark and chill, for there were no windows here to admit the light of the moon. There were odd gusts of cold wind in the castle corridors, doubtless the result of ancient stone walls in need of repointing, I told myself firmly. Still, my hands trembled upon the brave little flame, and I murmured under my breath, coaxing it to stay alight.

Suddenly, a malignant draught gusted, blowing out my candle and plunging the passage into darkness. My heart slammed painfully against my ribs and I could scarcely breathe in the stifling darkness. What had seemed chilly a moment before was now airless and dank, a suffocating blanket of blackness.

Without thinking, I began to recite an "Ave Maria" under my breath, marking off each syllable with a tentative step towards my room. So long as the prayer held out, so did my courage. I had not thought myself religious, and yet the words sprang instantly to my lips when I was in the grip of terror.

I had just formed the words *"mortus nostrae"* when my foot scraped against the stout oak of my door. I pushed it open and almost fell inside, so eager was I to put the door between myself and the darkness behind me. I bolted the door and nearly collapsed with relief at the sight of the warm, cosy chamber. Frau Graben must have lit the fire, for the hearth glowed its welcome. I carefully relit the candle and fixed it into a holder next to the bed, letting it illuminate the darkest corner of the room.

It was but the work of a minute to wash myself and don the nightdress folded neatly on the bed. I had only the one, and I noticed a rent near the hem had been mended with small, tidy stitches. It had been washed as well and smelled of basil, and as I lifted it, a few sprigs of the herb fell from its folds. I placed them carefully under my pillow but did not retire at once to sleep. I was far too overwrought by the dark deeds of that night to sleep easily. I sat up for a long while thinking about the count. The night sky was bright with moonlight and thick with cloud, a wretched night to practise the astronomer's arts. He would not be on the observatory walk this night, I mused. Perhaps he was sitting before the fire, sunk deep into opium dreams. I could not blame him if he were. I should have craved oblivion too if I carried the burden of his memories. I longed to go to him, to offer him whatever feeble comforts I could. But I was painfully aware of how badly I had already behaved with him, and although I regretted nothing, I picked my way carefully on the stony path to sin.

At length I settled with my writing things to send a letter to Anna. It was another letter of omission, for there was so much I could not speak of. How could I explain to her the horrors I had seen here, the monsters that I had been told walked abroad? Even as I wrote, the pleasant, homely sounds of pen scratching upon paper and fire falling to ash were underscored by the howling of wolves in the depths of the black forest beneath my window. How could I explain to my sweet, prosaic sister that evil stalked this place in the shape of undead men? And how could I confess to her the feelings I harboured for the count? Anna was a loyal creature, selfless and devoted. She would never understand the emotion that gnawed at me. It was not love, I could not give it so pretty a name. It was something far more elemental, a hunger I could neither name nor understand. I craved him, as Tantalus had craved water, and the more time I spent with him, the greater my thirst.

I could well imagine Anna's reply if I did unburden myself to her. She would counsel flight, swift and immediate. She would advise me to leave this place and never come back, to banish the man from my thoughts and bolt the door against my longing. She would scold me for permitting a few stolen kisses to overcome my scruples and my resolve. She would not judge me for my feelings, for hers was a romantic soul and she knew the strange and unassailable power of the human heart. But she would fault me for not resisting the pull of this man, and I could not find the words that would make her understand.

Our grandfather had taken us once—long before he became reluctant to leave his house—to call upon an eccentric friend of his who practised mesmerism. The gentleman cast his influence over the maidservant who brought our tea, causing her to warble like a nightingale and reveal her inmost secrets. It had been a cruel trick, I thought, and the girl ended scarlet-faced in embarrassment, clutching the coin her master gave her in recompense. And now I was that girl, powerless over some insidious power I could neither resist or refuse. I would do whatever he asked of me, I reflected coolly, and my detachment surprised me. I was not angry that it should be so, or fearful of what would become of me. With his power over me came the certainty that however I acted, whatever passed between us was fated to be and I was content to have it so.

I could not explain my willingness to succumb to his influence. It did not settle with my character or my intellect, and I wondered that I did not oppose it more. Had the setting, beautiful and sinister, overcome my scruples? Was the dark magic of the Carpathians exerting its invidious influence? Was it simply that, denied proper companionship for so long, I wanted to belong to another? Or were the romantic trappings of the situation merely masking my own baser desires? I had not thought myself a carnal creature, but I imagined scandalous things when I was in the count's company and worse when I was not. I had touched his hands, the broad palms and the long, elegant fingers, hands meant to stroke and caress. I had kissed his mouth, the firm lips that tasted of fruit and smoke. I had felt the length of him pressed against me, muscle and sinew, hard where I was soft, and I thought of the flesh beneath. He was a testament to the tailor's art, his clothes beautifully made and perfectly fitted to his form. I had seen the fabric ride the hard thigh and muscled calf to the long, straight expanse of his back and the breadth of his shoulders, the places I longed to cling to. I thought of the firmly marked brows and the small cleft in his chin, as if nature herself had best marked where to kiss him.

And yet none of these parts could account for the attraction of the man himself. For all his physical charms and his elegant ways, it was his mind that captivated me most. He was a creature of mystery, with fathomless secrets, as enigmatic as a Grecian sphinx, a conundrum no mere mortal could hope to solve. He was so strange a combination of superstition and sophistry, of courtliness and cunning, I could not make him out, and the riddle of him teased at me, pricking my curiosity to obsession. I could tarry here a thousand years and still never know the truth of him, I thought in exultation. It was maddening, for he had begun to intrude upon my thoughts to an alarming degree. But to sit and think about him, to untangle the Gordian knot of his character, was a glorious diversion. He was providing me with inspiration for my work and for my own imagination, and it occurred to me that this man could well provide me the greatest adventure I would ever know.

But how could I confess such truths to Anna when I could scarcely own them myself? How could I possibly explain to her all that I had seen? I knew her well. Anna would counsel me to fly at once, leaving behind the horrors I had beheld. She would not, could not, comprehend the power of the count's allure. And there were no words to make her understand.

Frustrated, I gave her a tepid and bloodless account of my stay at the castle, speaking of nothing important and concealing all that was. I gave my love to my nieces and nephews and I asked after William's parishioners. I wrote about Anna's garden, sympathising with her complaints about the wind that had stripped her prize rosebush. And I mentioned the dreary weather, omitting the wolves and the strange deeds we had done in the crypt. It was a lie, that letter, and I did not like to send it. But I knew Anna would worry if I did not, and so I wrote on, telling her a little about my book and that I meant, for the first time, to see my work published under my own name. I felt reckless in this place, a new boldness had crept into my work and my feelings, or perhaps it has always been there and merely wanted the spur of independence to urge it on. Whatever the cause, I felt myself—the passive girl Anna had known and loved—slipping further away the longer I tarried in Transylvania, and I wondered as I signed it with a flourish if I had said too much. There was nothing to alarm her until the last, when I spoke forthrightly of my ambitions, and the tone was so unaccustomed, I worried it would distress her. But I could no more unpen the words than I could have held back the tides. I knew Anna cherished hopes that my sojourn abroad would teach me tractability and that I would come home to marry Charles and settle to comfortable domesticity. I hated that my plans must divide us, but it seemed better she understand me now than later. With a wistful sense of having burnt my boats, I sealed the letter and put it aside for the post.

It was very late then, and my bones ached with fatigue as I brushed out my hair and plaited it firmly, tying the ends with little silken bows as I had done for Cosmina. I blew out the candle and slipped into bed, falling almost instantly into a deep, restless sleep.

Not surprisingly, I dreamt of the count. We were in the garden, but a different garden, for this one was beautiful and well tended, with soft grassy lawns and great knots of flowering plants and fruit trees, their branches heavy with lush fruit that bowed them nearly to the ground. We trod a narrow path in this garden, admiring the beauties of it. And then he reached for me, gently at first. But then he became urgent in his attentions, demanding even, and I wound myself about him as he buried his hands in my hair, his mouth hot against my neck. And although I had never yet spoken it aloud, I murmured his name, trailing a whisper over his skin.

Suddenly, with that drifting awareness that only the dreamer has, I was awake and yet not so. The man in my arms stilled and withdrew from me. I made a small sound of protest, but he put a finger to my lips, a finger cold as the grave. I slid back into slumber and if I dreamt again, I did not remember it when I wakened.

I awoke the next morning with a heavy head, my limbs leaden. I stretched slowly to waken myself, and as I did, I realised the careful, tidy plaits in my hair were undone. My hair was loose about my shoulders, the ribbons scattered over my pillow. I stared at them as if they were phantoms, scraps of unreality. I put out a finger to touch one, half expecting it to dissolve into the thin grey air. But it was real enough and cold, cold as only silk can be when not warmed by contact with the flesh. I took it up and saw that it had been carefully unpicked. The knots had been undone from both of the ribbons, the hair unwoven.

11

I sat up in bed, knees drawn to my chest, arms hugged tightly about them. The ribbons had not fallen from my plaits, that much was apparent. Only two possibilities remained. Either I had unbound my hair in my sleep or someone else had done so.

I thought of the dream I had had, reliving each moment of it in the cold light of day. There had been an embrace with the count, a moment of abandon when I had given myself up to his caresses. And then his hands in my hair, fingers twisting through the weight of it. Had I been dreaming of something that actually happened? Had I—or someone else, I thought with a shudder—been unbinding my hair when I dreamt of the count doing so? Was it possible that something that had actually happened in my room had invaded my dreams?

And if so, then what *had* happened? It was not impossible that I had undone the knots myself. I was not given to somnambulism, but I might well be capable of unbinding my hair ribbons in my sleep.

But what if I had not? My door was bolted, as it had been the night the dog had appeared in my room. What creature of flesh and blood could pass through stone? I thought of the ruddy, gloating corpse of Count Bogdan in his coffin and felt my stomach turn to water.

I rushed from my bed and dressed hastily, coiling my hair tightly into place, thrusting each pin as if it were a stake to contain a malignant creature. My hands trembled, but my resolve was firm, and I left the little room in the tower determined to keep my wits clear and my heart stout.

I worked in the library alone for some time before I was interrupted by Clara Amsel, sent to find me on behalf of the countess. The older woman looked pale after the ordeal we had suffered the night before, but if I expected our mutual experience to bind us closer, I was mistaken. Frau Amsel had never shown a sign of desiring better intimacy with me, and she looked at me with scarcely concealed dislike as she disclosed her errand.

"The countess is unwell today and Dr. Frankopan insists she keep to her bed. Still, she wishes to see you," she finished, with a glance of interest at the sheaf of papers I had stuffed beneath the blotter.

"I would be very happy to see the countess," I told her. "I will need a moment to tidy my papers and then I will find my way to her," I said by way of dismissal. But Frau Amsel was not to be dismissed, and instead she stood by, a plump, silent sentinel as I tamped the pages of my manuscript together and secured them in my morocco writing case.

I left it upon the writing desk and followed her, wishing I had insisted upon taking a moment to wash my hands or neaten my hair. There was something rather grand about the countess that made one feel grubby and mean.

Even her room was majestic, I realised, as Frau Amsel rapped upon the door and waved me in. The room was decorated with silver-gilt embellishments and hung with lily-green silk, a lovely combination, but a chilly one on a cold, sunless morning. A fire roared upon the hearth, and the countess was covered in a multitude of coverlets and heavy furs.

"My dear Miss Lestrange, how kind of you to come," she said rather breathlessly.

"It was kind of you to invite me," I returned.

She waved me towards a chair, a pretty affair of silver-gilt, embellished by feathery carvings meant to depict the wings of swans. A tapestry portraying the courtship of Zeus and Leda warmed one long wall, and upon another hung a portrait of a young Count Andrei next to a painting of a pair of beautiful young women. Andrei wore the traditional robes of a Transylvanian boyar in his, but the girls clung together in magnificent court gowns of white tissue, their skirts billowing together like a pale silken sea.

The countess followed my gaze. "My sister," she said, with a touch of wistfulness. "Cosmina's mother. That was painted the year of our debut in Vienna."

"Cosmina is very like her mother," I observed, noting the same high, white brow and thoughtful blue eyes.

"Yes, it comforts me to look at her sometimes. I remember the old days and it makes me happy," the countess confided.

She fell silent then and I glanced about the room, noting that it wore the same settled air as my grandfather's room, the domain of an invalid with all the necessary comforts close to hand. On a wide table next to the bed were gathered everything the countess would require for her amusement or her care. Unguents and potions jostled with the latest novels from Paris and a stack of fashion papers. There was a basket of correspondence, the envelopes thick with coronets and coats-of-arms, and a pot of scented powder and a stack of fresh handkerchiefs rested upon an Orthodox Bible. Jostling them was a pretty ormolu clock laden with porcelain roses and thick with gilding. The paintings and tapestry were the only pieces of secular art permitted in the room, for the rest of the space was given over to mournful icons in heavily gilt frames.

"I wanted to thank you for your help yesterday with Andrei," she began, her voice uncharacteristically soft.

"Madame, I beg you will not mention it. I am not certain I acted for the best," I told her truthfully.

"But you did!" she protested. "It had to be done, and I am grateful for your support. I am surprised that an outsider would be so sympathetic to our ways," she added with a nod of approbation. "Even for Ferenc it is difficult, and he has lived among us for many years."

"I understand his family are Hungarian," I put in, grateful to steer the conversation from the events of the previous night.

The countess lifted a derisive brow. "Hungarians who have lost all sense of whence they come. They once loved this place as much as we, but they have sold themselves for the Austrian Emperor's favour. The Germans, they sit in their palaces in Vienna and think to understand us, but they never can. It is like asking a cow to understand a lynx. They do not speak the same language, they do not value the same things."

I gave her a rueful smile. "Rather like the Scots then, ruled from London by people who do not understand us at all."

"Precisely. And like the Scots, our troubles are of long standing, born in the mists of time. Long ago this land was settled by Romans, the warrior legions who wrested these mountains from the hill tribes and civilised them. In the middle ages, Transylvania was independent, ruled by ruthless princes who did what they must to keep the Germans and the Turks and their empires at bay. Always there were wars and bloodshed in these valleys. This castle was built by the first Count Dragulescu to hold the valley against either empire. He lost his life upon the highest battlement, defending his homeland."

"Dreadful," I murmured, thinking of the legend the driver had told me of the Devil's Staircase.

Her lips twisted again. "Dreadful was the fate of his wife, the first countess, a beautiful Wallachian princess, she whose daughter was sacrificed to build this castle. When the count, her husband, fell in battle, she knew she would not survive the siege of the Dragulescu fortress, that once the enemy breached the walls, she would be taken and used cruelly, as no woman ought ever to be used. But she would cheat them, she decided. She wished to die with her honour held high for all to see. She flung herself from the tower to the river below, where the silver water ran red with her blood."

I blinked. "The tower? The tower where I am lodged?"

"The very room."

I drew in a slow, shuddering breath.

The countess went on. "Can you imagine how desperate, how frightened, she must have been? To destroy herself, and with it, all chance at immortality in the comfort of God's presence?

"Of course," the countess continued, "she may well have thought of those Roman generals who were the first Roumanians, the sons of Jupiter, come to settle this land before the Huns. They knew how to die with honour."

"And how did the Dragulescus keep their home if the count was killed in battle?"

"The count had a younger brother who rallied his soldiers,

and at the last moment, the castle was saved. Many centuries later, when the Hungarians came to power, the Orthodox Dragulescus converted to Roman Catholicism and swore an oath of fealty to their Magyar masters."

I nodded towards the gallery of dismal icons. "But you are Orthodox."

"Devoutly. It is well for the Dragulescu men to maintain they are Catholic, and my son does, as did his grandfather and my husband. But the women are free to embrace the true faith, for all that they are of the Dragulescu blood. I am not a Dragulescu only by marriage, you understand. I was born of the blood, a second cousin to my husband, and the blood of dragons flows in my veins."

She pronounced the last words with relish, her eyes alight with some inner fire.

"Dragons?"

"Yes," she told me proudly. "The name Dragulescu comes from the Roumanian word for dragon. It is said that long ago a dragon lived in the belly of this mountain and we subdued him to make his mountain our own. Folk said we harnessed the dragon and rode him over the sky, raining fire upon our enemies. Even now, it is said he slumbers for a thousand years beneath the castle, waiting to be awakened should we have need of him."

"It must be lovely to belong to such a place with such history," I mused.

She nodded thoughtfully. "But with that belonging comes responsibilities that must never be shirked. One owes everything to the land and the people, everything," she finished fiercely.

Having seen for myself the hardship that such dereliction could cause, I could well understand the violence of her feelings. Such a feudal system could only possibly function if the lord and master oversaw his demesne carefully, involving himself in every part of his dependents' lives. They must be able to rely upon him, as fully as children rely upon a father, to decide upon which crops to plant, when to harvest, which animals to breed and which to cull. Their very livelihoods depended upon his choices, the very lives of their children. I thought of the shuttered school and the boarded church, the flooded fields and the pitted street. I thought of all that had been left to fall to ruin in Count Bogdan's time and how much labour and effort it would cost his son to put it right. One only hoped he was up to the challenge.

"And that is why my son must have the proper helpmeet," she added, with such delicacy that I might have missed the meaningful glance she darted me. A tiny furrow had appeared between her brows, and I realised then the difficult position in which she found herself. She was my hostess and must be hospitable; still more she was grateful to me for the role I had played in persuading the count to fulfill his duty. But I must not be permitted to entertain hopes, I reflected bitterly, and the countess's remarks were by way of warning me not to nock my arrow at that particular target. I was merely the granddaughter of an esteemed but impoverished scholar, and I earned my keep by means of my pen. I was unworthy of his attentions, particularly attentions of the matrimonial variety.

"Of course," I said faintly, wishing the interview over, but understanding I had no power to stop it.

"I had hopes he would marry Cosmina," she went on carefully. "The match would have finished what my union with my husband began, the bringing together of both branches of our family." She reached for a handkerchief and dabbed at her mouth, and I believed it was so she would not have to meet my eyes. "Andrei has proven difficult, and of course, his happiness is so important to me. It would grieve my mother's heart to think of him unhappily settled. But there is more to consider than his own inclinations. The name and the blood of the Dragulescus must not be degraded by his choice." The clock upon the table gave a little chime. "Oh, dear. It is time for my medicine," she said, waving the hand that held the great pigeon's-blood ruby. "Will you be so kind as to fetch Frau Amsel?"

I rose, and as I did so, I realised it was merely a clever stratagem on her part to change the subject. She had impressed upon me that I was an unsuitable match for her son and had done so in a way that had been calculated to bring embarrassment to neither of us, and the timing was calculated as well, I suspected, with the need for her medicine a suitable expedient to make certain the conversation would not be continued. It was cleverly done, and I could judge from the satisfied expression upon her face that she was pleased with the results. I had offered her neither argument nor resentment, and both of us knew I lacked the courage to re-introduce the topic once it had been so definitively retired.

I hurried to find Frau Amsel bustling in the door. Doubt-less she had been hovering outside, perhaps even listening to our conversation. She brushed past me to attend the countess, and I closed the door softly after.

My rapid departure and the countess's remarks left me feeling a little unsettled. A hasty glance out the window revealed that the sun had finally appeared, banishing the storm clouds, and I hurried to my room for my stoutest shoes and a warm plaid shawl. A brisk scramble down to the village might well prove muddy, but escaping the close atmosphere of the castle was worth any untidiness, I decided.

Just as I passed through the court and out into the paved area beyond, Florian called my name. His eyes were deeply shadowed, and I smiled at him in sympathy. Broken slumbers seemed to be endemic at the castle.

"Do you mean to be going to the village?" he asked.

"Yes. I wanted some fresh air."

To my surprise, he gave me a rueful, knowing smile. "I am seeing to the pigs, so I am bound that way also. We go together?"

His face betrayed nothing arcane, no hidden motive, and yet I could not help but feel a frisson of emotion, as if he were silently appealing to me.

"Of course. That would be very kind of you," I said, inwardly chiding myself for being fanciful. I had wondered if Florian nursed a modest affection for me, but nothing in his gaze seemed admiring. He was distracted, perhaps not unreasonably so, given what we had seen the previous night. It had made us comrades of a sort, and when he offered his arm, I took it with a greater sense of ease than I had felt in his company before. Whether from his innate courtesy or his desire to improve himself, he insisted we converse in English rather than German, and although it hampered us a bit, I appreciated his efforts.

We said little during the descent, for Florian had judged it correctly, and the way was slippery with mud and rotting vegetation. At the foot of the mountain was a path I had not yet taken that paralleled the river, winding past the odd farm and dark copse until it ended at a piggery. It was a ramshackle stone building, mended and patched to keep the pigs warm and dry, and beyond it lay a large field, carefully fenced and furnished with a good stone trough and a tidy mud puddle for the fat porkers. There were a goodly number of the animals, snuffling and rooting about the field, and several of them let out squeals at Florian's approach.

"They are handsome animals, your pigs," I offered.

Florian smiled, his boyish face lit with pride, and his accent grew thicker with his enthusiasm. "The best in the valley. Almost ten years to make such a herd," he observed with satisfaction.

"It must be very gratifying," I said, thinking out loud, "to apply one's self to a project and see such substantial results."

"Count Bogdan trusted me only to keeping the pigs. But I always think I do this well and he will give me more to do."

"And did he?"

Florian shook his head. "No, miss. Count Bogdan trusted no one. He tell me he gave me the pigs because he does not care if they live or die. But I care."

"And they are thriving now," I pointed out.

"Pigs are simple. They have only to be growing fat and content," Florian said, pointing at the largest of his sows, a great solid creature with a train of plump piglets scampering after.

"We ought to envy them that, I suppose. Tell me, do you have more responsibility under the present count?"

I am not certain what made me ask it, but Florian did not seem to mind the intrusion. "Count Andrei does not think so much about these things. Farmers pay the rents, and this is all the count is caring about. He gives me the harvest this year," he said, his complexion flushing with pride. His eyes were downcast, but it was apparent he was deeply pleased to have been given such responsibility.

"Perhaps the coming of Count Andrei will be the making of you," I said lightly.

He did not respond, but gave a low whistle. A tame pig trotted up to have its ears scratched. Florian hummed a folk song as he rubbed at the pig's head, and I ventured a question I had been longing to ask.

"Florian, what do you make of the ceremony in the crypt? Do you think Count Bogdan will rest now?"

His hand faltered on the pig, then resumed its gentle stroking. "I pray God he will. All that must be done, it was not done," he said carefully, "but perhaps what is done is enough."

"I confess I am rather glad it all stopped when it did. I do not think I could have borne seeing a man's heart taken out—" I broke off, sickened at the thought.

Florian gave me a sad smile. "It is their way, miss. I have lived here very long time. Roumanians are different to Germans. The magic and monsters are being real here. They say the waters of the Carpathian rivers must be your heart's blood to understand it."

"I want to understand it. It is a very beautiful land," I told him truthfully.

"Then you must stop the thinking that Transylvania is like other places. It is different here. See what is. Not what you are wishing it."

It was rather good advice, I decided. We left the piggery then and made our way to the village proper where, at Florian's suggestion, we stopped to take refreshment. The village looked no better than it had during my previous visits; indeed it looked rather worse, for the recent storms had churned the sole street to a muddy expanse passable only at great risk to one's shoes and hems. An enterprising soul had placed a bit of wood over the worst of the puddles and we reached the inn with scarcely more dirt than we had gathered at the piggery.

We were greeted by the innkeeper, a tall, thin man with a short, plump wife. He welcomed us heartily in German, speaking to Florian with some warmth and greeting me cordially, if not familiarly. Then he withdrew, shifting smoothly to Roumanian to call orders to his wife.

A few members of the local peasantry had also stopped to pass the time. They had fallen silent at our arrival, and though Florian nodded gravely to each of them in turn, they rewarded him with the merest inclination of the head in reply. To me they exhibited nothing but furtive curiosity, no friendliness or welcoming sally was forthcoming, and I wondered how much the villagers knew of the castle business.

The innkeeper and his wife alone greeted us with anything approaching warmth, but their custom depended upon good feeling, I reflected with some cynicism. They must pander a little to keep their business in good standing, and it was only after I caught the innkeeper's wife flicking me a nervous glance that I realised the root of their worry: we were castle folk, and if we reported any ill feeling to the count, it would be a simple matter for him to see to it that the inn was shut, depriving the innkeeper and his family of their livelihood.

I darted a quick glance at Florian, thinking on Dr. Frankopan's concerns about the dangers of loose talk. It would not do for any of us to share too freely the dark happenings at the castle with the innkeeper. Doubtless his position gave him the opportunity to spread a great deal of gossip in the valley, and I made a note to mind my tongue in his presence.

Florian, in spite of the cordiality of the innkeeper's greeting, fell into a melancholy mood and said little. I asked him about his time in Vienna and his love of music, but even those topics did not rouse him, and after few more attempts to engage him, I was forced to admit defeat. He was preoccupied and turned in upon his thoughts, and it struck me then how similar he was to the villagers. For one of the castle folk, Florian seemed for all the world a simple farmer. He cared about his pigs and he dressed like a peasant, with the same tight white trousers and embroidered shirt rather than a gentleman's tweeds.

Eventually, I tired of making conversation and amused myself by looking about the inn, careful to avoid the avid glances of the other patrons. It was a modest little establishment, only the front room of a private family home, but neat as a pin, with a row of polished metal tankards hanging from the ceiling and an immaculate blue-tiled stove sitting in the corner for warmth. But as I looked more closely, I saw that several of the tankard hooks were empty, as if their occupants had been sold off, and the clothing of our host and his wife, while clean and tidy, bore the hallmarks of long use, the colours faded with much washing and telltale patches at the elbows and knees.

The innkeeper's wife came then bearing mugs of dark beer and platters of sausages and ham, cheese and bread. She brought pickled cabbage and beets and a great bowl full of mushroom soup. The other patrons ate nothing and drank only beer or the local plum brandy, and for an uncomfortable moment, I wondered if we had been served the family's supper. But it would be an unthinkable breach of courtesy to send it back, and I nodded to her in thanks. She bobbed a clumsy curtsey, and as she left I saw strapped to her back a peculiar contraption, a little wooden box where a swaddled infant slept.

"How clever," I observed. "It would keep the child close to the mother and not interfere with her work. Like the Indians in America."

"Have you been to America?" Florian asked.

"No. Indeed, apart from my time at school, this is my first sojourn out of Scotland, although I mean to travel more. I find I have a taste for it."

"I do not know why there is travel," he said, his expression one of genuine puzzlement. "To love one's home, one could not leave it and be happy."

"And do you love your home so much?" I asked, reaching for another crisp, sizzling sausage.

"I speak of Austria," he said softly.

"Of course, how stupid of me. You were but a child when you left, yet still it must be home to you."

"Many things may make a man's home," he told me, his face

sober, even anguished. He paused for a moment as if gathering his emotions close, then continued, his mien lighter and
more conversational. "I hate this place when we come, but I
learn to love Transylvania. We have everything here, here there
is mountains, sky, forests. And we have the best music."

"You have never heard a bagpipe," I put in teasingly, the
remnants of my Scottish pride pricked only a little.

"But I have!" Florian protested. "We have here a bagpipe,
and the flute, made from the shinbone of the sheep, with
music so sweet, it would charm the leaves from trees."

A spirited debate on the merits of Scottish versus Roumanian music followed, and I discovered through the innkeeper
that Florian was rather famous in the district for the sweetness
of his tenor voice besides his other musical accomplishments.
The innkeeper's wife and I prevailed upon him to sing for us,
and the innkeeper fetched a sort of lute, pear-shaped and rather
medieval-looking, to accompany him. The other patrons,
whose conversations had never risen above guttural whispers,
fell entirely silent and assumed expressions of mournful interest
as he began to sing.

We settled in to listen to him, and I was entranced from the
first note. He sang in Roumanian, and I longed to understand
the words. The innkeeper's wife leaned near to me, her lips
close to my ear as she translated into German.

"He is singing the *miorita,* a sorrowful song of three shep-
herds. One learns that his two friends are planning to kill him.
He does not resist, for it is his philosophy to accept death. Just
before he dies, he asks them to carry a message to his mother,
to tell her he has married a beautiful woman—Lady Death."

I felt a frisson of emotion at her words, but she went on,
murmuring softly as Florian sang the shepherd's lament. *"I have
gone to marry a princess, my bride. Firs and maple trees were my guests;*

my priests were the mountains high; fiddlers, birds that fly; torchlight, stars on high."

When he finished we applauded and the innkeeper's wife daubed at her eyes with her apron. It was very like the songs of the Highlands, full of woe and lamentation, and I wondered if poverty and oppression were necessary to create such music.

He sang again, a more cheerful song about death dancing through a field of flowers—the souls of children who had died—and by the time he finished, I had had my fill of Roumanian music, no matter how beautiful the melodies.

He must have caught something of my mood, for he gave the lute back to the innkeeper and gestured for me to rise. "We will go now to reach the castle before dark," he advised.

He settled the bill with the innkeeper and accepted the muted blessings he and his wife insisted upon giving. I did not know if this was a Roumanian custom or if we were particularly vulnerable as we were returning to the castle, but I was glad of the gesture. The rest of the company watched us in heavy silence, and for the first time, I felt the weight of it, an ominous thing. Not to speak in the presence of others struck me as the purest form of aversion, but even as we took our leave, I saw one or two of them cross themselves Orthodox-fashion and cast us pitying glances.

I raised the subject as soon as Florian and I gained the muddy road. "The local folk do not seem hospitable toward strangers," I ventured.

"They hear what happens at the castle."

"So soon?"

Florian shrugged. "Gossip travels on the wind. Of course they hear. But they will say little to castle people. They belong to the master. He makes life good or bad for them."

"You mean the count?"

His mouth worked, but he said nothing.

"Florian, let us speak plainly. The count could make life better for his people, and they resent him because he has not?"

He gave a single short nod, but even as he acknowledged the truth of what I said, his words denied it. "It is for him to rule as he is pleased."

"Rule? He is a nobleman, but he is no prince."

"I say again, Transylvania is different place. The old ways are the only ways. The count rules. What he wants, he will do. The peasants are tired. They are hungry and poor. He can be helping them. He does little."

I felt a swift stab of fear. "Might they rebel then, if they are angered enough by his neglect of them?"

He shrugged. "Count Bogdan was not good. They do nothing. They drink sorrow and wait for the better times. They are sad now because Count Andrei, he is not better."

"He has only been here a few weeks," I argued, wondering even as I said the words why I felt compelled to defend him. "There has scarce been time for him to make changes to improve their lot."

Florian met my eyes then, and I was struck once more by the fathomless sorrow I saw there. "They know the *strigoi* walks here. It is an omen. Evil things will happen." Florian looked at the sky, noting the angle of the sun. "We must go. It grows late."

But however I pressed him, he sank once more into his solitude, and I took his arm in silence as we started up the mountain path. The dying afternoon was a beautiful one, with the great blaze of turning leaves flaming over the valley. Gold and scarlet grasshoppers leapt in the dying grasses whilst bronze beetles winged their way to sanctuary for the night. The sun warmed our faces and the crisp air was full of birdsong. It would have been perfect, but for the fact that the hand I held was not the count's, I reflected ruefully.

Suddenly, a roll of thunder echoed over the mountaintops. A cluster of dark grey clouds had gathered in the east and was rolling slowly towards the mountain.

I must have started, for Florian hastened to reassure me. "Do not fear. We are safe yet. Thunder sounds from far away. But some say it is Scholomance," he added. "Do you know the Scholomance?"

"It is a bit of folklore," I said, casting my mind back to my grandfather's library. "It is a very old superstition, is it not? I seem to remember a lake."

Florian nodded. "In the mountains south of Hermannstadt, there is lake, deep and black. Here the Devil has school for teaching dark magic. There is taught secrets of nature, language of animals, magic spells. The Devil gives learning to ten pupils. When learning is finished, the Devil says to nine to go home. But the tenth must stay with the Devil. He must ride a dragon and he prepares thunderbolts for the Devil. He brews thunder in the black lake. When the weather is fine, his dragon sleeps under the black lake."

He paused and stared upward at the high stones of the castle, the sharp pointed towers piercing the sky above. "Here the people say, one time in a hundred years a Dragulescu goes to the Scholomance to learn the Devil's ways," he finished bitterly.

I took a deep breath and wrapped my shawl more closely about my body. For some unaccountable reason, all the talk of the occult and curses had overcome me, and I felt bowed with foreboding. "I think I have heard quite enough about the Devil for one day."

I started up the Devil's Staircase and Florian followed. We did not speak again.

12

―――❧❧❧―――

That evening we were a smaller company at table, for the countess had kept to her room and Frau Amsel dined with her. The count was distracted, eating nothing but pouring out several glasses of amber Tokay. Cosmina bravely attempted to keep the conversation light and engaging, but although the count replied to her pleasantly enough, the conversation eventually faltered, and when the meal was at last concluded, she excused herself and went directly to bed. Florian followed soon after, and I made a motion to withdraw, but the count intervened.

"I have something to show you in my workroom," he said, and although his tone was conversational, there was no mistaking the note of command.

Wordlessly I followed him up to the workroom. The candles had been lit and Tycho slumbered peacefully on the hearth.

"Come and see what I have found," the count said eagerly. I went to the worktable where he had taken up a pretty box of pale wood inlaid with darker wood in an intricate pattern. The front of it was set with a series of knobs, half a dozen, and when he raised the lid I could see they were attached to corresponding rods carved with symbols. A table of similar symbols had been incised on the lid of the box.

I put out a tentative finger. "It is very curious. I've never seen the like. Is this ivory?" I asked, touching one of the rods.

"It is. It is a device for making astronomical calculations. The rods are fashioned of bone or ivory, and the whole of it is known as Napier's bones after the astronomer who designed it."

"A macabre name," I observed.

He slanted me a knowing look. "It is the fatal flaw of Transylvanians that we have a fondness for the macabre. Surely you discovered that last night."

"I cannot begin to understand what happened last night," I said slowly.

He waved to the sofa by the fire. "Sit. I will try to make sense of it for you."

I had intended to make my excuses, plead a headache or some other trifling indisposition and effect an escape. But as always, the power of his personality persuaded me to something I had not intended.

But I was determined to preserve some vestige of formality, and as I perched upon the edge of the sofa, spreading my skirts wide between us, I saw his lips twitch in amusement.

He settled himself as far from me as the narrow sofa would permit.

"You think us barbaric," he began.

"I do," I acknowledged. "But it is a barbarism I would know better. I do not come from a modern city. Edinburgh is a place where ideas are exchanged and philosophies are born, but no one looks to us for the latest fashions or the most modern conveniences. The Highlands are more backwards still, with folk content to live as they have for a thousand years. And yet Transylvania is a place apart. It is nothing so simple as manner of dress or speech or whether a railway has been put through a valley. It is an acceptance of mythology and feudalism, the two of them tied together in such a way as I cannot separate them, warp and weft of the same peculiar cloth."

"You think we nobles keep the stories of monsters circulating in order to keep the peasants under our thumbs?" he asked, his tone mildly amused.

"Not deliberately, but I think it suits both master and serf to preserve the old ways. And the worst of it is, all of you and the land itself, conspire to make me believe it as well."

"Is it so terrible to believe in the dark and terrible things you have been told of? Fear and passion walk hand in hand, you know. We are afraid of being destroyed, being possessed, and yet we crave it. What child has not thrilled to ghost stories whispered under the bedclothes by the dark of the moon? And what man or woman has not longed to be lost in the wood and found again?"

I shook my head. "You speak in riddles and I do not understand you."

He leaned forward, his grey eyes quite black in the shadowy room. "Then let me speak plainly. You are afraid here and you do not know what to believe. I have told you I will protect you. You have only to trust me and you will be free to enjoy your fears."

"Enjoy them!"

He gave a little shrug. "Everything may be enjoyed in life, my dear Miss Lestrange. Even fear. It wants only a change in one's perspective."

"And what ought my perspective to be?" I demanded.

"That this is an adventure," he replied, leaning closer still.

He was more animated than I had ever seen him, alight with something that nourished and strengthened him. Had he given over taking opium for something stronger still? Or had he begun to feel his power as master of this dark place?

He raised his head slightly, as if catching the scent of me in the air. "You are not thinking as a writer or as a woman," he chided. "You are trembling and shrinking like a schoolgirl from your fears. If you embraced them, faced them down, you would see the opportunities that lie before you."

"What opportunities?"

"To create. To find pleasure. To live," he replied, moving closer still.

But as he spoke, I thought of the villagers lacking even fresh water and my indignation rose within me. I said nothing, but arranged my skirts again, spreading them carefully between us as a boundary he must not breach.

"Stop fussing with your dress. You are vexed with me," he said, directing that piercing gaze at me. "Why?"

"I am a guest in your home. It is not my place to be vexed with anything you choose to do," I said evenly.

He laughed, a sharp mirthless laugh. "You do not believe that." He gave a tug to his neckcloth, as if it were wound too tightly. "Come, we have endured too much together for pretence. Tell me why you are cross with me and I will tell you why you are wrong."

This last bit of arrogance pricked my temper beyond recall. "I am cross because I find we have no point of connection. I thought there was some sympathy between us, some common feeling, and I learn instead that you are everything I have been taught to despise." I warmed to my theme and carried on, heedless of the words themselves. "You are a libertine and a rake. You take pleasure in everything and responsibility for nothing. You have wealth and opportunity and you squander them both upon idle pleasures. You are the master of this land, and yet you lift not a finger to ease the burdens of its people."

He gave me a slow, lazy smile. "I had no idea you were such a revolutionary, my dear Miss Lestrange. Shall I build you a barricade from which to denounce me? Or would you prefer a tumbrel to carry me through the streets to my destruction?"

"You have very kindly and quite thoroughly proven my point. I lay the most serious charges of defect of character at your feet and you laugh. You are amused by my scorn rather than abashed at your own failures."

"Because you do not scorn me," he said evenly. "You scorn yourself because you see me for what I am and still you cannot help but think of me."

I gaped at him, but before I could form a proper response, crafted of equal parts logic and disdain, he continued on. "I know all these things about myself, and if you will but call it to mind, I am the one who first revealed them to you. It should come as no surprise to you now that I am an indolent creature of pleasurable habits. I freely confessed to you I am a hedonist, given to frivolity and idleness. Do you think to wound me with the arrows I myself placed in your quiver? Carry on, my dear. You are welcome to try. But I am immune to your barbs, and in fact, I suspect they strike you more deeply than they ever could wound me, because I am content. It is only you who wish me to be better than I am."

"I wish you to be what you could be," I rejoined. "Nature has gifted you beyond compare, and you throw these gifts back at her because you cannot be troubled to exert yourself on anyone's behalf but your own."

"Really? I remember exerting myself rather a lot last night and at your insistence," he countered, his eyes bright with mischief.

"I am sorry for that," I returned. "I had no notion of what I was asking of you."

"And yet I complied," he mused, stretching his legs out comfortably, his hands laced behind his head. "I complied solely upon your request. You command me and I obey, and yet I am castigated for failing to exercise my power to better those less fortunate. I could say the same of you."

His tone was bantering, but his words were arresting.

"You will not speak seriously with me. I ought to have known it was a mistake to attempt this."

I rose, but he was quicker, placing himself directly in my path with a smoothness and speed that seemed almost inhuman.

"Let me pass," I said. The top of my head scarcely reached his chin, and even as I said the words, I knew them to be futile.

"She gives an order, and yet I do not feel the force of it," he said softly, bending his lips to my ear. "She could command me to any crime, lure me to any sin, and yet she does not put out her hand to direct me."

"Let me pass," I said again.

"More hesitant yet again," he said, moving his lips still closer to my ear. "I would do anything you asked of me, Theodora, do you not know that? You have only to stretch out that little hand to save me. You could destroy me with your goodness."

He took my hand in his, reverently, sacredly, turning it over in his as a pilgrim might a holy relic. And then he pressed his lips to the palm as his other arm stole about my waist.

"I cannot think," I said stupidly, and I felt a strange giddy lassitude come over me. I swayed, but his arm held me fast.

He guided me to the sofa, and I knew that he had been quite wrong. I did not command him. I was powerless before him, and whatever he asked of me, I would surrender to him.

He pressed me down into the soft velvet cushions, murmuring my name over and again, chanting it like an incantation. I twisted my hands in his hair, begging mutely. He complied, kissing me over and again, introducing me to pleasures I had never imagined, for who could imagine paradise who has never yet wandered there?

He braced himself to pull away his coat and waistcoat, and it was then that I saw the first scarlet drops seeping through the white linen wound about his neck.

A chill ran through me, and I felt my heartbeat hard and fast in my throat as I stared in horror.

"What is it?" he demanded. Seeing the direction of my gaze, he put his hand to his neckcloth. His finger came away red, and he stared at it.

"An accident, when I shaved," he said, but his complexion had gone white as marble, and he thrust himself away from me. The word *strigoi* hovered unspoken between us, souring the air.

"Go now," he said harshly. He turned from me, and I rose, hesitating. Even then, I did not wish to leave him, even then, when the first seeded doubts about what he was began to flower.

He glanced once over his shoulder. "I will save you even if you will not save yourself," he said, his voice low and menacing. "Go to your room and bolt the door. Hang the basil and say your prayers. *Go now!*" he roared, and I gathered up my skirts and fled from him.

The next morning I found a note pushed under my door, a small scrap of paper with two words slashed across in thick black ink. *Forgive me.* I read it over a hundred times and carried it in my clothes, resting against my skin. It was my talisman, my consolation against the doubts that beset me. I had made up my mind that vampires did not exist, that Dr. Frankopan's tales of *strigoi* were the ramblings of a frightened old man. But the events in the crypt—the strange and otherworldly appearance of the corpse—and the circumstances of my last parting from the count had shaken my certainty. I had seen the blood upon his neck and I had heard the desperation in his voice. Whatever I believed he was, it was nothing to his own anguish. Had his father, that monstrous revenant, attacked him directly? Had he made something dark and unnatural of his own child? When I lay alone in my bed in the depth of the night, with the low howls of the wolves passing on the wind, I could almost believe it.

And yet by the light of day, it seemed impossible. Aurelia's death could be put to a wandering maniac—perhaps the work of an itinerant or the savagery of the Popa men who roamed the mountains claiming to be wolves. The castle, for all its battlements and fortifications, remained unlocked. A man wanted only the physical strength to manage the Devil's Staircase and the stealth to gain entry after the household was fast asleep. Perhaps Aurelia had even arranged an assignation with the fellow and things had gone terribly wrong, I decided. It was certainly a more palatable solution than the notion of vampires.

The Transylvanian *strigoi* was simply a device, I reasoned. It was a relict of grief and a longing for the departed to come back again. It was achingly sad, a simple people's response to the suddenness and finality of death. It spoke of the desire to cling to the dead, to keep them alive in one's memory, walking the earth, searching for a way to break the bonds of mortality. Taken alone, it was merely a tragic bit of harmless folklore, put about by unlettered people who had seen little of the world and knew nothing of life beyond their mountains. I knew from my grandfather's writings that every primitive culture boasted a type of vampire, and I knew too that such things were never found amongst civilised folk. There were no revenants in cities. Only in the imaginations of the country peasants were they to be found, incarnations of bereavement and loss and fear, and in so remote a place as Transylvania, even the educated might be seduced into believing.

And it must be acknowledged that the suggestive atmosphere of the castle played its part. It was as Gothic a ruin as any to be found in sensational novels, although I understood well enough why most of the vast castle had been left to decay. The mountains were thick with forests, but it would take acres of trees and dozens of men to fell enough wood to keep the fires blazing through the winter in the castle. Far cheaper and much less bother to simply lock the doors and leave the empty wings to moulder away. The furniture and ornaments, the hangings and books were all costly, doubtless purchased in more solvent times. Such things were expensive to keep in good repair. It would require a sizable staff to keep the castle in good order, the books supple and free of dust and worm, the furniture clean and the moths chased away, the instruments and weapons polished and gleaming. The castle was a pale shadow of what the place must have been at one time, bristling with soldiers, bright banners flying from the turrets, perched proudly upon the mountain.

Now it was merely a sad old relict of a more feudal time. There was nothing sinister in that save the passing of years, I decided. It was a house tragedy had touched, but perhaps with the old count's passing, a new era could begin. Perhaps with encouragement, Count Andrei would refurbish the place and fill it with light and conversation and music. It could be lovely again, and surely a gentleman with a connoisseur's eye who spent the better part of his time in elegant cities was just the person to bring sophistication and modern thinking to this old horror.

But it was pointless to hope for such a thing, I reminded myself. Count Andrei had demonstrated his negligence quite thoroughly. He cared little for his castle and less for his people. To wish him to feel otherwise was futile and would only lead to my own disappointment that a man of such possibilities and such natural gifts would scorn them all. I even began to pity him, for while I used logic and reason to dismantle the stories of vampires, I thought of the tormented look upon his face as he ordered me from his room. He had believed he was protecting me from himself, but I did not fear him. By the cold light of day, I saw that he had fallen prey to the superstitions of this place, but I had not, I persuaded myself. There were things I could not explain, but neither could I lay them at the feet of vampires and call it truth, and so long as I did not hold the truth, I could not leave. He might believe he had been made monstrous by his father's efforts, but I did not, and as the days stretched on, I became increasingly convinced that I must wake him from this nightmare and persuade him once more of his own mortality even as I fought the urge to flee.

The next fortnight passed quietly. By day I wrote in the library, my solitude unbroken, and my afternoons were spent with Cosmina. I saw little of Florian and nothing of the count. The latter suited me. My feelings towards the gentleman were so tangled, so indefinable, I could not think upon him with anything approaching equanimity. Perhaps I ought to have left the castle then. I could have taken myself to London or even to Anna's and finished my book in more congenial circumstances. But when I lay down to sleep or put aside my pen and closed my eyes, I thought only of the count, of the storm of emotions he had raised within me. I relived every moment that had passed between us during that interlude upon the sofa, how his mouth had lingered over my pulses, the warmth of his breath raising the blood hot and fast just beneath my skin. The pleasures had been exquisite, yet even in my inexperience I knew they were the merest taste of the banquet he could spread before me. To remain in such a place with such a man was to court disaster, I told myself firmly, and yet I could not leave him. *I will protect you,* he had sworn. I believed him. Had he not sent me away for my own protection? In the face of my doubts and fears, I trusted him still.

Even if I had mustered the will to leave, I should have had a difficult time persuading Cosmina to accept it. Once or twice during the fortnight, I hinted at such a thing, and she fell immediately into such a passion of reproach and pleading I could not refuse her. We walked often down to the village so that she could play the Lady Bountiful in the countess's place. We carried baskets of scraps from the castle table and little oddments to give them ease. Florian sometimes caught fat brown trout from the river for their suppers, and Cosmina spent much of her time knitting warm caps for the children and shawls for the old women. The weather was growing colder, the air clear and sharp, and each day the morning sun rose upon a landscape that glittered under the first frosts. The pigs in the piggery were growing fat and tall, and the smell of woodsmoke filled the valley from morning to night.

The whole of the valley began to take on a settled air as if preparing to tuck itself in for winter, and with the change in weather, the occurrence of sickness rose. Dr. Frankopan was too often abroad with his patients to call frequently at the castle, and Cosmina did her best to bring comfort and aid to the little hovels where folk could not spare the coin for his attentions. She cared deeply for the villagers, and in her affection for them, she often neglected to care for herself. Whenever she could be spared from attending to the poor of the valley, she devoted herself to the countess, reading aloud with a hoarsening voice or scurrying down to the village to bring some new embrocation from Dr. Frankopan. Not unexpectedly, Cosmina took a chill and grew thin and pale, rather too much of both for my liking, and I began to fuss over her. I saw that she rested better and ate more in my company. She took care of the countess, and in turn, I took care of Cosmina, reminding her to wear a hat on the occasional sunny afternoon in the garden or to take the strengthening tonic prescribed by Dr. Frankopan. In a frank moment, he revealed to me that it was nothing more than a bit of good beef tea, boiled down and flavoured with herbs and wine, but he felt that Cosmina needed a bit of cosseting.

"She is beset by nerves," he told me seriously. "This business with the *strigoi* is difficult for one of her temperament. The best remedy for overset nerves is the company of those who are sturdy and strong," he said with a meaningful look at me.

I felt ashamed then, that I had neglected her rather badly since my arrival. I applied myself to her care, and we spent many happy afternoons stitching together or picking the strange black-skinned apples that grew in the castle garden.

As ever, the countess's health waxed and waned, and when she was strong enough she joined us of an evening to dine and play piquet. Even Tereza resumed her duties, although she never smiled, and I noticed she wore a vial of blessed water about her neck.

And so the days passed, days when I grew more comfortable at the castle, days when I felt as if I had sipped from the river Lethe, forgetting those I had left behind and the life I had once known. It began to feel as though I had always lived in this mountain fastness, always dwelt in this strange and beautiful land. And even the occasional letter from Anna did nothing to recall me to my previous life. Her existence was an easy and peaceful one, and it seemed far removed from the life I now led.

One morning, a few weeks after the unsettling events in the crypt, Cosmina ran me to ground in the library, fairly dancing in excitement and dressed for an outing, a pretty basket looped over one arm.

"Oh, I am so glad I have found you! You must come, hurry now—I've brought your shawl," she ordered, urging me from my chair and thrusting my plaid into my hands. Her colour was higher than it had been for the past fortnight, almost hectic, but her eyes were shining, and I was pleased to see her looking so well.

"Where are we going?" I demanded.

She grasped my hand and tugged me along behind. "We haven't time to tidy your papers. You can do that later. If we tarry we will miss him!"

We hurried into the early afternoon sunshine of the court. It was a glorious day; a bright golden haze lay over the valley and it was unseasonably warm.

"The pedlar is come! We have expected him for weeks, but he was held up in Buda-Pesth. Hurry now, Clara is just ahead there."

I saw Frau Amsel moving heavily down the Devil's Staircase, red in the face and puffing. Out of courtesy, I slowed my steps.

"Frau Amsel, the way is difficult, is it not? I think we should descend more safely together."

I proffered an arm, which she took with a grudging nod.

"Florian usually helps me, but he is very busy today with work for the count," she advised me. I could smell the distinctive aroma of plum brandy upon her, but her steps were steady and firm.

Cosmina walked hard upon our heels, impatient to descend, but she need not have hurried. A knot of village women had assembled to wait for him as well, and it was fully a quarter of an hour after we arrived before the pedlar drew up in his gaily painted wagon. He was a shifty-looking fellow with sharp features and lank, greasy hair, and he gave us a jovial smile which did not touch his eyes. But he bargained fairly, and after perusing his wares—the pretty painted tin cups and the strings of bright beads and the dainty little looking glasses—I put out my hand to touch a length of fabric. It was violet, the colour of half mourning, and almost appropriate for my state of mourning. It had been woven with a pretty pattern of small black roses, barely noticeable on the field of purple. Too late I remembered I had not stopped to collect any coins before I left the castle.

I turned to Cosmina, dropping the length of fabric. I meant to ask her for the loan of the price just until we returned to the castle, but before I could speak, Frau Amsel swept the fabric into her arms.

"I will take this," she said, fixing me with a challenging stare.

The pedlar, whose sharp eyes I suspected missed very little, put his thumbs into his braces and rocked back upon his heels with the air of a man who intended to make the most of an opportunity.

"I have only the one dress-length, and I have carried it the length of Hungary. Which of you will give me the best price?"

Frau Amsel thrust her hand into her pocket and withdrew a faded, washed-leather purse. She sorted through the coins and produced a handful.

"Here, this is what I will give you," she told him, flicking me a triumphant glance. She seemed certain of victory, and well she ought, I mused, for I had no coin to counter the offer and no desire to brawl with Frau Amsel, although she had clearly decided to dislike me.

"I think this lady wants it more," I said softly. The pedlar looked disappointed; doubtless he had anticipated a better price, but there was none on offer, and he accepted with an unctuous smile. He wrapped the fabric into a paper parcel and tied it with a bit of grubby string. Frau Amsel scarcely waited for the knot to be secured before she left without a word. I turned to Cosmina, lifting my brows.

She had seen the exchange, but merely waved a hand. "She is an odd creature. She was doubtless afraid you would carry off what she fancied. Although it was rather stupid of her, for she is frightful in purple. It would have suited you much better."

I shrugged. "No matter. I am in mourning in any event. Let me see the beads you have there. What a pretty shade of blue. They quite match your eyes."

She beamed happily and chose a few more things, counting out her coins happily while the pedlar wrapped her purchases in paper bundles, pleating the paper to make tidy little packages in the shape of animals.

"How clever," I said, admiring the little monkey he had just fashioned.

With a few quick movements of his fingers he created another, this one a dog with rather familiar features. He presented it to me with a flourish.

"I thought you might like a little tribute to your dog," he said.

"My dog? I have no dog," I told him, but even as I said the words, I felt a familiar weight press against my leg. "Tycho!" I rubbed at his silken ears. "You curious thing, did you follow me here?"

"He must have," Cosmina said. "He seldom leaves the count. It seems you have made a conquest," she said. Her tone was light, but her colour had faded and she looked a little breathless.

"We have walked too far," I chided her. "You are only just out of bed after that nasty cold. I ought not to have let you come."

She gave me a gentle smile. "You could not have prevented me. He comes only four times a year, and it is always a wonderful treat. I will be fine. I am a little tired, that is all. A short rest and I will be good as new."

"Perhaps something to drink at the inn," I urged, and she complied, letting me carry her basket full of parcels and guide her to the familiar iron gate with the horse's skull.

The innkeeper's wife hurried out and motioned for us to sit at a pretty little iron table in the shade of a great elm. We settled there, and she hurried back with a tray of cold plum wine and a plate of small sweet biscuits. We drank and ate slowly, Tycho at our feet, and after half an hour or so, Cosmina seemed restored. She sat with her back to the tree, lifting her face to the dappled shade. She was so pale I could see the blood moving in her veins, and I thought of the countess, lying wan and feeble in her magnificent bed. I thought too of Cosmina's mother, lost so young, and I wondered what weakness ran in the blood that the women of their family proved so frail.

As if sensing my scrutiny, Cosmina opened her eyes and smiled. "You needn't worry so. I am not as fragile as all that."

"Of course not," I said stoutly. "A little rest and you will be right as rain." I hated the sound of my voice, jovial and hearty, as if I could promise her restored health, when the truth—if I could bear to own it to myself—was that I feared for her. She tired herself on behalf of the villagers and her aunt, and I wondered if she could be persuaded to temper her efforts before they took too sharp a toll upon her.

She peered into the basket and picked among the parcels until she came to a tiny one in the shape of a mouse.

"This is for you," she said almost shyly, pressing the little mouse into my hands.

"How thoughtful of you!" I tugged at its tail, unfolding the clever paper to reveal the strand of polished blue beads, each scarcely larger than an apple seed.

"I chose them for you, not for me," she told me. She motioned me forward and I knelt before her to let her clasp the necklace about my throat. "How pretty they look!"

I turned, running a finger over the beads.

"That is just how you used to worry the rosary of your mother's, do you remember?" she asked suddenly.

"Oh! I had quite forgot. Fancy your remembering that," I murmured, feeling the unpleasant tug of memory.

"I remember how upset you were to have lost it that day. We were on a picnic, I remember. With Fraulein Möller. She took us to the little waterfall in the woods. We were meant to be sketching birds, I think. But we ate a picnic in the meadow and told stories and ate too much of the marzipan she had brought for a treat. I made daisy chains and you gathered the flowers for me. And the afternoon was so warm, we dozed off in the sunlight, with the bees and the butterflies dancing about us. And when we woke to leave, you found you had lost your rosary. You were so unhappy, I remember the day was quite spoilt."

"I did make a terrible fuss," I admitted ruefully. "I remember we were very late back to the school because you and Fraulein Möller helped me to search and we were all lectured quite sternly by the headmistress on punctuality."

"I did not mind," Cosmina said loyally. "I only minded because we could not find it, and I knew it hurt you to lose it."

"It was the only thing I had of Mama's," I recalled.

"And it was blue, I remember that," Cosmina said with a fond look at the necklace she had bought me.

"Yes, it was. The colour of the Madonna's robe." I touched the necklace again. "How like you to remember it, and to give me this. Thank you, Cosmina."

She bent swiftly to press her cheek to mine. "I am so happy

you are here," she said in an odd, choked voice. "I want you to be happy here as well."

"I am," I told her truthfully.

Just then a voice hailed us and we looked to the gate to find we were not alone. Florian stood there, muddy to his waist, but looking rather happier than I had seen him.

"Florian, whatever have you been doing? Playing in the piggery?" Cosmina asked, her tone touched with coolness. Perhaps she resented the intrusion upon our private moment, but there was no call to be rude to poor Florian. He flushed deeply.

"No, Miss Cosmina. I have been seeing to the digging of the new well."

I looked up sharply. "The new well?"

He nodded. "Yes, miss. The count, he gives orders for a new well. There is digging for many days now, and today the water comes."

I realised then that a commotion had been rising outside the peaceful garden. I rose and went to the gate. On the street, folk were scurrying to and fro, bearing pitchers and pails, and over and again I heard the word *apǎ*.

"Water," Florian explained with a smile. "They are still wary, but happier." I canted my head at him, but he did not elaborate. He looked at Cosmina and an anxious frown settled between his brows. "Are you ready to be going to the castle? I will leave now to take you."

"Escorted by you, muddy as a dog? I hardly think so," Cosmina said with a sharp laugh.

He flushed again, a deep, angry red and turned on his heel to leave us.

I resumed my seat beneath the elm. "It is not like you to be unkind," I said mildly.

Cosmina's pretty features wore a pained expression. "It is a greater unkindness to encourage him. In Vienna he might well have been someone. Here he is no one. Like me."

A thread of bitterness stitched her words together, and I sipped at my wine, choosing my phrases carefully. "If you truly believe that both of you have so little worth, why not encourage him? He is a nice enough young man."

"I told you I do not wish to marry," she said almost angrily. The tips of her nostrils had gone quite white and she was breathing very fast. "You ought to understand. You have no one, you want no one, and you are content it should be so."

I thought of Charles and the future he had offered me, and I thought of the count and all his maddening ways, and I had never felt the want of a confidante so keenly. I longed to unburden myself to Cosmina, to tell her that I had been offered—and very nearly accepted—marriage to a man I did not love, and that I spent my days thinking about a man I could not have, a man who had scorned her as a woman ought never to be scorned.

She was watching me closely, and for an instant, the words trembled upon my lips. But I had kept my own counsel too long to confide so easily. I merely smiled and rose, brushing the leaves from my gown.

"It grows late and I think you are more tired than you will own."

If she was disappointed that I made her no confidences, she did not show it. She rose, too, and I took up her basket and whistled for Tycho and we began our long ascent up the mountain.

13

The count did not appear to dinner that evening, and as Cosmina was quite tired from our excursion to the village, the meal was a simple and short affair. We each of us retired early to our own pursuits. I meant to write for the rest of the evening, but I could not settle to it, and the scribbles I made were messy and slashed with my pen where I crossed out passages that displeased me. I had meant to write a passionate scene between two lovers, a scene of declaration and devotion, and the words failed me—failed me because I did not know what words folk used at such a time, I thought in disgust. I had no experience of such things, and even an imagination as broad as mine could falter. I longed to know what they would say and feel, what sweet sighs would pass between them, what caresses they would exchange. Of course I could not write the whole of such things, but if I could not imagine the entirety of the act, how could I comprehend its effects? And from there my thoughts drifted from my characters to the events of the day.

The count was the source of my distraction, for as Cosmina and I had passed through the village upon our return, I had looked more closely, reckoning the changes I found. A party of men was draining the river meadow for good pasturage, and a father and son were perched upon ladders, giving the school a fresh coat of paint and prying off the boards that had held the shutters fast. There remained an air of sleepiness about the place, but between the pedlar and the new improvements, something indefinable had changed. I noted there were yet branches of basil hung at the windows and here and there charms against evil had been newly painted. The people themselves seemed happy, but warily so, as Florian had said. They still feared the *strigoi* then, but they were pleased that the new count had finally bestirred himself to take an interest in their well-being. The question was why? Why had Count Andrei at last begun to improve the lot of his people?

The question plagued me. Alternately I hoped I might have been the cause of it and ridiculed myself for my foolish fancies. The count had spoken plainly enough of his feelings towards women. They were playthings, pretty toys to while away his hours of boredom and to be discarded once he tired of them. When he married it would be to some dull creature whose blood ran blue and who could give him sturdy sons with an excellent pedigree. If I interested him—and I conceded it seemed so—it was simply because he had few other diversions at the castle. Had we encountered one another in Paris, he would not have spared me a second glance, I told myself firmly.

But we are not in Paris, I thought by way of reply. I believed in free will, but I could be persuaded to fatalism. Perhaps we were here together at this time because it was supposed to be thus. I could never be more to him than a fleeting indulgence, but I realised with a sudden cold shock that I was not certain I wanted more from him.

Before I could think too long upon it, I rose and mounted the narrow stair to his room. I groaned to see the door ajar, for if it had been closed, I think I would have lacked the courage to knock upon it. But it stood open just far enough for Tycho to catch my scent and come to the door.

I peered past him to find the room empty, but the door that led to the workroom stair was also ajar, beckoning. I patted Tycho absently and passed through the room, gathering my skirts to mount the twisting stair to his workroom. He was standing at the longest of the tables, his sleeves rolled to bare his forearms, his neckcloth and collar discarded. He was bent to a task, and as I moved closer I could see he held a feather in one hand and a tiny piece of clockwork machinery in another. A lock of jet hair fell over his brow, but he did not seem to notice, so intent was he upon his work. I stood for a long moment before he spoke, and when he did I started, for he had not turned his head and I had not realised he was aware of me.

"It is an orrery," he said, nodding towards the intricate pieces scattered the length of the table. There were long, slender rods and several spheres and half spheres in various sizes, some painted in beautiful colours, others more muted, and the tiniest daubed with silver paint. At the end of the table rested a slab of inlaid wood and a collection of legs, and scattered over the table were an assortment of clockwork gears and complicated mechanisms. "A model of the solar system. When it is put back together, a simple crank will set the whole of it into motion, the entirety of the universe captured in a tabletop."

I moved forward and watched as he dipped the end of the

feather into a bowl of oil and, with a precise and delicate touch, applied it to the gear.

"Another piece of your grandfather's?" I asked him.

He nodded, intent upon his work. After a moment, he gave a little sigh of satisfaction and put the feather aside. He wiped his hands upon a bit of linen and turned to face me, his arms folded over his chest. The light fell upon his bared neck then, and I saw no scar there, not even the palest mark to blemish the smooth expanse of olive skin.

"I am sorry to have disturbed you," I began.

"It is a welcome intrusion," he replied with cool gallantry. He was watching me closely, assessing me, I thought, and I felt myself grow hot under his scrutiny. I wished he would return to the orrery, and to cover my confusion, I moved to the other side of the table.

"Is this Venus? It must be. What else could be so bright—"

"Do not touch it," he cautioned. "The paint is not yet dry."

I drew back sharply and put my hands behind my back.

"You are ill at ease tonight," he observed. "Is something amiss? Some trouble with your room perhaps?"

He was playing the host now, and I felt my courage wilt miserably within me. I could not possibly say the things to him that I wanted to say. I murmured an excuse and made to leave. He returned to his work, but as I reached the door, he called after me.

"There is a length of fabric upon the sofa. I believe it belongs to you."

I glanced towards the sofa and felt my heart give a peculiar lurch.

"That is the dress length that Frau Amsel purchased from the pedlar today," I said in some confusion.

He had picked up his feather and another clockwork gear. "It is yours," he repeated.

"I do not understand you. Has Frau Amsel changed her mind?"

"Frau Amsel has come to understand that her behaviour towards a guest in my house was intolerably rude," he said mildly, never taking his eyes from his work.

I gathered up the length of fabric and went to him.

"It belongs to Frau Amsel," I said quietly.

He put down his work and turned to me, his gaze inscrutable. "Do you find that you do not like it after all?"

"Of course not. It is lovely," I began.

He turned away from me. "Then it is yours."

I did not stir from my position. "She paid for it."

"She has been recompensed," he returned.

"You cannot mean you paid her for it?"

"Naturally. She will be bothered enough by her disappointment. There was no need to punish her purse as well."

I struggled to understand him. "That you took the fabric from her astonishes me, but that you can speak of it so calmly is incomprehensible. She paid for the cloth. She has a right to it."

He dropped the feather and turned to fix me with such a look as I had never yet seen upon his face. "I am master of this castle and lord of this land. No one has a right to anything that I wish for myself."

There was no possible response to that, so I did not attempt to make one. Instead, I placed the fabric upon the table and dropped the lowest and gravest curtsey I could manage and turned to leave.

Once more he recalled me at the door. "You will not keep it then?" he asked evenly.

I turned back to him, hands fisted. "You wish me to help you upset a poor old woman? How could I possibly keep the cloth when I know what was done to retrieve it?"

"That poor old woman is vicious as a viper, and you would

do well to remember that," he said calmly. "She took the fabric from sheer malice, she told me as much when I taxed her with it. She does not like you and she knew you wanted it, so she took it. It was childish and unworthy, and she violated every rule of hospitality in treating you thus. In disrespecting you, she disrespected me, and that is unacceptable. I gave her the choice of permitting me to pay for the fabric or resigning her post and leaving the castle at once for her transgressions. She was grateful to take my money and be done with it."

I felt the hot rush of anger ebb a little, even as I wished to hold fast to it.

"It still seems wrong to be so high-handed," I said, my voice sounding feeble even to my own ears.

"And did you not identify this as a feudal place?" he asked.

"I did," I admitted. He took up the fabric and put it into my hands.

"Take it."

"I cannot possibly. I am still uneasy about the method by which you acquired it," I told him with some asperity. "And even if that were not true, I could not accept a gift from you. It is not proper."

"Proper? I think we have passed beyond the pale of propriety, Miss Lestrange." He put his head to the side, and I saw that his eyes were clear and alight with some anticipated pleasure. "You will not do this to please me when I have done so much to please you?"

"Please me?" I paused and suddenly my bodice felt uncomfortably tight, constricting me. Had he made the improvements in the village at my urging? "The digging of the new well?"

"And the pasture, and the school, and the church," he added, numbering them on his fingers.

"You did not do those things to please me," I said faintly. I could scarcely hear my own voice over the drumbeat of my pulse in my ears.

He leaned forward, his lips brushing my ear. "Didn't I?"

I closed my eyes at the sensations that assaulted me. "You have owned that you do nothing you do not wish to do. It pleased you to make those improvements."

A warm exhalation passed over the flesh of my neck, summoning and warming the blood beneath. "It pleases me to please you," he murmured.

A single fingertip stroked downward from jaw to collarbone, tracing the pulse that surged and fluttered there. His other hand came around my waist firmly, possessing, even as his lips coaxed. *I ought go,* I thought stupidly. *It is not too late to turn back. Now, I will push him aside and take my leave.* Instead I lifted my chin, exposing my throat to him as he lowered his head. Fear rose within me, choking and hot, but still I stood in the circle of his arms, yielding, trusting. I felt the graze of his teeth against the soft flesh of my throat, and I waited, bracing myself for the pain of the piercing that would follow.

But it did not come. Instead he covered my mouth with his own and thrust his hands into my hair, wrenching aside the pins and plaits as he pressed me against the worktable.

His kisses were a revelation, for I had never imagined such things. Rather than frightening me, his abandon challenged my hesitation, and my passion rose with every proof of his.

He broke off suddenly, his lips so near to mine I could still feel the warmth of them. He put a fingertip to the first of my buttons, twisting it.

"Your gown buttons in the front, like a maid's," he said, his voice low and soft.

I swallowed hard as his fingertip brushed the bare skin above. "I have no maid. I must dress myself," I replied.

"Shall I be your maid?" he asked, sliding his fingers behind the décolletage. My knees failed me then, and he held me firmly against him with one arm as his other hand continued its work at my buttons, sliding intimately under my chemise.

"What if it were true?" he murmured against my lips. "Everything you hope and everything you fear. Is that what you have come for?"

"Yes," I said, opening to him.

He slipped each button from its hole, and with each another of my doubts slipped away. There was no space for them, crowded as my head was with the feel of him, the scent of him, the taste of him still hanging upon my lips. I had merely sipped of him yet, and I craved the whole.

"'What will you say tonight, poor solitary soul, to the kindest, dearest, the fairest of women?'" he murmured. It was Baudelaire, a lingering line from the poems he had given me. "'There is nothing sweeter than to do her bidding; Her spiritual flesh has the fragrance of Angels, and when she looks upon us we are clothed with light,'" he added.

He punctuated the poem with kisses, tracing his lips over my skin with every syllable. "'Be it in the darkness of night, in solitude, or in the city street among the multitude, her image in the air dances like a torch flame.'"

He drew back, the smile of Mephistopheles touching his lips. "Do you remember the rest?"

"'I am your guardian Angel, your Muse and Madonna,'" I said obediently, my breath coming in short gasps.

"Yes, I think you are my Muse," he said, clasping me to him and gathering me up as if I were a small child. I had not realised the strength in him. I had looked at his elegant clothes and taken him for a plaything of fashion, but the man who carried me to the little sofa and bore me down into the cushions was no idle creature. He was hard and fit, and when I drew his clothes away with impatient fingers, I could have wept at the beauty of him.

The pleasures we took upon that little sofa I could never have anticipated. He was neither tender nor rough, for although he coaxed responses from me, he had his own joys of me as well, and I was glad of it. The thought of playing the student to his tutor would have been unbearable. But we were equals, demanding of and rendering to each other the fullest of physical pleasures, and I realised how fortunate my choice had been. Had I surrendered myself in the marriage bed, my own satisfaction would have been illicit, a thing to be stolen from my husband. With a lover, it was a holy thing, a sacrament to the act itself, celebrated by the ordained. This liberty to do and choose whatever I liked made me bold, and my boldness pleased him and there, upon his grandfather's velvet sofa, he engulfed and consumed me and burnt me to ash to be reborn.

The act itself I cannot remember, not clearly, for the pieces have broken and fitted themselves together again like tumbling shards of kaleidoscope glass. I remember the feel of his back, the long silken muscles sleek beneath my fingers. I remember the little cries and the sweetly whispered words, those that urged and those that begged, and above it all, the astonishing duality of the act itself. The physical was so much more primitive than I had expected, and yet the emotions were exalted. I had expected release and relief and pleasure, but not tenderness. I had not expected to care for him.

And when it was over and his head rested upon my breast came the rush of sweetness. I knotted my fingers in his hair, thinking of Samson, and how a man is never so vulnerable as when he sleeps in a woman's arms. And I kissed him then, as I had not kissed him before. I had always waited for him to press his lips to mine, but as he drowsed, sated and entwined, I put my lips to his brow, as if to mark him for my own.

After a little while, he roused and stretched and poured out brandy for us both. "A restorative," he said, with only a trace of mischief.

I had wrapped myself in the length of dress fabric, preserving the vestiges of my modesty.

"You oughtn't cover yourself," he told me. "It is a crime against nature." He tugged at the cloth and I pushed his hand away.

"Stop," I said, but the word carried no force.

He regarded me thoughtfully. "You do not see yourself as I do, Theodora. There is much to admire. You are a woman of quiet charms, but charms nonetheless."

I sipped at the brandy, steeling myself against the fiery sting of it. I said nothing, but he did not seem to require a reply.

"Ah, you are looking sceptical again," he said lightly. "You think me a poor connoisseur, but I assure you, I speak with a master's eye." He put a hand to my hair, stroking it and twining a lock about his palm. "Your hair is lovely, almost as black as the wing of a raven. And your eyes are most arresting, so wide and so bright. Those eyes see everything, do they not? Sometimes when we are at table and your gaze is fixed on your plate, I imagine you still see everything that passes. Tell me, can you look into the heart of a man with those eyes?" he asked suddenly, his tone lightly mocking.

"I am no more perceptive than any other woman, and I daresay less than most," I replied.

"What do you perceive in me?" He dropped his eyes to the glass he turned in his hands, studying the ebb and flow of the brandy.

I hesitated, casting about for the right words. "A wounded thing. I think you have been hurt much in your life, and you do not want people to know it."

He lifted his brows in surprise, but did not speak and I went on.

"I think you are kinder than you would own to yourself, and I think your spirit is gentler than you pretend. You have taken up a carapace of coldness and sophistry to protect what you do not wish to expose."

"And what is that?" he asked, his tone a shade less jovial than before.

"Your most secret hope," I said, dropping my voice to a whisper. "Restoration."

"What a pretty picture you paint of me," he said softly, tracing the length of my neck with his thumb. "Everyone else sees me as a man to be envied, but you see the worst of me."

"Not the worst of you," I hastened to say. "Only the most vulnerable. A wolf in a trap will snap and snarl at whoever comes near to him out of fear he cannot protect himself."

"And I am a wounded wolf," he finished with a mocking smile.

"You may laugh at the metaphor, but I find it apt."

"As do I," he capitulated. "But I ought to warn you that what you have seen thus far is the merest sheep compared to the truth of me."

"Do you think so little of yourself that you wish me to share your low opinion?"

He drew away from me a little then, and I felt the coolness of it. Neither our minds nor our bodies touched, and though I had felt the connection between us, it was lost.

"I put no value upon my stock," he said, his tone dropping a little. "I see myself as I am, and you would do well to lose your illusions."

"Will you take them from me?" I teased, thinking to draw him in with good humour.

But he did not smile, and the eyes that had looked upon me

with warmth and approbation had turned cool and appraising. "I ought to. For your own good. I gave you the measure of my character early on in our acquaintance, but I have found it is a peculiar affliction of women that they will believe what they want of a man and ignore what he is, no matter how base, how vicious. A woman sees in a man only what she wishes to make of him," he added bitterly.

"Perhaps it is rather that we see what you might make of yourselves. You had no inclination to better the lives of your vassals, and yet you have done so. Does that not make you improved upon what you were?"

Something stirred in his eyes then, some flicker of cruelty that ought to have warned me.

"You think me caring and disingenuous? Even after I told you what I am? Shall I tell you again? I am a seducer of women, child. I take what I want, where I want, and I will employ any stratagem to secure it." He moved forward, gripping me by the shoulders. "Look at me, Theodora, and without wishing me to be other than I am. See me, and be warned."

"You do not frighten me," I told him, the trembling of my hands belying my words.

"Then why do you shiver? Am I not a horror story to frighten the stoutest heart?" he asked, dropping his head to my neck once more. He put his lips to the pulse at my throat and I felt the pressure of his teeth, poised above my heartbeat.

"Yes," I whispered into his hair, "and for that I pity you."

Instantly, he reared back, his hands still gripping my shoulders, his complexion dark with fury.

"You pity me?" he rasped.

"I do. There are stouter walls built round your heart than round this mountain. You take women for pleasure but not companionship, and any intimacy besides the physical causes you pain. Oh, I do see you for what you are. You are a man who wants to be understood, to be taken for all his flaws and all his failures and loved in spite of them. You despise my sex for our follies, and yet yours is the greater for at least we will take love where we can. You would throw it back and scorn the gift of it."

"You do not love me," he said, his colour fading to paleness. "You came here for the purpose of being seduced. Do not lie. I smelled willingness upon you the moment you entered the room. Do you think I have been blind to your sighs, your trembling, your longing glances? You are curious and passionate and you will use this night as fodder for your imagination, but do not mask it with the veil of love and think yourself better for it," he said. "We are cut of the same cloth, Theodora."

I felt a chill at his words, abashed that he had taken the measure of me so keenly. "At least I do not plate my heart with the cynic's armour. I believe I will love, and I will be loved, but you dismiss it out of hand as so much foolishness with your taxonomy of women and your scientific seductions. You reduce us all to playthings and formulae, to be won with calculation and guile. That is the real foolishness, for if no woman ever sees you, how can she begin to love you?"

"I do not require love," he said stonily.

"We all of us require love," I replied. "You think me childish and silly for clinging to the promise of it, but it is human to want happiness, and if there is happiness without love I am not convinced of it."

I paused then, watching the play of emotion across his face. I could not decipher it, but I knew he warred with himself, as if something I had said had thawed some part of him long-frozen and removed from the rest.

After a moment he put his hands to his temples. "I shall wake from this and find you are a pipe dream, sent to torment me for my past sins."

I put my hands over his. "I am no dream." I kissed him then, offering him my warmth. "I am here. I am real," I said, kissing him again. He embraced me, returning my kisses feverishly for a moment, until he wrenched himself away. He brought my clothes and dressed me, tenderly as any mother will dress a newborn child. I knew it was dismissal, and I felt only tired and much older than I had when I entered the room in search of my own destruction.

At the door, he cupped my face in his hands. "Do not bombard my defences, little one. They are all I have, and I find myself in danger of growing too fond of you. Believe me when I tell you it would be fatal for us both."

He kissed me one last time, and I felt the finality of it in his lips. "We will not speak of this again," he said as he opened the door. "It would doubtless improve my reputation, but it would ruin yours, and I am still gentleman enough to care," he finished. He closed the door, but gently, and I returned to my room, a more experienced and much more confused woman than I had been when I left it.

14

To my surprise, I slept deeply and dreamlessly that night—whether from the brandy or my physical exertions, I could not say—and I rose the next morning feeling much clearer in the mind. I had gone to the count's room deliberately, and although he was the experienced seducer, it was I who had gone to him. My courage had failed me once or twice, yet when the moment came, I had seized it. I was fully a woman now, and I felt the difference of it. So many things that had been veiled from me were now revealed, and although my experience must remain secret, I knew I should never be the same. I had gone boldly to claim that which I wanted, and in doing so, I had thrown down the barriers of my diffidence. It seemed astonishing to me that I had ever considered making a home with my sister or a life with Charles Beecroft. I was another person then, a child; I had existed only as a possibility. But now I truly lived; I was creating the life I intended to have for myself and I was filled with the power of it all.

Perhaps I should have left the castle that morning. I wonder how much of what followed would have come to pass had I not remained. But I felt the pull of the place and of the man himself, even if our parting had not been a romantic one. It was my own fault, I decided. No man likes to have his weaknesses prodded, and I had been ruthless in my examination of his. I believed what I told him, but I also realised that he might never rise equal to the task of reclamation. So much at the castle had been left to fall to ruin, so much beauty wasted and decayed. Little wonder the master of the place should prove the same, I reflected. But how I longed to try. I had seen the satisfaction to be had in restoring the village; how much greater the satisfaction in restoring a soul! I romanticised him, but it was to be expected. I was young and foolish, and he was my first lover. I could no more have left him then than I could have cut out my own heart.

Besides, as I reminded myself stoutly, I had promised Cosmina to stay. Guilt pawed at my stomach over the question of Cosmina. I knew she did not want the count for her own; she harboured no secret passions, nursed no girlish dreams. She was repulsed by marriage, and I strongly suspected would have been horrified by the act I had embraced so fully. There was something cool and untouched about Cosmina, and it occurred to me that even if she were to marry and bear a dozen sons, she would always remind me of the Madonna, remote and beautiful and above the squalid and the mundane. I was grieved to find that the little necklace of blue beads that Cosmina had presented to me was gone, lost somewhere in the workroom, and I determined to find it as quickly as possible.

I meant to visit the workroom during the day, but my book intruded. I wrote for hours in the library, Tycho resting at my feet as I scribbled, and when I emerged, it was to find I was

very nearly late for the evening meal. I hurried through my ablutions and joined the company in the great hall, surprised to
find the countess holding court.

"Good evening, my dear," she said, inclining her head slowly.

"Good evening, madame. How nice to see you," I returned,
rather breathlessly.

Frau Amsel stood at the countess's shoulder, hovering pro-
tectively and refusing to look directly at me, as if I were a
basilisk. I did not mind; if she were as vile as the count suggested, then I should prefer to keep my distance. Florian looked
exhausted from his efforts in the village. His hair was newly
slicked with water and he rocked a little on his heels from
fatigue. Cosmina was still a trifle paler than I would have liked,
but she greeted me with a warm smile. I did not dare look
directly at the count, but I fancied he was regarding me
thoughtfully, and I felt the heat rise in my cheeks at the memory
of what we had done together.

The meal was rather more formal in view of the countess's
presence, and when it was concluded we repaired to the library
for an evening of piquet and music. It was a pleasant enough
time, or would have been, were it not for the things that went
unspoken. There was much we might have said to each other,
and much that we concealed.

But the evening passed and when the clock struck eleven,
we rose to retire. Just as we reached the great hall, a tremendous thud echoed throughout the room. Cosmina gave a little
gasp, and the countess's hand flew to her heart.

"Someone is at the door," said the count.

After a long moment of breathless silence, the sound came
again, harder this time. At the count's side, Tycho stood, watchful
and bristling slightly. The count nodded almost imperceptibly,
and Florian moved forward and threw open the door. Lit from

behind by the pale starlight, a man stood silhouetted in the doorway, his shadow looming long against the floor, almost touching our feet. He stood there for the space of several heartbeats, then moved out of the shadows and into the room.

He was just above average height and solidly built. He was dressed for travelling with a long coat of chamois over country tweeds. He carried a small leather bag in one hand, and a wide-brimmed hat shaded his face. The candlelight was deceiving; for the space of a heartbeat I thought there was something familiar about him, something in the way he held himself, but how could that be? I was a stranger in this place, and with the exception of a handful of villagers, I had no acquaintance.

He turned his head, surveying the company from under the brim of his hat, saying nothing. Then, with an exclamation of satisfaction, he tore the hat from his head.

"Theodora!" cried Charles Beecroft.

I stared at him, wondering what sort of mad dream I had conjured that I should see Charles in Transylvania, in the Castle Dragulescu of all places.

But he was real. I could smell him, horse and sweat and leather mixed with something sweet like honey.

"Charles," I said, moving forward. Behind me I could feel the count stiffen like a pointer. "Charles, what are you doing here?"

Charles puffed a little. "What am I doing here? Isn't it perfectly apparent that I have come to see you?"

I turned swiftly to the countess. "Madame, may I present Mr. Charles Beecroft of Edinburgh, my publisher. Charles, this is the Countess Dragulescu, my hostess. And her son, the Count Dragulescu, master of the castle."

Charles bowed, a trifle awkwardly to the countess, but she inclined her head graciously.

"You have come a very long way, Mr. Beecroft."

"Aye, I have. And I apologise for disturbing the household at this hour. It took a bit longer than I expected to ascend the mountain." He smiled at her, his gentle, winsome smile, and I could see that she was charmed.

Charles turned to the count. "Sir, my apologies to you as well."

The count regarded him coolly, canting his head as he assessed him.

Charles looked abashed and turned to me. "Does the fellow have no English? What language does he speak? My French is fairly abysmal, but I could try."

"He speaks English," I said, *sotto voce*. "His excellency was at Cambridge."

"Indeed?" Charles raised his brows, and I knew he was not pleased to hear it. He had been schooled before his family had risen to prominence in publishing, and his own education had been spotty. It was one of his few shortcomings and one that Charles felt keenly. He fixed the count with a smile I did not quite believe. "I must again extend my apologies for the intrusion."

The count smiled coolly. "Accepted. If you will excuse me, I wish to retire." He gave me a significant look, then turned on his heel and left us, the dog trotting after him.

Florian and Cosmina hovered near and I took the count's departure as a chance to introduce them. The countess was still watching Charles carefully.

"You must be tired, Mr. Beecroft. You will of course remain as our guest here."

"Oh, I couldn't, madame," Charles protested. "That is very kind of you, but I only wished to see Theodora as soon as I arrived. It was impetuous of me, and as I say, I misjudged the distance to the top of the mountain. I can easily hire a room in the village."

I stared at him. Charles, impetuous?

The countess merely waved her hand. "I will not hear of it, and the villagers are nervous of strangers. You will stay here for the duration of your visit, Mr. Beecroft. You will be a welcome distraction," she added.

If Charles thought her choice of words odd, he gave no sign.

"That is very kind of you, countess. I will accept then."

"Excellent. Miss Lestrange, will you be kind enough to show your friend to the room next to Cosmina's? It is always made up. I think he will be comfortable there. Come, Cosmina. You may light me to bed. Florian, bolt the doors, and Clara, I should like some milk."

They departed, but I noticed Cosmina, lingering a bit behind, casting the odd speculative glance at Charles. When she had gone, I turned to him.

"Charles, what—"

He stopped me short, his voice clipped and cold, unlike I had ever heard it.

"Theodora, I have not slept in three days. My last meal was yesterday morning. I am filthy, I am starved, and I am in an extremely bad temper. We will talk later. Now be a good girl and show me to my room."

I obeyed, lighting him to the room the countess had specified. The hearth was swept and freshly laid, and it took but a moment to kindle a bright fire to banish the chill from the room.

"You ought to have something to eat," I told him.

"In the morning."

I hesitated at the door. "If there is nothing I can get for you, then I will bid you goodnight."

"You look different," he said suddenly. I turned back. He was sitting on the edge of the bed, one boot still on, the other in his hand.

"So do you, Charles." I went to him and knelt swiftly, drawing off his other boot. I put them aside, a little distance from the hearth so as not to damage the leather. I took his hat and his coat from the bed and placed them on hooks by the window. I drew the curtains closed and by the time I was finished, he was fast asleep, sprawled over the bed, fully clothed.

I took up a coverlet, another of the great furry robes that abounded in the castle, and draped it over him. He murmured something unintelligible, but it sounded like my name.

The next morning I went to Charles's room just as Cosmina was approaching his door with a tray for breakfast.

She did not seem entirely pleased to see me.

"I thought your friend might be hungry. It is the day for laundry and poor Tereza is run off her feet this morning."

"How kind of you," I said, embarrassed that she should wait upon Charles. She was of the family, after all, and it was my fault he had come. If there was a burden to be borne, it ought to be mine.

"Let me take that." I lifted the heavy tray out of her hands, but she released it a trifle reluctantly. She turned and tapped her way down the corridor as I kicked lightly upon the door. Charles answered, rested and in good spirits it seemed. He was half dressed, wearing the same breeches and boots of the night before and a clean shirt open at the neck. He held a razor in one hand and a towel in the other.

"Thank God," he said upon seeing the tray. "I was about to gnaw upon the bedposts." He waved me in and went back to his ablutions, shaving carefully as I watched.

"You will forgive the impropriety, I am sure," he said lightly as he caught my gaze in the looking glass. I turned away and began to uncover the dishes.

"There are bread rolls and a maize porridge called *mămăligă*. It is rather tasty. The maid ought to have brought it, but she has not been herself of late. Her sister died a fortnight ago." I was chattering from nerves. This new Charles was a stranger to me, cool and aloof where my Charles had always been kind and undemanding.

He turned from the looking glass, wiping at the traces of shaving soap with his towel.

"I will pour out the coffee. It is Turkish-style, quite thick and very bitter. Cosmina did not bring sugar. I will go to the kitchens for you and fetch some."

"Theodora," he said, his voice low. I did not look at him.

"There is new butter for the bread rolls. You might like a bit of that, and here is some honey for the porridge."

I reached for a spoon for the little honeypot, but he took it from me. I put my hands behind my back and stepped away.

"I ought to be rather angry with you, you know," he said mildly as he sat to his breakfast.

"Angry with me? Whatever for?" I plucked irritably at the withered basil tied to the window latch.

"You have been here the better part of six weeks and you have not written a single line."

"I wrote to Anna." I heard the note of sulkiness in my voice, but I could not help it. Something about Charles's presence had aroused my petulance.

"And Anna wrote to me. She was not at all pleased to hear about the dead maid, and she said your letters have been peculiar. She wanted me to come and take matters in hand."

"Matters here are not yours to take in hand," I retorted, now thoroughly annoyed. I did not like the familiarity with which Charles referred to my sister. It bespoke a conspiracy between them I could not like.

"You've no call to be crabbit," he said mildly.

I took a deep, slow breath and strove for patience. "I am sorry. I did not mean to be ill-tempered. Not when you have come so far to fetch me."

He folded his arms over his chest and raised his chin, affecting a rather mulish expression. "Sit down, Theodora. I cannot think with you flitting about. And I did not come to fetch you."

I obeyed and took a chair, sagging into it in my relief. I had feared a scene, imagining myself a reluctant Helen, dragged back to Sparta by an importuning Menelaus. "But why else—"

"Oh, I came to see you, partly to ease Anna's mind, but also because there is unfinished business between us."

He went to his leather bag and withdrew a notecase. He dropped it into my lap and resumed his seat, rubbing his hands together in anticipation as he looked over the food.

"What is this?" I asked. The case was thick with Scottish banknotes.

"The proceeds of the sale of your last two stories," he explained, spreading the bread rolls thickly with sweet butter. "You did not leave your bank details. Most irresponsible," he finished severely. "But the money belongs to you and have it you shall."

He continued to eat, chewing serenely while I fumed.

"That is absurd," I said finally. "You might have sent it to Anna or held it yourself. You could have made arrangements with any of the Imperial banks and I could have collected the funds in Hermannstadt," I pointed out.

"That horrible little hole I travelled through last week? Don't be absurd," Charles rejoined. He sampled the *mămăligă*. "You are right. It wants a bit of honey." He spooned on a modest amount and tried it again. "Better. Besides, I told you, Anna was worried. I thought it far better to come and see you for myself, and allay her worries. I would have already come and gone had it not been for the disasters along the way."

"How long have you been away?" I asked.

He made a gesture of impatience. "Forever and twice as long. I was actually in Vienna attending to business when Anna wrote to me. It ought to have been an easy matter to travel here, but my pocket was picked," he said. "I lost my money and my papers. I could not purchase a ticket on proper railways then, not in the Austrian Empire, so I had to travel illegally. I fell in with a rather dashing crowd of Gypsies who let me ride with them as far as Zagreb."

I felt a little faint. "But if you lost all your money, how was it you still had mine?" I asked, brandishing the notecase.

"I carried your money in my bag for security. My own funds were upon my person, and before you ask, no, I was not going to spend a pound of your money," he said firmly.

"Of course you wouldn't." Charles would have sooner starved than touched a penny of what did not belong to him.

"Once in Zagreb, I met up with a shepherd at the market who promised to take me as far as Belgrade. From there I met up with a band of travelling musicians who were bound for Klausenberg."

"Klausenberg is a day's journey too far," I told him, rather unhelpfully.

"Yes, I realise that now, but at the time, I simply wanted to get out of Belgrade. I could not rest unless I was always pushing onward. In Klausenberg, I met a farmer who said he would take me a few miles down the Hermannstadt road. And that is how it went. Every day, pushing onward, meeting someone kind enough to get me a little further on my way."

"Charles, I am so sorry," I murmured. "I never imagined that what I did would lead to this horrible journey for you."

He stared at me, his eyes showing some hint of the old spaniel softness. "Horrible? It was the adventure of my life."

"Adventure?"

"I rode with brigands in Serbia. I slept under the stars. I drove a herd of sheep to market. I have met the most extraordinary folk. I have never felt so alive in my entire life. Not that I wish to repeat the experience," he finished with a warning look. "It has all been quite too wholesome and rough, and I am ready to be back amongst the civilised. I expect it will make for some rather good conversation at my club," he added with a nod of satisfaction.

I sat in silent stupefaction. "I suppose it will at that. Well, you have given me my money and I will be happy to make you the loan of it for your return journey. The Dragulescus will loan you a horse and a man to guide you back to Hermannstadt. That is the nearest train station. You can replace your passport there as well, I imagine."

I rose, but he put down his spoon. "Not so quickly, if you please. I may have completed my errand, but I cannot leave you without making certain you are quite all right. As I said, you look different to me. Tell me about the death in the castle and about this count fellow."

I told him, haltingly at first, then more quickly as I warmed to my theme. I was so relieved to have a confidant that I told him more than I had intended, with the solitary and notable exception of my feelings for the count.

Charles's expression grew increasingly thunderous as the conversation wore on, particularly when I made mention of the *strigoi* and the savage lupine habits of the Popa men. When I finally reached the agreement we had all made to keep Aurelia's death secret, he could contain himself no longer.

He dashed his spoon to the table and burst out with, "Is that all? A vampire killer stalking the castle? Are you quite certain there aren't any banshees in the stables? A werewolf in the library? Oh, I forgot, the werewolves are outside in the forest. How stupid of me!"

I rose and spoke with as much dignity as I could muster. "If you are not going to be serious, there is no point in having this discussion."

"I *am* serious, Theodora. What has happened to you? You know this is nonsense. You are a student of folklore. You know that every people has its superstitions, and you know them for what they are—tales to frighten children. You know there is a logical and rational explanation for everything that happens. That is what separates us from these poor superstitious folk who live their lives in fear of the bogeyman. You've a fine mind, my dear. Use it," he instructed tartly.

"You do not understand! You did not see that body, that awful body. I tell you it was not a human responsible for what happened to that girl. It was something less than a man. And how else can you account for the death? You must at least allow for the possibility of some supernatural agency."

"I could offer half a dozen possibilities," he replied, his tone calm and reasonable. "And none of them supernatural. For instance, one of these wandering Popa fellows. They have the whole countryside convinced they are wolves, but I say it is a tremendous fraud. What married man would not like to leave his family and carouse with his brothers? Perhaps their antics got out of hand and they killed the girl. Perhaps a wandering pedlar or Gypsy did the deed. Perhaps it was an accident or suicide. Perhaps her sister, this Tereza, was jealous over a trifle and decided to dispose of her."

I shuddered. "How cold you are."

He pulled an indignant face. "I am pragmatic, Theodora.

And so you should be. You are an Edinburgher. You were raised with the tales of Burke and Hare, stealing bodies from graveyards and murdering unsuspecting folk to sell their bodies to the cadaver schools. You know that man is capable of any horror towards his fellow man, and that may be doubly true of women. The most fiendish creatures I have ever known have worn skirts and the Devil's own smile."

"What about the corpse of Count Bogdan?" I demanded. "How can you account for the state of it, plump and rosy and brimming with blood? It was unnatural."

"Was it?" he asked. "Theodora, I have never seen a corpse some weeks dead, but my youngest brother has. During his medical studies, he told such tales as would frighten the heart of the stoutest man at the brightest noon. His stories from the dissecting room are larded with folk who gasp and moan and roll their eyes when they are touched—some even weeks after their deaths. It is all quite normal to a rational mind."

I considered what he said. It seemed so reasonable couched in those terms. But he had not yet felt the pull of the black forests of the Carpathians, and he had not yet listened to the howling of the wolves under a silver moon.

"But what if it is just possible? This is not like other places, Charles. Things happen here that do not happen elsewhere. I cannot explain it except to say that what I have seen defies science."

He fell silent a moment, stroking his chin as he thought. His hands were pale and soft, nothing like the hands of the count, with the wide smooth palms and the long, deft fingers.

"But even if your premise proves true, and there is no supernatural force abroad in this place, it would make no difference to my situation. I have promised Cosmina that I will remain, and I mean to honour my promise."

He pushed his coffee away. It must have grown stone cold in any case. A skin wrinkled the top of it.

"I cannot leave you here until I have satisfied myself that you are in no danger."

"I cannot leave," I told him firmly.

"Theodora, I never thought you stubborn, but this—"

"It is not stubbornness," I corrected. I hesitated. "It is the book."

Charles's attention was pricked. He sat forward in his chair, the last of his breakfast forgot as his eyes sharpened.

"Go on."

"I have begun it. And it is by far the best I have ever written. It will be the work that establishes me, solidly. It will be the foundation of everything I want to achieve. But I cannot write it without this place."

He stared at me in disbelief, shaking his head slowly. "It is as if you are bewitched," he said heavily.

I shrugged. "Perhaps I am. You always did say the best writers are half-mad," I reminded him.

He gave me a gentle smile, but still his objections remained.

"Theodora, you are so caught up in the madness of this place that you cannot even see the absurdity of it all. A girl has died, and you are willing to believe it was some monster who did the deed. Your imagination is quite overwrought."

"I cannot explain it, Charles. I only know that this place has fired my imagination like no other. I must stay to finish what I have begun."

"It is a most unique situation," he admitted finally, glancing about the room. "I can well understand why it moves you so."

I said nothing. I had learned from long experience that it was best to sow the seeds of an argument and let Charles bring them to fruition himself. Charles often found himself at odds with his own nature. His chivalry warred with his more mercenary tendencies, and at this moment, the prospective husband challenged the man of business. Protect the woman he hoped to marry, or encourage her to remain in peril and write a book he could use to make his mark? I prayed the merchant would prevail.

To my astonishment, he nodded. "Very well. I understand why you cannot leave. It does certainly present you with an opportunity for a novel you must not lose."

Relief surged in me, sharp and painful as a lance.

"Then you will leave me here?"

He shook his head. "I cannot in good conscience. Neither as your publisher nor as your friend, and I still cherish hope someday to be more."

I opened my mouth, but he waved a hand. "Do not reply. I know well enough what you will say. But you must know the offer stands, and it always shall. I accept that for now you have rejected me, and we will not speak of it for the present. You will continue to write and you will remain at the castle."

"And you?" I ventured.

He smiled, and for the first time, it reminded me of a crocodile's smile.

"I will remain with you."

15

If I was annoyed at having a chaperone, I did my best to conceal it. Charles was entirely capable of creating enough of a distraction that I should be forced to leave the castle, and it seemed a tremendous victory that I had been able to persuade him I should stay. He told me with a bland smile that he meant to spend the morning exploring the castle, and I left him with a feeling of sharp unease. I tried to settle to my work, but every time I lifted my pen, I thought of him falling into conversation with the count and my stomach gave a little churn as if I had just boarded a ship and not yet found my sea legs.

After a pleasant midday meal, Cosmina proposed a visit to the village. She wished to call upon Dr. Frankopan and suggested that Charles might like to see more of the valley. He accepted with alacrity, and it occurred to me that I had seldom seen Cosmina look quite so uncertain of herself. She had always been quieter than most of the girls of my acquaintance, but she had worn a mantle of self-possession. Now, as she looked at Charles, once or twice I detected a hesitancy. I wondered if she were perhaps forming a *tendresse* for him in spite of her protestations against men and marriage.

We ventured down to the village, and all the while Cosmina kept up a patter of entertaining narrative about the castle and its legends. Charles was intrigued; I had known him too long to mistake that intently arrested air. He was doubtless fitting Cosmina's chatter into the conversation he and I had shared over breakfast, and it was with only the slightest touch of annoyance that I noted he helped her over the roughest going while leaving me to pick my own way down the Devil's Staircase.

In the village, Cosmina pointed out to him the fresh improvements, and Charles surveyed it all with great interest.

"It seems as if the new count is making rather excellent progress," he commented blandly. "Is he not here to oversee matters himself?"

I said nothing but bent swiftly to fuss with a bootlace. The less I said upon the subject of the count, the better. Charles pricked like a pointer every time his name was raised, and it seemed inevitable he would discover my feelings for the man himself. I only hoped such a revelation could be postponed until long after we had both quitted the place.

"Count Andrei does not often go abroad during the day," Cosmina told him. "He prefers to keep more nocturnal hours."

I rose to find Charles had turned to me, his brows lifted significantly. "Really? What a singular fellow."

"Not at all," I returned, rather too sharply. "He is by way of being an amateur astronomer. He could hardly practise the astronomical arts during the day, now could he?"

Cosmina cut in to point out the graveyard just then and Charles turned away, but his expression was speculative, and I chastened myself. I should have to be far more careful if I expected to keep my feelings for the count concealed.

We walked on to Dr. Frankopan's little cottage in the woods, and I was pleased to find the old gentleman at home. We were greeted with great warmth, and when he discovered we had a visitor with us, his usual fuss became an outright furore.

"How do you do?" Charles asked politely.

"How wonderful, how wonderful! A Scotsman, I do not think I have ever met such a creature before," he exclaimed, much to Charles's chagrin. Like many educated Scots of English descent, Charles had taken pains to banish both Scottish colloquialisms and accent from his speech, although they did creep in from time to time.

I smiled behind my hand, and Charles glowered a little at me as we were hurried to comfortable chairs beside the fire while refreshments were sent for. Madame Popa served us with a sullen humour, and I was not sorry to see her leave. If Charles connected her with the tale I had told him of the man who had taken to the mountains as a wolf, he betrayed no sign of it.

Dr. Frankopan gestured towards the tea things with alacrity. "Ah! Today the good Frau Graben has sent me a wonderful apple tart made from the apples grown in the castle garden. Have you seen the garden yet, Mr. Beecroft? An astonishing thing to find a place of cultivation so high upon the mountain."

"I have not. I have only just arrived last night," Charles explained.

"Oh, you must see it, you must!" Dr. Frankopan advised. "Of course, it is not so tidy as it was in the old days, but there is still beauty there in the ruins. And you will see the little trees that produce the famous black apples."

"Black apples?" Charles looked a trifle alarmed as he poked a fork cautiously into his slice of the tart.

"Only the skins," I reassured him. "They are quite extraordinary-looking, small and purplish-black like plums. But the flesh is very white and sweet."

These were the apples Cosmina and I had picked and I knew from experience that they were delicious, although not prepossessing in appearance.

"Like something out of a faery tale," Charles said, giving me a significant look.

"Precisely, precisely!" Dr. Frankopan said happily. "The whole place is like something out of a faery tale. You will find much to interest you here, sir, if you are not averse to country pleasures."

Charles strove for diplomacy. "I confess I am a man of the city, Dr. Frankopan, but I am determined to learn the error of my ways. I do already see it is a most remarkable place."

"It is, it is," Dr. Frankopan agreed.

With that we fell into conversation about the village and the valley and a little of life beyond, for Charles had the most recent news from Vienna, and the afternoon was one of the most pleasant I had passed since coming into Transylvania. It struck me as I watched them that Charles and Dr. Frankopan were similar men, holding several virtues in common. They both were kindly and worked hard. They were agreeable and decent and they both conducted themselves in such a manner as to help those they could.

It also struck me that they were both solicitous of Cosmina. When it became apparent that she was sitting in the draught from a poorly fitted window, Charles insisted upon changing his seat for hers, and more than once I caught Dr. Frankopan watching her with a little furrow of worry ploughed between his brows. He was still concerned for her health, I realised, and I wondered if there was something more seriously amiss with her than I had known. But she seemed stronger than she had the previous week, and every day her colour rose and she was able to walk further and with more purpose. Even now, roses bloomed in her cheeks, and I was glad of it.

Charles seemed to enjoy the afternoon as well, and as we departed, Dr. Frankopan pressed him with an invitation to come again, alone or in company, whenever he chose.

"I am an old bachelor, you will not disturb me," he assured Charles.

"We are the pair of us old bachelors then," Charles said rather too heartily.

We made our way back to the castle then in the waning afternoon light, the drooping sun casting long golden shadows over the valley, gilding the scene to a burnished tranquility. Cosmina drifted ahead, picking an armful of leaves to place in bowls, and Charles fell into step at my side.

"Well?" I asked. It was a testament to our long friendship that the single word was sufficient.

He paused, thinking. "I have finally realised what it puts me in mind of. Do you remember those curious children's books we published last year? The metamorphoses books?"

I nodded. They were some of the most delightful books Charles had produced. Each had been crafted with clever turn-ups so that the turning of a page produced a feature that popped to life, a bird on the wing, a castle tower rising above a forest ridge.

"That is what this place reminds me of. A metamorphoses book. A turn of the page and something new and wonderful springs to life. Most unexpected," he said, his voice dropping curiously.

And when he spoke, his eyes lingered on the graceful figure of Cosmina in the distance.

★ ★ ★

I was not jealous of Cosmina, I told myself firmly. It was absurd to place any importance whatsoever upon Charles's apparent interest in her. There was no attachment; Cosmina's antipathy would see to that. But it did not escape my notice that she managed to be just at hand to place herself next to Charles at dinner. And later, when the household adjourned to the library for quiet entertainments, Charles hurried to help her with the arrangement of her silhouette table.

"It is not often that I use the table," she told him as he lit the candle and placed it opposite the screen according to her instructions. "But visitors here are so rare a pleasure, we try to commemorate the occasion with a silhouette, to bring pleasure to us in the lonely hours after they have gone. I thought I would cut one of you and one of Theodora, to remind us all of this night," she finished, her colour becomingly pink.

Charles preened a little and seated himself on the other side of the screen from Cosmina and her sharp little scissors. She took up a piece of black paper and began to cut, her eyes darting between her work and the still shadow thrown upon the muslin.

Florian watched the interplay with a sullen air and began to work a mournful little melody upon the harpsichord until the countess called to him.

"Florian, my dear boy, play us something more cheerful. We have had enough of sorrowful things," she commanded with a kindly smile.

He obeyed, spinning out a pretty tune that was so soft and coaxing, his mother began to nod over her needlework, and it was still possible to hear the gentle rustle of the fire and the heavy sleeping breaths of the dog settled upon the hearth rug.

Only the count seemed unaffected by the soothing music,

for he took a chair close to mine, ostensibly to look over the castle guest book I had unearthed. I turned the pages slowly, reading over the spidery scrawls of ink, once black but now faded to pale brown upon the foxed pages.

But the count was not a man to be ignored, and as Cosmina and Charles fell into conversation, he spoke, his voice low and soft and pitched for my ears alone.

"It will never do."

I puzzled over a rampant signature that scrolled over the better part of a page. A baroness of some sort, visiting from Buda-Pesth a quarter of a century ago. The castle had been a hospitable place then, for each page was filled with signatures of the great and good, and the further back I turned, the more exalted the names.

"What will never do?" I murmured. I had found an archduke, and just below, the illegitimate son of a pope.

"You and that fellow," he said, darting his eyes at Charles almost imperceptibly. "It is absurd."

"I do not understand you," I said primly.

"Don't you? Come to me when he is abed."

I caught my breath at the brazenness of his command, but still I kept my eyes fixed firmly upon the decaying page before me.

"I shall not."

"Do not hiss at me, my dear. I mean only to talk with you. It was an invitation to converse, nothing more."

I dared a glance and was surprised to find his eyes alight, whether from amusement or malice, I could not say. He was an enigma to me, this curious nobleman from Transylvania. I could not say from one moment to the next what he believed, what he held dear, what he would not do. More than an enigma, he was a chameleon lizard, always changing his colours just when I had learnt his disguises.

But even such a man as this could not command me, I decided, summoning my tattered pride.

I opened my mouth to refuse him, but just then he put out a hand, barely touching my arm. "Please?" he asked.

He was humble, as I had seldom seen him, and I wondered if this was a fresh stratagem of his to throw me from my complacency.

"I cannot," I said firmly. And to show that I meant it, I closed the book and rose to walk away.

Cosmina's silhouette of Charles was a remarkable thing. It managed to convey the features of the man, but it captured something indefinable as well, some essential part of him that I would have thought unknowable without conversation and expressions. I looked at the flat shadow snipped from the ebony paper, and I saw the friend, the publisher, the erstwhile suitor. And something more. Cosmina had captured something rather dashing about him as well, and I realised this was how she saw him, not as the stiff and stuffy man of business, but as the congenial gentleman who had engaged her attention.

"It is very like," I said finally, and Charles looked mightily pleased.

He gave way for me to take my turn behind the little screen, and I saw that the count had settled himself behind a chessboard. I had not seen it before; the pieces appeared very old and fashioned of marble, burnished to a sheen with long use. As I watched in some trepidation, the count invited Charles to a game and they began to play. All the while, Florian kept up his gentle melodies while his mother drowsed and the countess read, occasionally putting out a slippered foot to stroke Tycho's back.

"What a pleasant man your friend Mr. Beecroft is," Cosmina said softly as she began to cut the silhouette.

"Yes, he is rather."

"Have you known him long?" I wished I could gauge the strength of her interest, but her expression was hid from me by the muslin screen.

"Years, actually. I must have met him when I was eleven, perhaps twelve. His family firm published my grandfather's books, and his father and my grandfather were great friends. They were both of them Englishmen settled in Edinburgh, so they felt the kinship of living abroad, I think. When his father called, Charles and I were left to amuse ourselves in the corner while our elders talked."

"And yet you never mentioned him at school. Curious." Her tone was speculative, but I could hear the decisive snips of her scissors.

"I cannot think why I should have," I told her honestly. "He was simply a person I knew. I only saw him once or twice each year until I came home from school and Grandfather fell ill. He called one day with some business or other for Grandfather and the poor old dear was asleep. Charles and I talked instead and he discovered I had written a few little stories. He asked to see them, and took them away to read. A week later he returned with an offer to see them published in a magazine, with an eye to grooming me to write a book."

My recollection was true and the events innocent enough, and yet I felt as if I were a penitent, called upon by her confessor to recount her crimes. I glanced at the muslin screen, but Cosmina was nothing more than an alteration in the light to me—no form, only the suggestion of a presence. In contrast, I was clearly revealed to her, every inch of my profile and expression laid bare. I felt naked and exposed, and I disliked it.

"Are you almost finished?" I asked.

"Very nearly, my dear. Hold quite still. I am at the neck and it is rather tricky as your hair is so heavy just there. Still, it would be worse if you were wearing your necklace," she added, and I started, realising that I had quite forgot to retrieve the beads from the workroom. I should have to go to the count for no other reason than to reclaim my property before Cosmina detected my foolishness.

"Oh!" she exclaimed suddenly, her voice a study in woe.

"What is the matter?" I said, my voice a trifle too sharp.

I rose from my chair to see what the trouble was. Cosmina sat, black paper in one hand, scissors in the other.

She looked at me in dismay. "You moved so quickly, you startled me and I have quite ruined it."

She gestured towards her lap where the tiny black image of my head had fallen to her skirts, the neck as neatly cut as if by a guillotine's blade.

16

That night my sleep was broken by dreams of the count again, and the following day I felt thick-headed and dull; even Charles commented that I did not seem myself. Cosmina fell ill again, a relapse of her cold, and I did not see her, although Dr. Frankopan called and said he had given her something to help her to rest. Charles accompanied him back to the village, where the good doctor promised him a hearty meal at the inn, and I roamed the library, too distracted to settle. In the end, I decided a rest in my room would clear my head, but as soon as I entered, I realised someone had been there before me.

I was aware of my pulses quickening, as if I feared someone still lingered, watching me.

"I am not afraid," I said stoutly. Almost as soon as I had said the words, my eyes fell to the table and I counted myself a fool. Coiled there was the string of blue beads I had misplaced. Since I had not gone to his room to retrieve them, the count must have returned them to me. Still, I could not rid myself of the feeling that someone had been in my room for a longer period of time than merely returning the necklace would have required. I searched my things carefully. Nothing had gone missing; nothing seemed actually disarranged. And yet I could not be completely at my ease in that room, and in spite of my fatigue, I took up my plaid shawl and made my way out of doors for a little fresh air.

Florian was about, and I was struck suddenly by the change that had come over him in the past few days. He no longer wore simply the long linen shirt of the peasant, for he had changed it for a properly tailored affair with cuffs and a collar. He wore a bit of faded silk wrapped and tied at the throat as a sort of neckcloth, and his boots were freshly shined. He had gained authority and it suited him, although his eyes were still the saddest I had seen.

"Good day, Florian. Where are you bound?"

He nodded towards the garden wall. "The last of the apples must be picked."

"May I help?"

He said nothing but passed me a basket, and beckoned me to follow him. We worked for some time in the ruined garden, picking the last of the sinister black apples with the sweet flesh. A light wind had blown up, tossing the tops of the stunted trees and bearing upon it the scent of woodsmoke and pine. The sun was warm upon my face, and I soon discarded the shawl, draping it over a sprawling tarragon bush.

Florian hummed as he worked, a piercingly sweet and sad tune, like a lullaby for a dying child, and I found tears pricking my eyes as I picked.

"Are you well, Miss Theodora?" he asked.

I nodded and summoned a smile. "I am tired is all. I slept poorly last night."

"Do you fear the *strigoi?*" he asked suddenly.

I hesitated, and then gave him honesty. "I do not know. I cannot think what to believe. One moment I am convinced that these monsters are real, the next I am chastening myself for a fool."

"Will you leave this place?" he asked, and although it was only for a fleeting moment, I saw something hopeful spring to life in his eyes.

"Eventually. I have promised Cosmina to remain for some time yet. Perhaps through Christmas."

"And when you go, will you be taking Miss Cosmina with you?"

I thought of the immense sadness in him, the chivalrous little attentions towards Cosmina, and the brusqueness with which she dismissed him. And I understood him a little better, or so I believed.

"You would not like for her to leave," I said kindly. I had meant to offer him some comfort, to explain that I had no intention of asking Cosmina to leave with me, not least because I had no place to offer her.

But before I could, he burst out in impassioned speech. "Because it is good she should go. You take her far from here— and soon. When your friend leaves, Mr. Beecroft, you take Miss Cosmina. Save her."

And with that extraordinary pronouncement, he turned upon his heel and left me in the garden, staring after him and pondering all that he had just told me.

I took one of the devilish black apples and shined it upon my skirt as I seated myself on a crumbling stone bench. It seemed clear to me, piecing together the revealing bits I had heard since my arrival, that Cosmina was in some danger. Perhaps from the spectre of the *strigoi,* perhaps from some inherent weakness in the blood of the Dragulescu women that seemed to afflict the countess and Cosmina in unequal measure. And Florian, in spite of Cosmina's indifference to him, thought warmly of her and wished her to be protected. They had been children together, and it was natural that his feelings towards her should be cordial ones. She was the nearest thing he had had to a sister, and although time and maturity had given them both an awareness of the differences in their expectations—she was the ward of the countess whilst he would never rise above hired steward—it was understandable he should look to her best interests. It only saddened me that I could not accommodate his wishes. I had no home of my own, still less did I have a place to offer Cosmina. It vexed me that I could offer her neither sanctuary nor solace; indeed, I could scarcely look at her without thinking upon my impropriety with the count and how she might view the matter.

As if conjured by my thoughts, the man himself appeared in the garden. I had not heard him approach, and when he spoke my name, I started up, the unbitten apple rolling from my grasp.

He retrieved it and polished it upon his lapel. "I did not mean to startle you, but you were so deep in thought. I called your name twice."

He extended his hand, holding out the apple upon his palm. I took it, feeling for all the world like an unchaste Eve.

"You seem low of spirits. Has your friend been bullying you?" he asked, but the nonchalance of his tone did not deceive me. He lounged against the tree, affecting an air of casual interest, one booted ankle crossed over the other.

"Charles? He would not know how," I told him. "He manages, he does not bully."

"And does he mean to manage you?"

"I cannot think that it should make any difference to you

what becomes of me," I said. I bit into the apple with a sharp snap of the teeth, but it tasted like ashes in my mouth.

The count's eyes narrowed, and I saw suddenly that he was angry but determined to conceal it.

"You can say that after the letter? My God, you are a cold-hearted little beast."

I tossed the apple into the bushes for the birds to quarrel over. "What letter?"

"You really did not read it?"

"I tell you, there was no letter. What did it say?"

"It was by way of an apology," he said, watching me closely. "I have behaved very badly with you, and it has caused me to experience an emotion I have very seldom felt before. Shame."

I wished then that I had kept the apple. It would have furnished me with something to occupy my hands. I twisted my fingers together to stop them trembling.

"You have no call to be shamed. You spoke the truth. I did come to you for seduction and you obliged me. I bear at least as much guilt as you."

"I am your elder by half a dozen years and a lifetime's experience," he said, coming to sit beside me upon the bench. "I should have anticipated your feelings, but instead I found I did not even anticipate my own."

My pulse thudded hard within my veins. His leg was so near to my own, I could feel the heat of his skin through my skirts. A leaf could not have fit between us, but he did not look at me.

"You were right, of course. I have armoured myself against any soft feeling, and it was a point of pride with me that I have never been susceptible. You interested me, attracted me, from the moment I saw you standing in the great hall, so different from my expectation. I thought to find frost and instead I found fire. For all my experience, Theodora, you are unlike any woman I have known," he added with a small, wistful smile. "And so I plotted your seduction as I have so many others. I took the measure of you the moment I held your hands in mine to wash them in welcome, and I knew that the greatest weapons in my arsenal against you were exoticism and fear."

"Fear?" I asked. A cold chill had risen in the hollow of my stomach, an icy mist spread through my bones, carried in the blood that cooled with his every word. I had thought him cynical, but I had not realised the depths of his cruelty.

"You are a writer of romantic horror stories. What better adventure for you than to live one? I employed every machination, aroused every doubt, and used your own curiosity against you. I gave you glimpses of what I am, my blackest heart and my monstrous ways. I let you see just enough of me to whet your appetites for more, and then I assuaged the hunger. That ought to have been the end of it, and perhaps for you, it has been," he said bitterly.

My heart gave a painful, bruising leap against my ribs. "But for me," he added, "it was not. Can you imagine my surprise, my dismay, to realise that I have been snared in the jaws of my own trap? I have never thought about a woman once I have had her. It is not in my nature to be tender or to form attachments. And yet, there is something fine about you, something uncorrupted, for all that I have done to you. How is that possible? I asked you to destroy me with your goodness, and by God, you have done so," he finished, with so black a look as made me tremble more.

But boldness rose within me and I covered his hand with my own. "If you hold any regard for me, why must that be your destruction? A shared attachment can bring joy," I told him.

He grasped my fingers for a moment, so hard the bones protested, but then he dropped my hand, and I wished again for the pain that I might at least be near to him.

"There can be no joy for us," he said, his tone harsh with unhappiness. "I must do my duty, as you have so often pointed out. I cannot play King Cophetua to your beggar maid."

With this last bit of savagery, he rose and walked a few paces upon the path and back again before turning to me. "If only you had read the letter. My pen is more eloquent than my tongue. I made confessions to you there I cannot bring myself to say again in the light of day. You would have a better measure of me now if you had read it."

"I could not, for it was not there," I reminded him.

"But I put it beneath the necklace so you would see it."

"There was no letter," I said, slowly and distinctly.

Comprehension dawned upon his face. "Of course not," he murmured. "I apologise. If you will excuse me, I have something I must attend to."

He rose to leave, but before he quit the garden, he turned back. He said nothing for a moment, but his expression varied wildly between fear and hope and something indefinable. He strode back and collected me to him, raising me from the bench and kissing me without either preamble or permission. But this was no sweet lover's caress; there was desperation in his lips, and in spite of myself I was moved. I clung to him for a moment as he abandoned my mouth to kiss my temples, my eyelids, my brow. At last he drew back, and when he spoke his voice was rough.

"If only you had read the letter. Things are moving apace now. I do not know what will happen, but you must be safe. You will leave—tomorrow. I will speak with Beecroft and he will take you from here. It is impossible that you should stay."

"I do not want to leave you." The words left my mouth before I could guard against them. Hearing them, he groaned and kissed me again.

"Do you think I would send you away if there were any way to keep you? I am master here, but there are things beyond even my control. You will go because I say you will. I have never asked for obedience, but now I demand it."

"But—"

He gripped my shoulders, his fingers biting into the flesh so hard I would bear the bruises of it for weeks to come. "Do you not understand me? I cannot protect you now."

Realising the strength of his grip, he released me, his expression sorrowful, imploring, and yet with an air of command I dared not refuse.

"Who will protect you?" I asked him, putting a hand to his face. For an instant, he closed his eyes, giving himself up to my touch. Then he stepped sharply backwards and the moment passed.

"I will not see you again, Theodora. Leave at dawn, and do not think of coming back. You will not be welcome, and you will not be safe."

And with that last brutal pronouncement, he left me.

I went to my room and began to pack, and some time later there came a knock at my door. I hurried to answer it.

"You look disappointed," Charles said with an attempt at jollity. "Expecting someone?"

"Of course not," I said dully, turning back to my packing.

"I happened across that fellow the count and he said you changed your mind, that you wanted to return to Edinburgh straight away. I do not pretend to understand you, Theodora, but I must admit I am relieved. Of course, one hopes the book will not suffer, but I have put my mind to it, and I have recalled an acquaintance of my mother's who I think may do us an excellent service. The Duke of Aberdour has a wonderful old place up in the Highlands, all pointed towers and crumbling stone, just like this. Well, not precisely like this of course," he added with a sharp laugh. I heard him as if from a distance, through a veiled mist of misery. I could not quite take in the fact that I must leave this place. That I must leave *him*.

"Well, what do you think?" Charles asked, his question tinged with impatience, as if he had put it to me more than once.

"About what? I am sorry, I was not attending," I told him as I folded a shawl into the box. I had forgot the one I had worn into the garden. It was still doubtless draped over the tarragon bush. I made a note to retrieve it before I left and reached for the necklace of blue beads and a handkerchief in which to tie it.

"About staying with the Duke of Aberdour, of course," he said testily. "He is a terrible old flirt, fifty years old and he's already seen three wives buried. Still, you can manage him well enough, I daresay. The place is wildly atmospheric, and I should think it would suit your purposes. A very congenial place to finish the book," he told me, rubbing his hands together. There was nothing Charles liked better than a tidy solution.

"Very well," I said quietly.

"It is not like you to be so amenable." He regarded me suspiciously. "And it is not like you to hurry away from something that you find diverting. You are snappish as a dog with an old bone when something captures your attention. Why have you had the sudden change of heart, my dear?"

I was too miserable to summon a lie. "Because I have been told I am unwelcome. The count is sending me away."

"What?" Charles bolted upright. "Of all the arrogance! Who is he to—" He broke off as the truth of it was borne in upon him and subsided back into his chair. "I see. That is how it is. Well, I ought to have guessed. He is a singularly handsome fellow, and you are certainly comely enough to catch his attention. Lovers' quarrel, then?"

The words were spoken lightly, but they were laced with pain. And something made me quite savage then. I carried enough of my own burden; I could not shoulder his as well. I flung a book into my travelling case. "Yes. That is precisely the nature of it. I am dismissed, for reasons I cannot understand or support. I do not know what excuses I will make to the others," I said suddenly, the sharp edge of anger dulled as quickly as it had been whetted.

Charles cleared his throat. "I think it best if we simply say that I have business in Edinburgh, and it concerns you. I will affect an air of mystery and say I cannot disclose the details, but you must fly at once to retrieve an opportunity that must not be missed. I had a letter today, forwarded me from Vienna. It was a note from Mother, but if I wave it around, no one will look too closely and it will be easy enough to convince them of its importance."

I bent swiftly and kissed his cheek. "I do not deserve a friend-ship such as yours, Charles, but I am heartily glad I have it."

He blushed a little. "Yes, well. We are quitting this place, and that is good enough for me. I had the most curious discussion with Dr. Frankopan today, and it has put me right off this village and the castle as well."

"I suppose he told you the same stories he told me about the *strigoi?*"

"Yes, and ghoulish tales they were as well. Quite chilled me to the marrow, I do not mind telling you. Tale after tale of wives throwing themselves from towers and deals with the Devil and things that are dead but not dead. But then Madame Popa served us a sort of plum brandy that has played havoc with my head. I found myself telling him all sorts of things, confi-dences and such." He darted a look at me, and I knew well enough what the subject of those confidences had been. "And we talked of our disappointments in life. Did you know his family disowned him? That is why he lives in a tiny cottage here, in the land God forgot."

"I thought you liked this place," I remonstrated gently.

He shrugged irritably. He seemed restless and ill at ease, as if the Carpathians—so seductively sinister to me—had proven too much for him. He reached into his pocket for a sweet and sucked at it, most likely for comfort, I surmised.

"I do like it, or at least I ought," he told me. "But I am so puzzled by it all. It does put me greatly in mind of the High-lands, you know—all majestic scenery and superstitious peasants. But I have always been able to laugh at the High-landers. Here, I would not dare to make sport of them. Here, I begin to believe it," he finished, his voice nearly inaudible.

I reached a hand to cover his. "Frighteningly easy, is it not? I hope now you understand what came over me."

"Understand? Theodora, a wolf howled from the woods as I was sitting and having a quiet drink with the doctor. A wolf, boldly walking abroad in the middle of the day! Who would credit such a thing?" He gave a shudder. "It is a place where quite anything could happen. And I do not blame you for any foolishness you may have indulged in whilst here," he added, a trifle sententiously. Whether he referred merely to my over-blown imagination or to my liaison with the count, I did not dare to wonder. But something else he said tugged at me.

"How curious that Dr. Frankopan was disowned by his family. He spoke of them to me as if he is still recognised. His brother is a nobleman living in Vienna."

"And content to let stand the provisions their father made when Dr. Frankopan was disowned," Charles revealed. "He was given the hunting cottage and a tiny allowance, but apart from that, he was entirely cut off from the family proper. No visits to Vienna, and none from them. Letters are exchanged once per year, at Christmas. And that is the whole of it."

"That poor man! How lonely he must have been for all of these years."

"Yes. Apparently, he gave up his family for love of a woman. The Frankopans did not approve of his beloved, and when the doctor wanted to offer her marriage, they were intransigent. They insisted he take a long sea voyage, doubtless hoping the attachment would not last. But before Dr. Frankopan returned, the poor creature died. He never forgave them for sending him away, and they never forgot he chose her above them. He has been here ever since."

"How tragic for him—and how providential for the people of this valley. They would have had no proper medical care without him," I pointed out.

"I suppose. Still, a hard consequence for a love that did not last," Charles returned.

"A hard consequence indeed."

Charles left me then to pack his own things, and when I had finished, I went to Cosmina's room to break the unwelcome news to her that I must leave. I rapped lightly upon the door and she called for me to enter.

"Oh! I did not realise you were not alone," I said rather awkwardly, for the countess and Frau Amsel sat next to the bed, and the three of them looked for all the world like the weird sisters upon the heath, waiting for MacBeth.

"Do come in," Cosmina begged. "I have been so bored, and Aunt Eugenia was kind enough to read to me. She is feeling stronger today."

The countess placed a ribbon in the book that lay open upon her lap, and Frau Amsel began to collect her needlework.

"We will leave you now you have Miss Lestrange to keep you company."

"If you would delay a moment, madame, I must speak with you as well."

"Oh?" The lightly marked, aristocratic brows rose. She was not accustomed to doing another's bidding, that much was apparent. But she obliged me, settling herself back into her chair. Frau Amsel unrolled her needlework with an air of malevolent anticipation.

"I am afraid that my friend, Mr. Beecroft, has had a communication forwarded to him from Vienna. He has urgent business in Edinburgh and must return home at once. And I must go with him."

"No!" Cosmina cried. Her hair, unplaited, spilled loose over her pillows, and her eyes were darkly shadowed and unnaturally bright.

"I am sorry, dearest. I have no choice in the matter. I must go."

Cosmina began to speak, but the countess interrupted her smoothly. "Cosmina, you must not importune Miss Lestrange. I am certain she feels quite badly enough to be leaving so quickly as it is."

The countess was perceptive, and the smile she gave me was almost kind. "We will be sorry to see you go, Miss Lestrange. When must you take your leave of us?"

"Tomorrow, madame. By first light. It is a long way to Hermannstadt."

"That it is. I will make certain Frau Graben prepares a hamper for your journey. The wayside inns can be quite impossible."

"That is very gracious of you," I told her, inclining my head. She returned the gesture, and I marvelled at how civilised we were being. But the countess could afford to be generous. I was leaving, after all.

Frau Amsel did not bother to conceal her glee. She smiled broadly and as she followed the countess from the room, she fairly radiated pleasure.

I settled myself into the countess's vacated chair, bracing myself for the inevitable scene which must follow. Cosmina had always been quiet, but she was capable of passionate rages when she was thwarted. I still remembered a fairly ridiculous scene over a penwiper at school that had resulted in a broken window.

"Are you very angry?" I asked.

She shook her head, and to my distress, a tear fell to her cheeks. "No, only sad. I have so loved having you here. But Aunt Eugenia is right. I must not be selfish. You have a life to lead, and it is far away from me."

I plucked at the bedcovers, pleating them between my fingers. "I do hate to leave you when you are ill."

She gave me a smile, a brave and trembling thing. "I will be well soon. It is just a cold, a trifling matter."

We fell silent then, and I was deeply relieved that she did not mean to make our parting a difficult one.

"Will you write to me? I mean really write to me? Once a month at least," she urged.

"Once a fortnight, and that is a promise," I told her. I rose and placed a kiss upon her brow. It was cooler than I had expected, and I was glad of it. "You've no fever now. Perhaps you will be out of bed soon."

"Tomorrow, I hope," she said seriously. "I should like to see you off. And Mr. Beecroft," she added, colouring slightly. I had forgot her fondness towards Charles, and I hoped she would not take his absence too much to heart.

"I would like that. You must rest this evening, and I will come to you in the morning even if you are still abed," I promised.

I took my leave of her then. I had no desire for company

that night, my last at the castle, and Frau Graben was kind enough to send up a tray. She had outdone herself, for the tray groaned under a variety of regional delights. There was a dish of vine leaves, stuffed with meat and rice and spices and smothered in gravy, and half a dozen others besides, as well as the usual accompaniments of pickles and breads and cheeses. I ate little, picking over the delicious morsels with only a feeble appetite. I ached to think of leaving this place, of leaving him. It would have been difficult enough to part from him under any ordinary circumstance. With such questions yet unanswered, it was insupportable. I did not know the extent of his feelings for me, or if indeed any such feelings existed. I did not know the truth of what he was, simply a man or something darker and more sinister. And perhaps most chilling of all, I did not know what he feared. Was it the possibility of his own destruction or mine that caused him to send me away?

Such questions teased and tormented me through the course of the evening, and finally I could bear it no longer. I went to the count's room, determined to break through his resolve at last. I understood the dangers of it; I had already seen that to prod him beyond endurance would cause him to strip the scales from my eyes and teach me unpleasantnesses. But I could not leave without seeing him one last time, and when I reached his bedchamber, I did not even pause to knock, but opened the door and walked straight in.

He was not there, but a fire burned upon the hearth, and the bed had been turned back as if he had expected to retire soon. I mounted the little stair to his workroom, surprised to find it empty. I had thought to find him there, tinkering with the orrery or reading one of his grandfather's almanacs. The night was windy and the sky full of cloud, unsuitable for astronomical pursuits. If he had gone to the observatory, he would only tarry a moment or two, and I decided to wait in the workroom for him. Before I could settle, I glanced at the window and gaped. I would have screamed, but my voice was stopped in my astonishment, for a great black shape hung at the window, pressing itself against the glass. It swung wildly, thudding hard against the window, and I realised it meant to break in, to gain entry to the count's room, and it was then that I recovered myself. I screamed, and before the sound of it died in my throat, the shape hurled itself against the window, destroying it in a shower of splintered glass. The form fell heavily upon the shattered glass with an inhuman groan, and it was only then that I saw it was the count, bleeding freely and insensible. I flung myself to the floor, heedless of the glass, and wrenched open his neckcloth that he might breathe more easily. I put my handkerchief to the jagged wound upon his cheek, but the snowy cloth turned scarlet as soon as it touched him. I ought to have gone for help then or fetched water or done any of a hundred useful things. Instead I knelt beside him in the midst of the destruction, willing him to wake, to speak.

After a moment—it may have been a moment, although it felt an eternity—I was pushed gently aside. "Let me see him, let me see him." It was Dr. Frankopan, with Florian and Charles hard upon his heels. I had not realised the doctor had even called again at the castle, but never in my life had I greeted anyone with greater pleasure.

I moved aside, but only a little. Whatever Dr. Frankopan did to him, I meant to help.

"Good God, what happened?" Charles demanded, but no one made him a reply.

The count stirred and emitted another deep groan when Dr. Frankopan touched his forearm. The doctor nodded. "As I suspected, as I suspected. His shoulder is out of place." He nodded towards Florian and Charles. "I shall require help to put it back."

Charles blanched but stepped forward. "Of course." Florian stepped forward as well, awaiting the doctor's instructions.

"I do not like to do this here, but the pain is extraordinary and the joint must be replaced before the muscles stiffen. Stretch out his arm, like this," he gave a series of detailed instructions, then turned to me. "I think you will not like to watch this. What we must do is most unpleasant."

"I will stay," I said, stubbornly, although I regretted it almost instantly. Unpleasant was not the word, I decided, for as they twisted and torqued his arm into the socket, he rose up and gave a great, guttural scream, then lapsed into unconsciousness again, pale as new milk, the blood still streaming from his face.

Charles was unsteady on his feet when they had finished, and even Florian, who had doubtless seen and done his share of unpleasant things upon the farm, seemed shaken and ill at ease.

"It is restored," said the doctor with some satisfaction. "Now, we must remove him to his bedchamber and assess the rest of his injuries before the lacerations can be repaired." Dr. Frankopan was a man changed, for he was cool and confident and thoroughly in command of the situation, even when the ladies of the castle appeared in the doorway. The countess gave a deep moan of anguish and would have sunk to her knees but for the support of Frau Amsel. Cosmina stood unsteadily, a dressing gown wrapped about her, her hair untidy and her feet thrust into slippers as if she had risen hastily from her sickbed. Frau Graben had even roused herself from her room next to the kitchens, but it was Tereza who commanded the household's attention. She pushed her way into the room, raising a shaking finger as she stared at the prone form of the count. She spoke in shrill and rapid Roumanian, but the horror and disbelief in her voice required no translation.

Florian related what she said, murmuring hastily to me in German.

"'I saw him,' she says," he told me. "'I saw him there upon the observatory. I was making the windows fast as I do every night before I retire. I was at the window in the opposite wing, and I saw him perched upon the edge of the observatory walk. *And then I saw him fly!*'"

The countess let out a great sob, and Cosmina reached for the doorframe to steady herself. Dr. Frankopan spoke up.

"What do you mean, child? Count Andrei did not fly. He fell from the observatory and was fortunate enough to fall through the window. He might have plunged straight to his death in the valley had he not caught himself," he said firmly. Tereza blinked at him and he repeated his argument in Roumanian.

But Tereza continued to utter the same phrases she had used before, and I had no need of Florian to know she would not be swayed.

"Child, he did not fly," Dr. Frankopan said patiently, saying the words over and again in Roumanian and German. "He fell."

"Or was pushed," Frau Amsel said, her voice overloud in the quiet room.

There was a gasp, and I think pandemonium might have broken out were it not for the fact that Frau Amsel was pointing to a bit of fabric snagged upon the broken window. She walked over and plucked it free, but I did not need to look upon it to know what she brandished in her hand. Clutched in her triumphant hands was the tartan shawl I had left in the garden draped over a tarragon bush.

17

I did not feel it when the countess slapped me, for I had gone quite numb, and it was only distantly that I heard Charles remonstrate with her angrily. The room spun and jerked around me, faces swam before my eyes, and the only constant was my own voice, repeating over and over again, "But I love him."

It was Charles who finally guided me away and took me to my chamber, and when we reached the room, he wrenched open the window and pushed my head outside, forcing me to drink in great draughts of the cold, crisp air until my head cleared. At last he drew me back in, and pressed a flask upon me.

"Good Scottish whisky," he said firmly. I drank deeply of it, and the room cleared at last.

"I do not understand," I said, my voice thin and feeble.

"Neither do I," he told me, his expression grim. "But it is best to stay here quietly until someone comes."

I did as he bade me, sitting upon my hands to stop them

shaking and listening to the little clock tick off the hours. The night was half gone when there was a rap at the door and Dr. Frankopan entered, his cuffs folded back and smeared with blood. *His* blood, I thought wildly, and for an instant I was certain the doctor had come to tell me he had died.

"Is he dead?" I demanded.

Dr. Frankopan gave me an odd look. "Dead? Of course not. He suffered a dislocation of the shoulder and some rather severe cuts and bruises, but nothing he cannot overcome with rest and good care."

I sagged into my chair, murmuring an *Ave* under my breath. If nothing else, the Carpathians would teach me religion, I thought wildly.

Dr. Frankopan drew a chair next to me and motioned for Charles to sit with us as well. "I have spoken to the countess, for it is she who rules during her son's indisposition. She apologises for her outburst and begs you will understand a mother's hysteria."

"She does not think me responsible then?" I asked, dizzy with relief.

Dr. Frankopan's response was carefully phrased. "She does not know what to think as yet. She wishes to make no decisions until her son has regained consciousness and can speak for himself as to what happened upon the observatory walk."

"Tereza!" I said suddenly. "Tereza must have seen that I was not there when the count fell. She may absolve me."

Dr. Frankopan shook his head sorrowfully. "Tereza saw nothing. I questioned her closely, and she saw nothing but the count."

I lapsed back into my chair, feeling a thousand years old. "What am I to do until the count rouses and can clear my name?"

He shrugged. "It would be best for everyone if you were

confined to your room. It would bring a greater ease to the family if you were not at liberty."

"I am to be held prisoner until he wakes?" I asked, incredulous. It seemed impossible, and I looked to Charles to support me.

"I think it is for the best," he said, to my astonishment.

"Charles! You cannot think that I—"

"Of course not," he was quick to reply, using the same tone one might to soothe a fractious horse or a fretful babe. "But this is a necessary expedient. I must insist that Theodora not be locked in without visitors," he said firmly to Dr. Frankopan. "She will receive regular visits from me, and writing materials and books besides. And anything else she should require for her comfort," he finished.

"Naturally, naturally. The countess wishes her to think of herself as a guest still," Dr. Frankopan said, his relief almost palpable. He had expected a fight then. But I had none left in me to give him, for all that mattered to me in that moment was that the count should live.

"Very well. I will sit quietly until I am bade to leave," I promised.

Dr. Frankopan took his leave then with Charles, and after the door was shut, I heard the turn of the key in the lock, the loneliest, most frightening sound I had ever heard. I was a prisoner in the Castle Dragulescu.

Charles was the first to break in upon my solitude the next day when he carried in my breakfast. I had finally lapsed into sleep just before dawn, and it was very nearly noon before he roused me.

"You needed your rest," he explained, when I scolded him for not waking me sooner.

"I know. And I know you are the only friend I have at

present. Pay no mind to my churlishness. I do not mean it," I finished helplessly.

He said nothing, but busied himself uncovering dishes and pouring out strong black coffee. The smell of it turned my stomach to water, but he had brought tea besides, and a cup of that with a nibbled bread roll comprised my breakfast.

"How is he this morning?" I asked finally. I had hesitated, both from the fear that he should have taken a turn for the worst, and out of the concern that speaking of him would grieve Charles. It is no easy thing for a man to measure himself against another and be found wanting.

But Charles was more a gentleman than I had credited him, for he brought me news of him and delivered it without resentment. "He does well enough, although he has not yet roused. Dr. Frankopan stays with him, and the countess comes and goes. Cosmina has been there as well, doing what she can. There is naught to do but wait until he wakes. His pulse is strong and his colour good, and although it was a shock of some magnitude to his mother to find that he is an opium-eater, Dr. Frankopan does not think the habit is of long enough standing to have damaged his constitution." Charles hesitated, then took a breath and plunged on, speaking rather more hurriedly. "He murmurs a good deal in his sleep, and once or twice he has called your name."

I finished my tea before I could master my tears enough to speak. "Thank you for that. It could not have been easy to tell me, but I am glad to know it."

"Do not thank me. Half of them seem to think it proof of your guilt—as if he speaks your name to accuse you. Still, I know you are guiltless, and so will everyone else once he wakes."

A sudden chill ran through me, stiffening my hand so that I nearly dropped the cup. "Charles, I am innocent, but someone else is not."

"What do you mean?"

I replaced the cup carefully onto the saucer and rose to pace the room. "They think I pushed him, but we know I did not. What if he did not fall or fly of his own accord? What if he was pushed, but *by someone else?*"

Charles absently took a sweet from his pocket and sucked at it, furrowing his brow. "I did not think on that. I suppose it is possible."

"Of course it is possible. Charles, I have been on the observatory walk. He did not fall. He was never careless and he is surefooted as a chamois goat. I would wager my life upon it— either something supernatural has attacked him or there was a deliberate and malicious attempt upon his life by someone in this castle."

"Perhaps the same person who killed the maid Aurelia?" Charles offered.

"Yes!" I whirled to face him, my conviction rising. "I am certain of it. The peasants would say it was his father, Count Bogdan, who tried to destroy him. But what if the superstitions and monsters are merely a diversion? What if there is nothing afoot here more sinister than simple human evil?"

"And whom would you suspect of the deed?"

I stopped pacing and thought, turning each of the castle's inhabitants over in my mind. "Frau Amsel," I said. "Aurelia carried the late count's child, a possible successor to the Dragulescu name and fortune. She was slain with her unborn child. If the present count died, who then would benefit? The countess would want a male to inherit, it is the way of things here. And who better than Florian, Frau Amsel's son, who already has a grasp of things and would keep the estate under the countess's rule? There would be no other direct heir of the Dragulescu line. She would have only to adopt him, and such things are easily arranged."

"Possibly," Charles said, his voice tinged with doubt.

"And she loathes me. It would give her great pleasure to dispatch me at the same time by putting my shawl in such a place as to implicate me. She could easily have slipped into the garden to retrieve it. And it was she who named me in the count's workroom when she retrieved my shawl."

I was hungry then, suddenly and ravenously hungry. I sat to eat the other things Charles had brought, dipping my spoon into the bowl of *mămăligă*.

Charles said nothing, turning my pretty theory over in his businessman's mind. At length he nodded. "It is a sound enough suspicion, I suppose. Although I notice you do not entertain the notion that another, even likelier suspect may have done the deed."

I took another spoonful of the hearty porridge. "Who?"

Charles sat back, managing to look simultaneously smug and uncomfortable. "The count himself."

I put down my spoon. "You think Count Andrei did this to himself? You are mad."

"Am I? Or perhaps you are simply unwilling to consider all possibilities."

I folded my arms and when I spoke it was with a stranger's voice, clipped and cold. "Go on."

Charles leaned forward. "You said yourself that the maid Aurelia carried a rival claimant to the estate. Who better to resent this than the sitting count?"

"Precisely," I replied by way of retort. "*The sitting count*. He had no need to put Aurelia's child out of the way. He had secured his inheritance as his father's lawful heir."

"But was he? How easy might it have been for the girl to produce a piece of paper, a bit of forgery with Count Bogdan's signature upon it, claiming responsibility for the child and naming it his heir? You said there was a quarrel between the countess and her husband. He meant to put her away and marry the girl. Perhaps he had taken steps to do so, irrevocable steps that would have disinherited your paramour."

I flinched at his use of the word "paramour" but I did not rise to the bait. "Surely the fact that Count Bogdan was dead put paid to whatever schemes the girl might have had to see her illegitimate child established as a Dragulescu heir."

Charles shrugged. "If she was cunning and ruthless, she might well have gambled upon her child's blood. Think how easily one might bribe a country priest or solicitor to draw up a bit of paper to stake her child's claim. She could promise them a hearty share of the estate upon settlement. Many a villain has been bought with less," he said sagely.

"I suppose it is possible," I admitted, though grudgingly so.

"Or perhaps the count simply bears the hot blood of his ancestors," Charles mused, "and thought to answer the insult done to his mother by dispatching the maid and her offspring. A colder plot, to be sure, but not impossible."

I did not answer this; I could not. Was it possible? Could he have killed the girl with no greater provocation than the knowledge that she had supplanted his own mother in his father's affections? It was monstrous; it could not be so. And yet, the possibility of it lived, like a monstrous thorny weed, pricking at my convictions.

"You are angry with me," Charles said at last.

I stirred the *mămăligă,* but it had gone cold. "I am not angry, only heartsick and longing to go from here."

He reached a hand to cover mine. "I will take you, as soon as it may be arranged, wherever you wish to go—to England to see Anna, to the Highlands, to Timbuktu. I will make it so."

His hand was warm and comfortable over mine, but I was

no longer the girl who could reasonably contemplate warm and comfortable. Still, I managed a smile and thanked him, and soon after he left me alone with my thoughts.

That evening it was Cosmina who brought my meal. She entered quietly and put the food upon the table and opened her arms. I went to her, resting my head upon her shoulder.

"I am glad to see you," I told her, my voice muffled. She put a hand to my head, cradling me close as one might a beloved child.

When she drew back, there were tears standing in her eyes. "I am so sorry, Theodora. I ought never to have brought you here. I hesitated to come tonight because I feared you would be angry with me."

"Angry with you? Whatever for?"

She grasped my hands in her own. "For inviting you to this place. For this," she said, taking in my little prison with a glance.

I had not drawn the curtains yet, and she walked to the window where the setting sun had already dropped beyond the mountains and the long shadows of evening were beginning to lengthen.

"There is a Scottish word for this time of day. You told me once, but I cannot remember it."

"Gloaming," I told her, coming to stand beside her at the window. "When the light has fled but the stars have not yet shown themselves. That is the gloaming, the loveliest and saddest hour of the day."

A ghost of a smile touched her lips. "And I thought only in Transylvania was there such poetry."

"It is a poetic place," I agreed.

"I hope you will remember it with affection," she said, her brow furrowing anxiously.

"Remember it? Shall I be permitted to leave then?" I asked her, a tinge of hysteria sharpening my tone.

She hastened to soothe me. "Of course! Oh, my dear, you must not believe this is anything other than the most fleeting of circumstances. Andrei began to stir this afternoon. It is only a matter of hours before he wakens and speaks the truth. Then you will be freed. It is simply that the countess is too fearful for his life to take any chances he might be attacked again."

"And she thinks I am a threat to him?" I asked evenly.

"She does not know what to think. In fact," Cosmina hesitated, biting at her lip, as if considering whether to share a confidence. "In fact, she fears it is Count Bogdan who has tried to destroy their son."

"Then why keep me here, locked away like some villain?" I demanded.

Cosmina spread her hands. "She is ill and confused and afraid. She believes the *strigoi* has attacked Andrei, but she also realises the truth may be more mundane. She will take no risks with his life, and even though she fears the *strigoi,* she must listen to the Amsels filling her ears with poison against you. Pity her, my friend. She only wants to protect her beloved son. Surely you can understand such a thing."

I relented a little. "Of course. But why should the Amsels have taken against me? And why do they say I would have done this terrible thing to the count?"

Her eyes slid away from mine and back to the view of the mountains. A single star shimmered low in the sky, and I knew it was Venus, shedding its benevolent light over lovers in the valley below.

"Frau Amsel says that you were driven to attack him when he spurned you after you enticed him to your bed."

I caught my breath against the wave of pain that washed over me. Whatever became of us, I had thought to have at least the memory of that night to console me in my loneliness. And now Frau Amsel had spoiled it for me, twisting what had been natural and pleasurable into something sordid and indiscreet. I could guess well enough how she had pieced the story together. The matter of the pedlar's fabric would have raised her suspicions. They could have been confirmed by a quick coin to Tereza, for the girl took away soiled linen and returned it clean. She was privy to all the secrets of the castle, I thought bitterly.

"It is true then?" Cosmina asked softly. She did not face me, perhaps to make it easier, or perhaps because she herself did not wish to see the truth of it writ upon my face.

"No," I told her, for that shoddy version of the facts would never be true to me.

"But you said you love him," she protested gently. "When he lay unconscious and bleeding. You said you loved him."

"Did I? I hardly remember now. But it does not matter. My feelings are my own. I do not speak for him. I can only vow to you that I would never have harmed him."

She turned to me then, her face half-shadowed and half-illuminated, a living silhouette. "I believe you, my friend." Her voice was firm, stalwart even. "I will be your champion," she vowed.

She embraced me again and gestured towards the food. "Eat. You must keep up your strength. I will come to you as soon as I have news of him."

And with that she left me, turning the key in the lock behind her.

I sat, although nothing tempted my appetite. I thought of what she had told me of the countess's fears, and I understood them perfectly. Had I too not wrestled with the question of whether something supernatural was afoot in the castle? Had I not swung wildly between the prosaic and the fantastic? I thought how much stronger my emotions would be were a beloved child at risk, and I forgave her then. I forgave her suspicions and her precautions; I forgave her my small prison and my large worries.

I even forgave her my dinner, I thought wryly as I picked over the meat. Frau Graben must have been distracted, for the joint was overcooked and leathery and bloodless. I pushed the food aside and closed my eyes, forcing myself to think calmly and logically. I returned to the beginning, to the death of Aurelia. I imagined the maid, lured to the room with the promise of what? An assignation? A bribe? Something had enticed her there; someone had preyed upon her avarice. Once there, had she known she was in danger? Had she attempted to flee? Or had she no sense of it, even to the moment when she was struck down? Had she been bled by a human hand or fed upon by a vampire's monstrous need? I imagined her lying upon the cold, stone floor and someone bending to take her life.

And upon this point my imagination failed me. I could not see the figure looming over her to finish the deed. Was it the seemingly gentle Florian? The stout and malicious Frau Amsel? *Was it the count?*

The question came unbidden to my mind, but once there, I could not dismiss it. Charles had roused my doubts, and logic prevented me from brushing them aside. I must face the possibility of it squarely. I knew so little of him. I had believed in the goodness in him, buried and blunted as it was. I had been so certain that there was honour in him, and a sort of old-fashioned courage that was so seldom seen in our modern times. He was a throwback to an age of mystics and warrior kings, imperious and implacable. And yet I had credited him with goodness as well, with a tender heart that was capable of being moved. Had he not undertaken to improve the lot of his people once he had been made aware of their need?

And yet I could not silence the small voice that whispered, *He only did so as a means to an end. The work would have cost him a few coins, a small enough price to woo a woman into his bed.*

I pushed the food aside and dropped my head onto my folded arms. I was tormented by doubts and questions, and until I had answers, I would not be free. What if he did not rouse? And if he did waken, I wondered with a horrible, creeping doubt, what was to prevent him from casting the blame upon me? If Charles was correct and the count's hands were stained with Aurelia's blood, what would prevent him from affirming Frau Amsel's tale that I had attempted his life? Perhaps it was a conspiracy amongst them all, I thought wildly. I was a stranger here, and a girl was dead. How much easier for them all if I were to shoulder the burden of blame.

This then was my darkest hour. The blue shadows of the gloaming had faded into the black and unforgiving night, and I sunk into a misery of the sort I had never felt before. It seemed hopeless in those dark hours, and I had no one to comfort me, not even Charles, for he did not come to me and I was alone with my fears. At length I gave way to tears, weeping into my arms, wetting the sleeves of my gown.

So bowed was I by my wretchedness, that I did not realise I was no longer alone until Tycho thrust a wet nose into my hands. I started, then began weeping afresh.

"Tycho, I do not know how you have come here, but I am glad to see you," I murmured into his fur. He turned his head and licked the tears from my cheek, and as he did so, I began to think more clearly.

"How *are* you come here?" I demanded, and so strange and fantastical were the things that had happened in that castle, I would not have been surprised had he made me a reply. But he merely continued on, licking my cheeks.

I rose and took him by the collar. "Lead on," I urged.

He turned and went directly to the tapestry stretched along one wall.

"No, I have not been so stupid as that!" I exclaimed, realising I had in fact been very blind indeed.

Tycho nudged at the tapestry and I pushed it aside, finding a doorway set into the stone. A tiny corridor led the way to a twisting stair carved from the rock—to the count's room, I had no doubt.

"Of course," I said, as much to Tycho as to myself. "The counts have always used the rooms above and would wish to visit their wives privately. A secret stair for the convenience of the master," I added with a rueful shake of the head. But this was not the time to ponder the implications of why I had been placed in this room, or the strangeness of my nocturnal visits. A more important development had occurred—Tycho had just revealed to me the path to freedom.

18

With some difficulty, I herded him before me up the tiny stairs
and back to his master's side. I waited behind, ready to scurry
back to my bolthole should anyone notice Tycho's reappear-
ance. I had noted the time, and the rest of the castle household ought to have been at supper. I could not wait until they
were all abed; I must take my chances now, although I dared
not contemplate my fate should I be found wandering at liberty.

I made my way slowly, one step, one breath, at a time until
at last I reached the top of the stairs. There was a tapestry here
as well, and I hesitated on the other side. Tycho had slid his
lithe body into the room, and it occurred to me that anyone
who did not know the secret geography of the castle would
assume he had been behind the tapestry the whole time,
perhaps snuffling out mice or old bones.

I stood behind the tapestry a long time, listening to my own
heartbeats drumming in my ears, but no other sounds pene-

trated the thick wool. At length I steeled myself to peer around the edge, and I gave a little sigh of relief. The count was tucked into his bed and was alone in the room, save for Dr. Frankopan, dozing quietly on the sofa in front of the fire. I dared not dwell upon the count, for the sight of him, swathed and stitched and lying motionless, had nearly caused me to cry out. The great bed and the perfect stillness of his repose bore too near a resemblance to a corpse laid out for burial; he wanted only a funeral wreath to complete his paleness. But his chest rose and fell with perfect ease, and I forced myself to carry on.

Dr. Frankopan slept as well, his slumbers punctuated by odd fits and starts and little snorts, and I was terrified lest he waken. The journey from the tapestry to the door seemed an eternity, but it could only have been a second or two before I had slipped through and gained the stairs without detection.

My hands sweated and the knob had been slippery in my palm, but I had managed it, and once outside, I hastened down the stairs as quickly and silently as I could. As I reached the bottom, I heard voices—Cosmina and Charles, and I froze, my very marrow stilled within my bones.

In a moment they would reach the corner and see me, exposed and defenceless upon the stairs, and all would be lost. Unless…

In a blind panic, I darted into the garderobe. There was not time enough even to draw the door closed behind me, so I threw myself behind it, counting upon the shadows to conceal me.

I heard them pass, so near I could have touched them, and I dared not even breathe until they were well upon the stair and out of earshot. They chatted seriously to each other, and I made a note of the fact that the countess and the Amsels would still be about, as well as the servants.

I crept from the garderobe to make my way to Frau Amsel's room, but even as I did so I turned my steps towards another.

I could not say what diverted me, but I walked as a lost soul, wandering in the night, will walk towards the faintest glimmer of light. Even then, I did not know what I would find when I reached my destination, but as I crept ever closer, I considered the question of trust, and where mine had been misplaced.

Charles and Cosmina were my friends, I reasoned, and yet when I heard them coming, I had instinctively hidden myself. Had I thought the matter over coolly, dispassionately, I would have reassured myself that neither of them would have betrayed me. But my basest instinct, the part of myself that was scarcely better than animal, desperate to survive, had fled from them.

I had been afraid. And as I moved through the shadows of the castle, I realised I always had been. I understood then that affection and fear can be entwined as tightly as lovers.

At last I came to the chamber I sought. It was empty and illuminated only by the light of the fire. I moved quickly, for I had little time, and my hands trembled as I searched. Fear and a rising hysteria were almost my undoing as I scoured the room and found nothing. But as I reached under the pillow, feeling blindly, my fingers closed over a piece of paper and something else, something smooth and cool that clicked softly between my fingers, and a third item I could not identify. I withdrew them all, and an eerie, unnatural calm settled over me. I understood, as I had not before, and I cursed myself for a fool.

"Have you found what you were looking for, my dear?" came the voice from the doorway.

I started, but Dr. Frankopan's expression was kindly.

"I was just waking when I saw you leave the count's room. I thought to follow you and see what you were about," he told me.

"Where are the others?" I asked.

"With the count. He will waken soon, I think. But I had to look to you as well. What fresh mischief brings you to this place?"

He came closer and I held out the things I had found.

"These are mine. She had no right to them, and yet here they were, under her pillow."

He took them from me. "A letter and a rosary?"

"The rosary was my mother's. I lost it, or thought that I did, when we were at school. Cosmina has kept it all these years."

He looked briefly at the letter. "It is a love letter," he said softly. "But it has been torn to pieces."

"And stitched back together," I noted. The paper had been destroyed and then carefully mended, held together by black silk stitches that ran like scars between the beautiful words. "It was taken from my room before I even saw it. I think," my voice broke upon the words, "I think she attempted to kill the count. She may even have killed Aurelia as well. Here, I believe this is proof of it." I proffered the third object and he took it from me with a pointed reluctance.

He sagged into a chair, his face very white, his spirit defeated. "Oh, dear little Cosmina. What have you done?" he murmured.

He said nothing for a long moment, and neither did I. We were both of us mourning the loss of the girl we had known and reconciling ourselves to the fact that in her place was a monster—a creature who stole and lied and destroyed. I thought of the odd little rages to which she had been prone as a girl. I had thought her willful and obstinate. Now I saw she was something far more dangerous.

Suddenly, Dr. Frankopan roused himself. "You must forgive me, my dear. I should not have doubted you, not for a moment."

"Of course," I told him, blinking hard against the sudden tears that sprang to my eyes. Someone else believed me. The relief was almost too much to bear.

"But you are not safe here," he said, pushing himself out of the chair. "No, you are not safe. Cosmina is a clever girl, and we do not know what tales she may spin to persuade the count and the countess that you have wronged them. We must get you right away, tonight. You will come to my cottage, and I will keep you safe until morning. If we are quick and quiet, no one will even know you have gone. I will bring word to Mr. Beecroft, and he can join you tomorrow. Thence, to Hermannstadt, and the *obergespan,* for the sheriff will know what to do. The time for pretending these things have not happened is past."

He thrust the objects into his pocket for safekeeping. "Come, child, come. There is no time to lose. They will not keep long to his room. We must flee now, while we have the chance."

He snatched up a cloak of Cosmina's for me and we hurried from the room. I followed him blindly, my hand clasped in his, and I felt such a welling of emotion, I could hardly endure it— relief at my liberation, and sorrow at what I had discovered about Cosmina's duplicity. But mantling it all was an over- whelming feeling of despair that I would not see the count again, for even as I fled my thoughts were entirely of him.

We gained the courtyard quickly and Dr. Frankopan pointed to the moon. "We do not even need a lantern. Gentle Selena lights our way," he said solemnly.

But as we picked our path carefully down the Devil's Stair- case, I realised the implications of the full moon. No sooner had we left the safety of the castle than I heard the howling of the wolves, the eerie sound carried on the wind.

"Make haste, make haste," he advised, springing down the steps with the speed of a man half his age. I followed, still clasping his hand, and more than once I would have fallen had he not righted me. At last we reached the village road, and I was not surprised to find the entire hamlet tucked snugly away for the night. Here and there a bit of woodsmoke escaped from a chimney, casting a hazy cloud over the face of the low-hanging moon. Little light spilled from the windows as they were shuttered tightly against the night and all that roamed abroad.

I clutched his hand even more tightly as we made our way along the forest path, for it was very dark, and the trees pressed in against us, breathing upon us in the shadows, it seemed. I heard rustling, but Dr. Frankopan told me it was only the wind; I saw eyes, but Dr. Frankopan told me it was simply the reflection of the moon upon the stones. I wanted to believe him, but when we reached the clearing and saw the cottage, warm light glowing from every window, beckoning us to safety, I nearly wept from relief.

He took me inside and shut the door, helping me out of Cosmina's cloak. "There, there. You have had a nasty shock. Go and sit by the fire. I will bring you some *pălinkă*. It will warm you through."

I obeyed, feeling so cold throughout I thought I should never be warm again, as much from misery as the wind.

"Here we are, here we are," he said, bustling in a few moments later with a tray and glasses. He poured out a generous measure for me and a smaller one for himself.

"Drink it up, child. You will feel warm soon. I daresay you are cold now from the shock of it all."

"I am," I told him, taking the *pălinkă* gratefully. I sipped it, but it was bitter and though I tried not to pull a face, little escaped Dr. Frankopan's attention.

"You do not like our local delicacy?" he chided with a smile. "No matter. It will do the trick, I promise you."

I took another sip. "I simply cannot take it in. Cosmina. All these years she was not the person I knew, the person I loved."

He nodded sorrowfully. "It is a difficult thing to have the scales drop from one's eyes."

"Yes, that is it precisely. I feel such a fool. She always used to say she was going to marry the count and live in the castle as his countess. I ought never to have believed her when she said that she was relieved when he refused her. She must have been so angry, so shatteringly angry."

"At him, for scorning her, and at you, for attracting his regard."

I think I coloured slightly at his last words, but there was frankness between us and I would not demur from the truth. "Yes. Any woman would have been angry, I think. But Cosmina was always possessive of what she cared for."

"Perhaps that is why she kept your rosary, a reminder of the friend she loved," he suggested.

I sipped again at the *pálinká*. It was better, smoother and easier to drink now I was accustomed to the taste of it. "Perhaps. I remember we had a row that day. She was angry because I spent so much time discussing poetry with Fraulein Möller. I thought her silly at the time, but now I believe she was jealous. She never liked me to have other friends, you know—none that were as close as she."

"And her feelings would be compounded if you formed an attachment with the man who refused to marry her," he concluded.

"Yes, of course." I subsided into silence and continued to drink, feeling warmer and a little light in the head.

"Why do you think she would have killed Aurelia?" he asked. "Do you not believe in the *strigoi?*"

"No. It is a faery story, meant to frighten children," I said, my voice louder than I had intended. "There is something more sinister afoot in that castle—a mortal murderer."

"You are certain?" he asked, his eyes suddenly shrewd.

"I am," I told him. "Someone killed Aurelia, someone attempted the count's life and meant me to hang for it. I believe that someone is Cosmina."

He said nothing, but merely watched me as I sipped at my drink. I continued on, warming to my theme. "Cosmina bore a grudge against the count and against me. What better revenge than to kill him and make me the scapegoat for her crimes?"

"But what motive would she have had for killing Aurelia?" he asked blandly.

I thought for a moment, but my mind was fogged with shock and fatigue and strong drink. It was difficult to put the pieces together, but I attempted it. "Aurelia carried a possible heir to the Dragulescu estate. If the count was killed, the child might stand to inherit, particularly if it were a son. Aurelia could have made an excellent case for Count Bogdan's estate to pass to his natural son rather than to the niece of his wife."

Dr. Frankopan said nothing, but sipped his own drink, letting me prattle on. "And another bird might well have been felled with the same stone. The rumours of a *strigoi* began with the death of Aurelia. Perhaps Cosmina meant to establish a perfect scene for Count Andrei's death. Everyone speculated that the revenant had returned to destroy his own son. If Aurelia was found foully slain by a vampire, and then Count Andrei suffered a similar fate, folk would merely put it down to the *strigoi*."

"Now that is a fanciful tale," Dr. Frankopan said, suppressing a smile.

"But possible. These mountains are thick with legends and ghosts. Everyone was ready to accept that Aurelia was slain by a *strigoi*. Why not Count Andrei as well?"

"I suppose," he said reluctantly. "It would have been a clever plot."

"Very," I agreed. "And she only altered it to put the blame for Count Andrei's death upon my head after she discovered the letter. That was when she decided to include me in her revenge. At one stroke, she would have been rid of me and of Andrei and ensured her own inheritance to the castle."

"And you are certain of this?" he asked, watching me closely.

"As certain as I am of my own name. It must be so, and I will see her brought to justice," I told him, heady with vindication.

He paused, then finished his drink. "That is unfortunate," he said finally. "If you had entertained the slightest doubt, there might have been hope for you. But not now."

"What do you mean?" I demanded.

His expression was sorrowful. "My dear child, I am fond of you—fond of you, indeed. But you cannot imagine I would ever let you do anything to harm Cosmina."

"But she is a murderess!" I protested.

"And she is my child," he countered.

I sat, stupefied, while he went to fetch a box upon the mantel. He returned to his chair and opened it, drawing out a miniature. He passed it to me, and I saw at once that it was the beautiful girl whose painting hung in the countess's bedchamber.

"This is the countess's sister," I exclaimed.

"My beloved Tatiana." He took the miniature from my nerveless fingers. "We met in Vienna. I saw her across the ballroom where she was dancing with one of the Emperor's nephews. She danced right out of her slipper and I brought it to her and drank champagne from it. It was the only time in my life I have been dashing," he added, a trifle ruefully. "I was her elder by some years, but she loved me, can you believe that? Ah, do not reply. It seemed a miracle to me as well, but love we did. My family would not agree to the match. They did not think minor Roumanian nobility was exalted enough to marry into the family of the Frankopans, not even Tatiana, the lovely Tatiana. She was an heiress, the eldest of the beautiful sisters Dragulescu, but even she was not worthy. We trace our lineage back to a senator of the Roman Empire, and we were expected to marry better." His voice betrayed no bitterness at the memory, only profound sadness. "I was sent away to recover from my disappointment, a sea voyage that lasted three years. When I returned, I learned that Tatiana had borne my child in secret. At first all was well enough. She had placed the child with a family outside of Vienna to foster it, and she visited, bringing presents and pretty clothes. But she grew sad and thin because she could not raise her own daughter, and because I never wrote to her."

He fixed me with a steely eye. "I did write to her, of course. But my letters were intercepted. Every last one of them. Tatiana had nourished herself on hope, you understand. Every month, she promised herself that I would come and marry her and claim her child. And every month, when I did not come, she slipped further into her sadness. Until at last, she no longer knew what was real and what was not. She was locked away in an asylum."

He paused and just when I thought he would give way to his emotion, he mastered himself and continued on. "I visited her, just once. She did not know me. She sat in her tiny cell, picking flowers only she could see and petting a pillow she said was a cat. She seemed happy enough, if one can be happy in that state. And you see, that is the real reason my family would not let me marry her. They knew there was a weakness in the blood of the Dragulescu women, a tendency to madness."

He waved a hand. "The countess is sound enough, for all her little hysterias. Her weakness is in her lungs. They are not sound, and she is not long for this world. But Cosmina, I thought she had escaped the troubles. She seemed so very normal. I used to visit her from time to time. I told the foster family I was a friend of her mother's for I was not permitted to take the child. How could I? I was a bachelor. I knew nothing of the raising of children. I had no money beyond the income my parents gave me. I was entirely dependent upon them. But I persuaded them to permit me to study medicine and to come to live here. And I worked upon Eugenia, finally convincing her to take Cosmina as her own, to raise her in the castle where I could see her often. Eugenia agreed so long as I promised never to reveal myself as Cosmina's father, for she wanted no interference. She has cared for her as tenderly as any mother, seen to her education and accomplishments. Did you know every penny has come from Eugenia's own pocket? She vowed to keep Cosmina's inheritance intact for her when she marries or reaches majority. She has done more for her than propriety and the law demand. She could not have loved her more wholly if she had borne her herself, and I could not grieve the woman who has reared my child by giving trouble. And so I promised, and it was a pact with the Devil, I think, for it has been the sharpest torment, to be so close to one's own flesh and blood and never to be allowed to reveal the connection. Never to take her hand and tell her the truth, never to look after her and protect her as a father should."

His eyes narrowed as he looked at me. "But I can protect her now. From you. I would never have moved against you had you not become her enemy. You have left me no choice, child."

"She is a murderess. I believe it and I know it can be proven," I said stoutly. "You must do what is right and let justice take its course."

"Justice? How is it just for that child to suffer for the sins of her fathers? If she is not wholesome in the mind, it is not her fault. She must be cared for and watched, which I can do. But I will not let her be taken to the sort of place where her mother yet lingers, not yet dead but neither wholly alive. That is no just fate for anyone," he returned, his face flushing with anger.

I made to rise, but suddenly the room began to spin and pitch. "I have drunk too much," I murmured.

But even as I said the words, I realised that strong drink was not the trouble.

"You have poisoned me," I said, gripping the arms of my chair.

"It is only a sedative," he corrected. He reached down and gathered me up, and I was astonished at the strength in him. I had thought him old and a little feeble, but he lifted me as easily as a dried leaf upon the wind. I wanted to protest, but I could not summon the energy.

"You will fall gently asleep and I will take you into the forest. The wolves will do the rest," he said softly. "Sleep now."

And then all was blackness.

I was cold, desperately cold, but apart from that I was not uncomfortable. I floated, neither here nor there, and waited for what must come. I did not want to die, but I had not the strength to resist it, and I lay upon the ground, my cheek pressed to the earth, the sharp scents of pine and leaf-mould filling my head. It was not a difficult way to die, I thought slowly. If only I could manage it before the wolves came. I imagined them, catching my scent upon the wind, creeping closer, ever closer, slavering jaws snapping down upon my bones and grinding them to dust.

I heard the howling then. They were calling to each other and to me. I could hear them, almost upon me, so near that I could smell the rough, animal scent of them. I wanted to scream, but the sound would not come. Something crept near to me, pressing a muzzle to my face, sniffing. I felt the snap of teeth upon my skirts and the slow, relentless pull as the animal began to drag me along the ground. And then nothing more.

★ ★ ★

I awoke to find myself in my room at the castle. I was restored to my prison then, I thought with resignation, but I could not be anything other than fervently grateful that I had escaped death. I opened my eyes to find Charles slumbering in a chair at my bedside. The curtains had been drawn, but I could see from the warm golden light at the edges that dawn had broken.

"Charles," I said, and my voice sounded like a rusted and unused thing.

He sprang to his feet, bending over me. "My God, you gave me a fright. How do you feel?"

"Bruised," I said, forming the word slowly.

He nodded. "Yes, well, you can blame Tycho for that."

"Tycho?"

At the mention of his name, the dog sprang up, placing his large head upon my bed. With a tremendous effort, I managed to put my hand upon his head.

"He found you before the wolves did. He would have dragged you entirely up the mountain, I think, had we not trailed him."

I moved my hand a little to stroke him behind the ear, but the effort was tiring and he seemed to sense it, for he licked my hand once and settled back on his haunches, watching me closely.

"You came to find me?" I asked. Talking was proving rather difficult as well, and my eyelids began to droop.

"Florian and I, at the count's insistence," Charles told me.

My eyelids flew upward and I winced against the light. "He is awake?"

Charles gave me a small, regretful smile. "Yes. And suffered no ill effects from his accident, it seems. He rages rather impressively, so I think he will be as he ever was. Aside from the scars, of course." A lesser man might have savoured the thought, but Charles was a stranger to smugness, and he had no pettiness within him.

"Where is he?" I asked, and Charles knew that I did not mean the count.

He hesitated. "You ought to sleep now. You are quite safe. He is not to be found. He fled as soon as he left you in the forest. Oh, Theodora, why did you run away?" he asked, his voice anguished.

I wanted to tell him, but my eyelids drooped again, and as I succumbed to sleep, I could not dismiss the notion that Charles was glad of it.

19

When next I woke it was evening, and Tereza brought water for me to wash and a tray of good, plain food. She helped me to dress, and when I had eaten all of the food and wiped my plate with the bread and eaten that, too, Charles came again.

"They are in the count's room. The entire household. Things must be discussed and you are summoned," he added apologetically.

The food that I had eaten sat like lead in my stomach, but I rose and smoothed my hair and followed him to the door. They were assembled as Charles had said, and to my astonishment, the count was dressed and seated in a chair by the fire. The countess and Frau Amsel had taken the sofa while Florian stood sentinel behind them. Cosmina huddled on the hassock at their feet and a pair of chairs had been brought for Charles and for me, completing the circle by the fire. Tycho raised his head when he saw me and thumped his tail by way of greeting, but he remained at his master's feet, guarding him, it seemed. When we had seated ourselves, I saw that Tereza and Frau Graben stood in the shadows, neither included in the circle nor apart from it.

I folded my hands together to keep them still. The count spoke first.

"I am glad to see you have suffered no ill effects from your experience, Miss Lestrange," he said formally. The same could not be said of him. He held a walking stick in his free hand, a heavy affair of ebony more suited to country pursuits than city idleness. He wore a sling at his neck, cradling his arm, and the wound upon his face slashed from brow to temple to cheek. The stitches were even and black, and rather than spoiling his looks, the effect was piratical and dashing. I had little doubt the Parisiennes would find him even more attractive with the addition.

"Thank you," I replied, and my voice sounded hollow to my ears. "It is good to see you as well," I added impulsively.

He inclined his head, but there was no warmth in him, only cool appraisal. "I have been apprised of the events that have passed, and I must apologise on behalf of our family that a connection of ours has attempted to harm you so grievously. The fault is entirely ours and we are abject in our sorrow."

The words were of the flowery sort the Eastern Europeans loved so much, a relic of their days of attachment to the Ottoman Empire, I thought. It was my turn to incline my head to acknowledge the sentiment and I did, gathering in the countess with my gesture to show I did not bear them ill will.

"Would you mind explaining to us why you sought the company of Dr. Frankopan last night?" he asked evenly.

And now we come to it, I thought. I could repudiate my convictions about Cosmina, even now. I had told no one save Dr. Frankopan my thoughts. The objects I had taken from her room were my only proofs of her instability. Without them, it was simply my word to hers, and she was nothing if not clever. It would be an easy thing to turn them all against me. She was, after all, as good as the daughter of the house.

I glanced at her, and she was watching me, her eyes large and sorrowful.

"I was afraid." I temporised.

The count lifted a brow to suggest disbelief. "Afraid of what?"

I hesitated again. I could say I feared the *strigoi;* I could claim I was afraid of them for keeping me locked in my room. I could choose expediency and hope to leave as soon as possible, putting all of the horrors of the place behind me.

Or I could choose to tell the truth and damn the lie.

"I was afraid of Cosmina," I said boldly, and stirring in the depths of the count's eyes I saw approval.

The countess gave an indignant sniff, and Cosmina put her hands to her mouth as if to smother a sob. Charles looked frankly astonished, and only Florian and Frau Amsel betrayed no emotion.

"Why were you afraid of Cosmina?" the count asked, leading me gently towards the edge of the precipice.

I looked only at him then, putting the others out of my mind. I spoke only to him, cared only for him.

"I think I always was. She used to fly into terrible rages at school. I told myself I never wanted to be friends with the other girls, but now I think back, I see I was afraid to befriend them—afraid of what she might do. I loved her as a sister, but I see now that I was always afraid, only I did not understand it was fear. I used to work so hard to make certain she was happy. I left off speaking to girls she did not like because I did not wish her to become angry. I studied German instead of French because she wished me to and I wanted to please her because she was my friend. At least, I believed she was. I found a rosary in her possession. It was the only thing I owned of my mother's and she stole it."

"Was there anything else?" the count prodded.

"A letter," I said softly. "A letter addressed to me that I never received. It was stolen from my room and when I discovered it, it had been torn to pieces and sewn back together."

I dared not look at Cosmina, but she had made no sound of protest. Doubtless she had discovered the objects missing from her room almost as soon as I had taken them.

"If we are to believe you, Miss Lestrange, then Cosmina is at worst a thief. You had only to confront her with the items and they would have been restored to you. Why did you flee?"

I twisted my hands together. They were cold, as cold as they had been when I had lain upon the forest floor, waiting to die.

"Because I was certain she had killed Aurelia. Under her pillow, with my things, I found the carving fork from the dining hall. It has been missing since Aurelia's death, and if it were compared to Aurelia's body, I believe the prongs would fit the wounds that killed the girl." I had seen it as soon as I had held the object in my hands, the two wickedly sharp prongs, a few inches between. If Cosmina had stabbed Aurelia with the thing, it would have rendered a wound precisely the same as a pair of very sharp teeth.

"No!" cried Cosmina. I looked at her then and her expression was one of outrage, her tone that of profound denial. She had been found out, and the shock of it was too much for her to bear. At the sound of her outcry, Tereza burst out sobbing and praying and Frau Graben hastened to calm her. The rest of the group said nothing, but I heard the countess's hiss of disbelief.

"This is an extremely serious charge," the count said soberly. "If you believed her to be a murderess, why did you not come forward?"

I flushed painfully. My flight had been foolish and ill-advised, and I had no excuse save that Dr. Frankopan had been sensible and persuasive and I had feared for my life.

"Dr. Frankopan insisted we leave. He said we could accomplish much more by leaving the castle and going directly to the *obergespan* in Hermannstadt. I believed he meant to help me."

"And instead he attempted your life," the count finished softly. My flush deepened.

"I trusted where I ought not to have," I said.

"And doubted where you ought not to have as well," he added. For a long moment, he said nothing, merely holding my gaze with his until I dropped my eyes to my lap. "Cosmina, Miss Lestrange believes you killed the maid Aurelia and ought to be brought to justice. What say you?"

I looked at her then, and her expression was blank, her voice soft and low. But under it all, I caught the note of rage, barely suppressed. "I can only say that I am sorry, profoundly sorry, that we have broken trust with one another. I cannot say how her things came to be in my room except that she must have put them there with an eye to discrediting me and blaming me for her own misdeeds."

Too late I saw the trap, springing neatly about me, catching me in its grim teeth. I could only sit, numbed to the horror of it.

"I did love Theodora, and I believed her my friend, but I see now I was deceived, and every lie she tells carries a seed of truth within it. She did lose a rosary at school, but I restored it to her when I found it and she has had it ever since. I do not know what letter she speaks of, nor have I seen the carving fork since it disappeared from the dining hall, but I think it is quite obvious she placed the things in my room, attempting to discredit me in the eyes of my family. We must thank God that she left her shawl behind when she attacked Count Andrei, or we would never know the depth of her villainy," she finished viciously.

Her facade was cool and almost entirely composed, but I knew something dark and violent seethed within. I thought of the time it must have taken her to stitch the love letter back together, the anger that must have raged within her as she set each stitch. I thought of the sharp blades of her scissors snapping my silhouetted head from my shoulders, and I knew what I must do.

"It maddens you, doesn't it?" I said softly. "Even now, you cannot stop thinking about it. You think about it every day, don't you? He refused you. You are not good enough for him because *he knows what you are.*"

She flew at me then, cursing, but the count had anticipated her, and raised his walking stick to block her. Florian darted forward, but the count waved him off.

"Cosmina, sit. You will not respond to Miss Lestrange's provocations," he said coolly. But even as he said the words, he gave me a nod, almost imperceptible, and I continued on.

"And you know what you are as well, do you not? You know the truth about your mother. She is not dead. She lives on, completely mad, locked in the same asylum where she has been since you were a small child. You know madness runs in the blood and you have waited for it to come for you."

She gave me a basilisk stare, as if she wished the flesh would melt from my bones, but I dared not stop.

"But did you know that you are Dr. Frankopan's child? He told me himself last night. You are his natural daughter, no more a legitimate Dragulescu than the child Aurelia carried. You do not belong here."

The words poured from my lips, goading her to some reaction that would betray her villainy. I laid at her door all of the crimes I believed her guilty of, but to my astonishment, it would be the most venal of them that broke her. I raised again the subject of my rosary. "It was my mother's. Why would you take it from me?"

"Because it was the only thing I had of yours," she cried, breaking her reserve at last. "That was the day that Fraulein Möller made such a pet of you, and you spent ages discussing the poetry of Heine with her, do you remember? But it was supposed to be *our* outing, *our* day. And you neglected me to sit and talk about poems with that stupid schoolmistress."

"And you took the rosary to punish her?" the count asked quietly.

"No, to make her look at me!" Cosmina returned, her eyes bright and lit with some unnatural fire. "We were friends and she ought not to have ignored me. When she thought the rosary was lost, she noticed me again. We were friends, and women must cling together in this world, for men are our destruction," she said, turning to the countess, pleading with her aunt to understand.

"And the letter?" I urged.

The beautiful complexion flushed, a stain of anger spreading across her cheeks. "Andrei should not have written it. It was wrong of him to write it. I had to take it away," she said stubbornly.

"And my son?" the countess asked, her voice even and low.

Cosmina said nothing, but the countess came at her, taking her by the shoulders and imploring her, "Tell me you did not harm my son. What did you do to him?"

Under her aunt's careful attention, Cosmina broke into sobs and the countess's hands fell away. "I did not think you capable of that, child. Not my Andrei. My son," she murmured, collapsing into a chair, her shoulder heaving as she coughed into her handkerchief.

Cosmina gathered her composure. She took a great, shuddering breath and squared her shoulders. She looked around the room, collecting us, and then spoke, slowly and distinctly. "Andrei is like a brother to me, and I would sooner die than harm a hair of his head. There is a *strigoi* that walks this place, and he came to claim his own son. You know this," she said, once more casting entreating eyes upon her aunt. "You know that Count Bogdan walks, that he demands the life of his son. You know these things. Why do you doubt me?" she asked, her tone persuading now.

The countess half turned from her. "I do not know what to believe."

"Believe she is a murderess," I said firmly.

It was this last that prodded Cosmina beyond endurance, for she flew at me again and this time the count surged from his chair, rising up to put himself between us and shielding me from her with his own body. "Cosmina!" he said sharply.

She paused, her hands outstretched, curled like claws, her eyes avid and hungry for vengeance. The count flicked one finger and Tycho sprang between them, baring his teeth at Cosmina, a low growl rolling in his throat.

"A word from me and he will tear out your throat," the count told her softly.

She darted her eyes to Tycho and then to me, perhaps gauging the distance between us and wondering if she could reach me before the dog reached her.

But she hesitated a moment too long, and in that second the count assumed control. He issued a command to Charles and Florian, never taking his eyes from Cosmina.

"Lock her in the garderobe," the count instructed them.

"No!" she cried. "I cannot stay there. That is where she died! She bled there," Cosmina protested, but the count would not be moved.

She twisted and writhed at first, and I watched Charles's expressionless face, knowing he hated what he must do. But neither he nor Florian faltered, and when Cosmina realised they would give no quarter, she calmed herself and allowed them to lead her docilely from the room. They removed her to the cold and comfortless garderobe, and as they did, the countess sat, ashen-faced, watching the devastation of her favourite niece. The two women exchanged wordless glances, and there was a *froideur* between them, a new coldness born of the countess's doubts and Cosmina's denials. I wondered if it would ever be mended, or if Cosmina had lost her aunt's affections forever.

We fell to silence until Charles and Florian returned, pale and unhappy. Charles gave a short nod to the count to indicate that his orders had been carried out, but Florian merely stood, his shoulders bowed, his woeful poet's eyes fixed upon the floor.

The countess turned to me. "I will never forgive you for this," she said clearly. Her eyes were dry and her expression stony. She was a woman who would hate implacably, and I knew I had made an enemy that night.

"I am sorry, madame," I said, and I meant it, for I had loved Cosmina too, and the revelations of the past day had been difficult to bear. I had not liked the count's methods, but I had understood them. Cosmina had to be shown for what she was, and her unnatural rages had persuaded everyone save the countess.

"Cosmina has stolen, and for that she must be punished. But I believe her. She is not responsible for the darkest deeds in this castle. It was the *strigoi*," the countess said stubbornly. "Count Bogdan walks this place, and he will come for us all."

Upon those chilling words we parted, and although the count gave me no looks of significance, no gesture of collusion, when he appeared in my room, I was not surprised to see him. He came to me by way of the tapestried stair, and stood, saying nothing but opening his arms in invitation. I went to him, putting my head to his shoulder as his good arm came to embrace me.

"I feel a thousand years old," he said, murmuring the words into my hair.

"What will become of her?"

"She attempted my life, and very likely killed Aurelia as well. She must be put away."

I drew back, searching his face. "You mean she will be gaoled? She will hang then."

"No," he said sharply. "I will not have the scandal of it touching my family. What Dr. Frankopan told you is true. Her mother is unwell, a weakness in the head and nerves. She has been locked away since Cosmina was an infant. I know Frankopan and others besides believe such weaknesses may be carried in the blood. If that is true, it is not her fault. She is a flawed and unnatural thing, but not evil."

"She has killed," I said, even then trying to convince myself that the girl I knew could have done such deeds, worked them out, coldly and maliciously, determined to end the lives of those she decided were unfit to live. "But it would give me no pleasure to see her hang for her crimes."

"I knew her as a child," he said, something almost pleading in his eyes as he willed me to understand. "I cannot turn her over to them. They will see only the deed and not the lost child. Even now I pity her."

I put a hand to his face, touching the long line of silken black stitches. "It does you credit," I told him.

He gave me a cynical smile. "You think so, but it is not merely for Cosmina's sake that I will not give her over to the authorities. My mother maintains her innocence, and I am not certain enough of my own conviction to persuade her. I know what I believe, but there is no proof of it, and without such proof, the matter would drag through the courts and the newspapers and we would all of us be mired in the mud of it. No, tomorrow Florian will go to Hermannstadt. There is a private clinic there, an asylum. It is the only choice."

"And they will simply accept your word for the fact that she is mad? They would lock her up on your recommendation alone?" I asked.

For a moment, the familiar *hauteur* settled over his features. "I am the Count Dragulescu. They will do as I say."

"And must she be kept in the garderobe until she is taken away?" I asked. "It is so cold there, and it is where Aurelia died."

The air of command did not alter. "She will remain there until she is taken. It is the scene of her crime, and it will not harm her to meditate upon her villainy."

But as soon as the haughtiness descended, it fled and his tone was gentler. "There is nowhere else that I can keep her to ensure our safety. I have sent a mattress for her comfort, and she will be given hot food whenever she wishes. It is the only way." He searched my face with tender and imploring eyes. "Will you forgive me?" he asked. "I could say I had no choice in how I brought the matter to light, but I did. I was ruthless, deliberately so. I used you to force a reaction from Cosmina, and I nearly destroyed you in the process."

"You did what you must," I said slowly. "But if you suspected her, why did you not confront her yourself?"

He paused a moment, as if searching for the proper words, and failing to find them, plunged on, taking honesty as his watchword. "Because I doubted you. I have known her tricks and lies and rages since she was a child. That is the truth of why I refused to marry her. Always there was something not quite human in her, although I never dared speak of it to anyone.

But I did not know how deeply rooted the madness was. I too searched her room, when I left you in the garden. I found the letter and the carving fork and the rosary, and I saw how neatly it might all have been done."

"You found them—and still you did not expose her?" I made to pull away, but he held me fast.

"Because I know her, I have always known her. She is capable of turning any circumstance, no matter how black, to her advantage. The objects alone were no proof, particularly since she would only say you had put them there yourself. And God help me, I doubted you. I had to know the truth."

I opened my mouth to remonstrate with him, and snapped it closed. Had I not doubted him for the duration of our acquaintance? I owed him a just response.

"I suppose I understand," I said slowly. "But my goading her into a rage has accomplished nothing. She confessed to theft, nothing more. She will never admit to killing Aurelia or to attempting to harm you. Even your own mother does not believe her guilty."

"But I do," he said with a grim note of satisfaction. "And I have the power to send her away."

"What of the evidence itself? Dr. Frankopan took it from me. If only we can find him." But even as I said the words, I realised the futility of it all. Dr. Frankopan would die sooner than see his only child swing from a hangman's noose. Doubtless the evidence against Cosmina had been destroyed, dropped into the river perhaps, to be swept away to the sea.

"He is missing and no one knows where he is bound," the count told me. "Without evidence, we cannot go to the authorities. It is for me to mete justice to Cosmina, regardless of what my mother believes."

We both fell silent again, and the strong sturdy rhythm of his heartbeat under my cheek comforted me.

"How did you know to send them for me?" I asked. "How did you know what Dr. Frankopan meant to do?"

He gave me a rueful smile. "I knew nothing. At first, we only knew you had disappeared from your room, that the door was locked and still you had escaped. To me, this meant either you feared someone in the castle or you were fleeing to escape your own misdeeds. Dr. Frankopan was the only person you knew outside the castle and he too had been missed. And then I remembered that before the accident, I had sent word to Dr. Frankopan that I believed I knew who was behind the villainy in the castle. I wanted to consult him about whether Cosmina could have struck the precise blow that killed Aurelia. I knew they often discussed medical matters, and she often helped to nurse the folk in the village under his direction. He would have known if she were knowledgeable enough to effect such a murder."

He touched the row of stitches in his face absently, and I wondered if they pained him. "But he never came. He sent word he was at a confinement, and that was the night I fell from the observatory."

"Fell or were pushed?" I asked gently.

"I do not know. I saw no one and I remember nothing, only the sensation of falling and the desperate lunge to catch myself. But as I lay in bed, thinking about you and the possibility that you had done this to me, I thought of my doubts about Cosmina, and I realised Dr. Frankopan was far likelier to play the comrade to her than to you. He has always shown partiality to her, and it did not escape me that my accident happened just a few hours after I gave him reason to fear for Cosmina. And I began to think if I had been deliberately pushed, then perhaps you were in danger as well. I sent out Florian and Charles and told them to take a piece of your clothing and Tycho. He found you, thank God," the count added fervently. "They carried you first to Frankopan's cottage, where they discovered the empty bottle of sedative with the tea things and guessed at what he had done. From there they brought you to the castle, hoping that with time the sedative would run its course and you would waken. You must rest now," he told me. "You have been through a terrible ordeal, and we will speak again later. There is much to discuss."

I obeyed, but when he left me and I settled into bed, I found I could not sleep. I thought of Dr. Frankopan, so casually capable of leaving me to die, torn apart by wolves. And I thought of Cosmina, savaged by the rage she carried. And the countess, who even now believed that some monstrous revenant stalked her castle. I hated and pitied them all, and I do not know which emotion surprised me the more.

The next day a flurry of letters came and went, and I saw little of Charles or the count, for without the use of his writing arm, the count depended upon Charles as his amanuensis, and Charles spent long hours at the count's side, penning the letters that would settle Cosmina's fate. Messengers came and went, village lads who brought letters and gossip, and by the second day, everything had been settled. I had been given strict instructions to rest and saw no one, although my thoughts turned often to Cosmina, biding her time in the garderobe below me.

Early on the second morning, she was summoned to the great hall where the count stood, Tycho at his side, looking for all the world like a feudal prince. The rest of the household had gathered as well, and a quiet and tractable Cosmina was brought to the hall. The countess was pale, but resplendently dressed in a gown stiff with jet embroidery, her chin held very high as she stared directly ahead. A strange gentleman stood at the count's side, and when Cosmina entered, he regarded her with a cool and professional curiosity. Her gown was creased where she had slept in it, and her hair was untidy, but she did not seem to notice, and her eyes darted strangely, as if the time she had spent in the garderobe had turned her wits entirely, as if the thin thread that had bound her to sanity had snapped once and for all.

"Cosmina, this is Herr Engel. He keeps a private rest home in Hermannstadt. He would like to take you there for a rest," the count said gently, but I was not deceived. He watched Cosmina as a dog will watch a viper, and she returned the look, cold and calculating.

"I am to be sent away?"

"For a little while," Herr Engel soothed. "Just until you have recovered your nerves, my dear."

It was a lie of course, and Cosmina smelled the untruth of it upon him. She laughed, a sharp and bitter sound that shattered the quiet of the great, vaulted room. "I am going away." She turned to collect us with her look. "I am going away and you all will stay. You will write to me, won't you?" And then she laughed again until she fell silent, and somehow her silence was worse than anything she could say. No matter how kindly Herr Engel put a question to her, she refused to reply, perhaps as a means to holding the reins of the situation.

At last he shrugged his shoulders and nodded towards the count. The count gestured towards Florian, who opened the doors to the courtyard where a group of village men had gathered. For an instant, it seemed as if a mob had come, and Cosmina's courage failed her. She staggered a little, but Herr Engel offered his arm in a very gentlemanly fashion, and she took it, raising her chin in a gesture of noble dignity very reminiscent of the countess.

At the doors they paused and Cosmina looked at him. "What about my things? Shall they be sent on? I should like my things." Her tone was anxious, and Herr Engel was quick to reassure her.

"We have all that you could require. And if there is something of importance, we will send for it," he soothed.

Mollified, Cosmina walked out with him, never turning back, never saying goodbye. I heard later that the party of villagers divided and seven strong men walked in front of her and seven behind, guarding lest she attempt to flee. The villagers noted the strangeness of the doctor's carriage, for it was a curious thing, with barred windows and heavy leather shades. And when Cosmina and her escort reached the carriage, he instructed his driver to lock them in together until they reached Hermannstadt.

The villagers had other things to spice the meat of their gossip, for Dr. Frankopan had not been found, but Teodor Popa had returned home, wearing a bright red coat that looked familiar to many. It had been badly slashed, and there were stains upon it that were dark and rusty, but Madame Popa was an excellent housekeeper, and it was not long before the fabric was clean and the rents mended and the brass buttons polished, and when Teodor Popa wore his coat in the village, no one dared to ask him where he had found it. The cottage in the woods remained shuttered and dark, and Madame Popa found employment with the innkeeper, whose wife was carrying again and could no longer manage her duties.

I saw little of the countess, for she did not seem willing to relent in her opinion of me, and every glance she threw my way carried condemnation for Cosmina's departure. She bore no such ill will towards her son, but I was not surprised. A mother's indulgence is a powerful thing, and she would not blame the count for his resolution to the situation, but rather I must bear the burden of guilt for bringing Cosmina's crimes to light.

For his part, Florian's sadness seemed permanently etched upon his face, and when he sought me out the afternoon before Charles and I planned to leave, I did not know what I should say to him.

We walked to the piggery together, for I craved fresh air and in spite of the cold of the drawing in of autumn, it was bracing and exhilarating. We did not speak until we reached the piggery, and even then Florian seemed to struggle for his words.

"I must ask forgiveness, for this is the Christian thing to do, and I have seen too much of the Devil in this place," he said suddenly, his face flushing painfully.

"Yes, there is too much of the Devil here," I agreed. "But what have I to forgive you for?"

He hesitated a long moment, watching a fat porker root in the ground for something tasty. When he spoke, he did not look at me. "I liked you, very much, when first you came here. But then Miss Cosmina says things, terrible things, and I began to hate you. She says them to my mother as well, and my mother, she tells me I must not speak with you. I told her I would speak with you, for you were a kindly person. My mother was angry with you because of this, and soon I believe the things that Miss Cosmina said of you."

It was a long speech for Florian, and I had no doubt, a painful one. I wanted to put a hand to his arm to console him, but it seemed an intrusion. "I understand, Florian. Either Cosmina or I must have been living a lie, and it is difficult to doubt the one you love."

He turned swiftly to me to deny it, but I raised a hand. "Let us be truthful in goodbye. I know you loved her. I did as well. There is nothing shameful in your regard for her, Florian. We do not choose where we will love."

He considered this a long moment, then turned back to his pigs.

"Will you remain here, now that she is gone?"

He shrugged. "To stay, I die. To leave, I die. Here I have memories. They cut me, these memories. But I am content to suffer. So I stay."

There seemed no possible reply to this that would not diminish the magnitude of his pain, so I fell silent for a time as well and watched the pigs, sleek and content.

"The improvements in the village will lighten the burden of your work," I said hopefully.

He shrugged again, an Oriental gesture of resignation. "Perhaps. But the villagers carry fear in the heart."

"They are fearful? Of what?"

"The *strigoi* at the castle," he replied.

"They ought not to be. I know the countess still believes that Count Bogdan walks, but no one else does."

"Tereza believes," he rejoined. "And she speaks with a loose tongue. She tells the people Count Andrei flew and Count Bogdan walks undead. The people fear the *strigoi* is come to them."

I did touch his arm then. "Florian, you must help to persuade them that this is nonsense," I said, feeling the hypocrite even as I said it. If I, an educated and modern woman had thought it possible, how much likelier were unschooled peasants to believe in such things?

"Is it?" he asked swiftly. He bent towards me. "I am glad you will be leaving. This is not safe, to be here."

"Florian, you cannot believe it. The Dragulescus have been patrons and friends to your family for so long. You cannot believe they are monsters," I told him, my tone sharp.

"I see the roof where Count Andrei falls. He says he catches himself, but it is not a possible thing." He paused, his mournful eyes bright with speculation. "I am believing he flew."

I felt the anger rising hot and thick within me. What hope did the count hold to banish the rumours if his own steward fed them? "Then I can only say I am surprised you would continue to work for him if you believe it. You should be shamed to take his money."

Florian gave me a fatalistic smile. "Folk here say, 'Better a mouse in the pot than no meat at all.'" His expression softened. "I am being a poor man. I must take any coin, even the Devil's."

I felt a prick of shame myself then, for I had forgot myself and the fact that Florian must work for his meat. I meant to earn my own keep, but I had Anna and Charles and other means of keeping myself from the workhouse. Here, there was not even that dread institution to provide for Florian should he leave the count's employ.

"We are neither of us free men, are we, Florian?" I asked finally. And I put out my hand to shake his.

That afternoon, I took my courage in my hands to go and bid farewell to the countess, for although she deplored my presence, the proprieties must be observed, and it was necessary to take formal leave of her before our departure. I found her in her bedchamber, sitting before the fire and stitching at a piece of tapestry bound tightly within its frame. She was working a scene from Greek mythology, a stretch of golden stitches forming a beach and a swathe of blue and green for sea and sky.

She waved me to the chair opposite and I took it, rather surprised that she even bothered with the gesture of welcome. I nodded towards the tapestry. "How lovely," I told her, and she fixed me with her cold grey eyes and gave a sharp little cough.

"The sacrifice of Iphigenia. Surely you know the story,

Miss Lestrange. The eldest daughter of Agamemnon and Cly-
temnestra, sacrificed by her father for a good wind to launch
the effort to retrieve Helen of Troy."

I realised then that her needle was laden with scarlet thread
and she was setting tiny, precise stitches just at the throat of the
graceful figure stretched upon a plinth.

"Yes, I recall it," I told her, finding the scene distasteful now
and unpleasant. "I have come to bid you farewell and to thank
you for your hospitality."

She pushed the needle into the fabric, setting another tiny
stitch into Iphigenia's throat. "Of course, Miss Lestrange. You
have been a most welcome and entertaining guest." The words
were the purest *politesse,* but there was no warmth in them.

Another stitch, this time a drop of blood staining the sand
crimson. I looked away, fixing my attention upon the painting
of the countess and her sister, the beautiful Tatiana.

"I am sorry about your sister," I said impulsively. "Dr. Frankopan explained what became of her. That must have been
very difficult for you. I have a sister myself, and I understand
the bonds of sisterly affection," I finished, rather pathetically.
The grey eyes lifted to mine and I saw resentment and scorn
there. She did not want my pity, and it was presumptuous of
me to offer it.

I rose and turned to leave, but even as I did so, something
tugged at my memory.

"Her inheritance," I said quietly. I subsided back into my
chair, conscious of the countess watching me closely even as
she worked. "Tatiana was the elder and it was she who inherited the fortune. It was to have passed to Cosmina upon her
marriage or her majority, her twenty-fifth birthday, I suspect.
That was why you were so eager to marry her to your son. I
could not imagine why any mother would willingly unite her

son to a girl who carried the taint of madness in the blood, but I see it now. You have had the control of her money all these years, and if she married your son, you would still have a claim upon it, would you not? But if she inherited in her own right, the entire fortune would be at her disposal. She could do as she pleased, even to taking the money from here and establishing a household elsewhere. And you did not want that."

The hand that held the needle stilled, and I realised she was watching me with a predatory amusement.

"You are enjoying yourself, Miss Lestrange, go on."

My mind was working feverishly, dredging up all the bits of gossip I had heard, recollecting the odd looks and the unexplained discrepancies I had noted.

"Cosmina stole my rosary and the letter, I believe that. And I think it likely she killed Aurelia as well. But the carving fork, her look of surprise when I revealed where it had been found. The imploring glances she sent your way. You conspired with her, didn't you? You had a greater reason to wish for Aurelia's death. You were an insulted wife, outraged and betrayed. And she carried the proof of that betrayal in her womb, a proof that might well cost your son a portion of his own inheritance."

It fitted together, so neatly I was astonished I had not seen it before. "I do not know how you persuaded her to do it, what promises or threats, by what tricks or cajolery, but she did. And you took the carving fork, did you not? For yours was the only other key to the silver. Cosmina cleaned it and returned it, but you took it away, and meant to keep it, for it gave you a hold over her to keep the instrument of Aurelia's destruction. What then? Did you fail to give her what you promised? I suspect you convinced her you could persuade Andrei to marry her, and you failed again. Is that why she attacked your son? To be revenged upon you both? And how cleverly it was done. If she had succeeded, she would have killed him and I would have borne the blame of it. She would have inherited her fortune and could have secured the castle itself as her own, with no one the wiser to her crimes. Only you would know she had destroyed Aurelia, and you would never reveal it. But she attempted the life of your son, the one act you could not forgive, and even as she stood in his room, imploring you to save her, you turned your cheek and offered her no succour. And now she has ended as her mother did, with no one to whom she can confess the truth and even if she did, who would believe her? For the Dragulescus are masters of all they survey," I finished, sickened by the tidy menace of it all.

I rose. The countess coughed again, more deeply this time, and when finished her colour was high.

"Do you think you will tell this to Andrei?" she asked pleasantly. She took up a dainty pair of scissors and snipped off the scarlet thread, putting her work aside.

"He has a right to know the truth," I said stoutly.

She laughed, an unpleasant and unwholesome sound. I thought of the madness that ran like a broken thread through the women of their family and I wondered to what extent the countess herself was damaged.

"My dear, my son will never believe you. He knows what Cosmina is. She is a creature flawed from birth. She has told lies and engaged in malicious and petty acts from the time she came to live with us. It is no great stretch to think she has merely expanded her repertoire to include the trick of murder. It is what he chooses to believe because it is logical and neat, and my son has a logical mind. It comforts him to fit things into tidy categories and fix them with a label, as an entymologist will label his specimens. He feels he understands Cosmina, and if you go to him, you will ask him to create a new understanding, a place where I am a greater evil than she and where you are to be believed above his own mother. What man is capable of that?"

And whatever villainy the countess was guilty of, none was greater than the piece of sophistry she had just constructed. Of course she was entirely correct. There was no proof she had ever coaxed Cosmina to become the instrument of her revenge—only the carving fork under the pillow and Cosmina's look of surprise had betrayed her. The structure of my argument had nothing sturdier than sand for a foundation, and I saw the whole of it blow away upon the winds of her scorn.

She rose and rang the bell. "Would you care for some tea, Miss Lestrange? I feel the need for some refreshment."

My hands fisted at my sides. "No. I will leave this place and I will not speak of this. But I see you for what you are. You are a monster," I said, my voice low and harsh.

Just then the door opened and the countess smiled over my shoulder, baring sharp white teeth. "Tereza, Miss Lestrange was just leaving. Will you—" But whatever she meant to ask was lost, for she broke off, putting her hands to her mouth, as if to stifle a scream. Suddenly she opened her mouth, and as we watched in horror, a river of blood began to flow, over her lips and onto the floor.

"*Strigoi!*" Tereza cried, pointing with a shaking finger.

Her scream brought Frau Amsel who ran to her mistress, taking up a basin to catch the blood. She turned to me, her eyes wide in her pale face. "Fetch the count! Go now! And take the girl!"

I turned and put an arm around the white and shivering Tereza, urging her to leave. As we quitted the room, I glanced over my shoulder one last time at the gruesome scene. The countess was covered in her own blood, for it had spilled from the basin, staining her hands and skirt and puddling upon the floor. Frau Amsel fretted and fussed and held the basin closer, but even as she did so, the countess raised her eyes over Clara's shoulder and met mine, her gaze calm and inscrutable. I hurried out with Tereza and found the count.

The next hours were tense and watchful ones. Without Dr. Frankopan, there was no physical nearer than Hermannstadt, and once more Florian was dispatched to the city to find a doctor and bring him back. In the meanwhile, the haemorrhage was stopped and the countess was dosed with a sedative left by Dr. Frankopan and sent to sleep. It was thought too dangerous to move her, and so the count emerged at last and told the rest of us to retire, for his mother rested and he and Frau Amsel would stay with her.

I ached for him, for his eyes were deeply shadowed and mournful, but he belonged to her then, and I left him to spend my last night alone in the Castle Dragulescu.

In the end, it was not my last night, for with the countess's collapse, our travel arrangements had been thrown in disarray and Charles and I were forced to postpone our departure one day further. It was not a pleasant day, for there was much whispering about the countess's condition and there were furrowed brows and dark looks among everyone in the household. Charles was fretful and nervous, ready to be quit of the place, and he chafed at the delay, even as I relished it. I had one more precious day to commit to my memory all that I wanted to remember about the place, and I wandered the castle, free of interference and interruption as I took my leave of it.

That evening, as the sun sank beneath the high peaks of the Carpathians, I wrapped myself against the rising chill and ventured into the ruined garden. I knew he would be there, and the burden of farewell lay heavy upon my heart. We had seen little of each other with all that had happened, and whatever idyll we had enjoyed together, it had come to an end. It remained only to say goodbye.

He did not turn as I approached, but Tycho pricked up his ears and gave a little whine of protest. I bent to scratch his head.

"He will miss you," the count told me.

"And I him. I owe him my life," I said, burying my face into the ruff of thick grey fur at his neck. After a moment, I wiped away my tears and rose.

"You must not weep," the count said with some severity. "How can I let you go if you weep?"

"And how can you not?" I asked, knowing the inevitable was upon us.

We walked for a little while then, deeper into the decaying garden. I could see the remnants of beauty there even yet, and I knew it could be made right again.

"I will restore it," he said, intuiting my thoughts. "I will make it right again. My grandfather would have approved."

"It will be magnificent," I said, seeing it in my mind's eye, beautiful and fertile and full of the promise of living things.

"I will make all of it better," he said, his voice firm with conviction.

"I know you will. You will be the saviour of this place."

He gave a short, bitter laugh. "I am no saviour, least of all of myself. And I very nearly destroyed you. I cannot ask you to stay. Not now. My mother is—" He broke off, then cleared his throat, continuing on in a voice rough with emotion. "She is dying. Consumptive, the doctor tells me, although she will not own it. She clings to her legends and her superstitions because they give her comfort, but she is dying, and it will not be quick and it will not be easy. I must do what I can for her. Alone."

I stared at him. Had I been wrong then? Was she simply a malicious old woman with a cruel sense of humour to play upon my fears? Or was she something darker and more evil still, a *strigoi,* feeding and then calling up blood to extricate herself from a situation she found intrusive?

"I did not realise," I said slowly.

"There is often consumption in the village," he explained. "She used to nurse the valley folk before she fell ill. I ought to have seen it when I came home," he said, his complexion darkening. "She was so pale and fragile. Her eyes were so bright. How did I not see?"

I thought of the symptoms she had manifested; the symptoms of a consumptive were very like those of a vampire. Even now who was to say which she was?

"How did I not see what she was?" he continued, and for an instant, something fierce and almost angry flashed in his eyes. Did he know then? Did he sense the monstrous evil within her? Whatever his feelings, he did not share them, but he recollected himself and gave me a joyless smile. "I must attend to her," he said smoothly. "I am the only one who can see to it she is taken care of as she must be."

Again that slight, shivering touch of something not quite right. Grief at his mother's ill health, or something darker? "I know," I said, summoning a courage I did not feel. I had not thought it would be so hard to leave him. "I must go. I have a novel to finish, and a life to begin."

He fixed me with those startling grey eyes. "So we understand each other, then."

"Not entirely," I said, breaking off a withered leaf so I did not have to look at him. "You see, I realise now it was all trickery. Everything you made me think about you, it was all just the sophisticated japes of an experienced seducer. You came to my room by way of the tapestried stair, you made me believe you were something more than human. I see it now."

"If you want apologies, I will make you none," he said fiercely. "I wanted you and I knew what to give you to make you surrender. Yes, it was calculated and deliberate, but it was not malicious. I had my conjurer's tricks and I used them well. Even now you do not know what to make of me, and I will not own what I am. I want you to think of me when you leave this place and wonder whether I am merely a mortal or something beyond. A better man would release you and want you to love another. I am no better man. I am selfish and flawed and I have nothing to offer you that is not broken or imperfect, including myself. And so I offer you nothing. But I will love you until the day I die, and no man will love you more."

He kissed me then, and I clung to him and we stood as long as we could in the shadows of his grandfather's garden, watching the first stars shimmer into life in the pale violet sky.

"When this is over," he said, his lips against my hair, "come to me in Paris. I will give you everything you could desire."

I opened my mouth, but he put a finger to it. "No, do not answer. Just think on it. You will live in luxury, I promise. You will dress like a countess, be the envy of everyone who sees you. I will keep you as you ought to be kept, with every wish and whim fulfilled."

I pushed his finger aside gently. "As your mistress," I said.

He regarded me a long moment in the dying light. "I can offer you nothing more. Not now."

"Then I will take nothing from you save your heart," I told him lightly, although mine seemed to fracture within my chest even as I spoke.

"But—"

It was my turn to speak and force him to silence. "You offer me all that you think you can give, and I thank you for that. But it is not enough. It never will be. I may not be worthy to be your wife, but I am far too worthy to be your mistress. To accept your invitation would mean to give up my work, for no kept woman can be a respectable authoress, and I mean to earn my keep by my pen. I know you will say it is not necessary, that you will keep me, and that would suffice for most women. But I am unlike most women, as you yourself have observed," I told him, lifting myself just a little. "And I will make my own way."

He put a hand to the nape of my neck and bent to rest his brow upon mine. "Go back to Scotland with Charles then, and write your book and know that I will be there. When the wind comes unexpectedly through the casement, you will hear your name and it will be my voice calling. When you blow out a candle, it will be my breath that rises with the smoke, curling once to touch your cheek. And when you weep—" he paused to rub his thumb over my cheek to catch my tears "—when you weep, you will taste the salt of my tears upon your lips."

He kissed me again and again until I thought I would die from breathlessness and longing. When we broke apart I looked to the night sky. Above us, a single star shimmered into life.

"Venus," I said, pointing with a trembling hand. "You see, you have taught me well. I shall not forget."

20

I did not forget, and it was the memory of that enigmatic and fascinating man that warmed me through the months that followed. I left Transylvania an older and marginally wiser woman, with a book of poetry in my pocket and the pieces of my heart resting beside. There was a new coolness to me, a reserve that none could penetrate, and my hauteur served me well in the new life I fashioned for myself.

I did not go to Scotland; there was nothing within its grey streets to lure me back. I went instead to London, where I wrote and walked and waited to be made whole again. To his credit, Charles was a prop to me, advancing funds against the sale of my book to permit me to take furnished rooms in a pleasant quarter of the city and visiting often in the capacity of friend as well as publisher. We had endured much together, and sometimes, when the hour grew late and the moon hung low, we spoke of Transylvania and the extraordinary time we shared there. It had finally occurred to me that the greatest mystery—whether the *strigoi* actually existed or whether Cosmina had been a murderess—could have been solved by the expedient of searching the garderobe for traces of blood. A human villain would have rinsed the blood down the sluice to create the fiction of a vampire; an actual vampire would have fed upon it. But it was far too late to make such conclusions now, and I knew the question would never be settled within my mind. Was the countess a *strigoi* who had committed her own murder and seen her niece carried away for the crime? Or was she a consumptive old woman who had formulated a murderous plot? I should never know, and after a time, I realised I did not wish to. There were times I did not wish to think upon my time in Transylvania at all, and others in which I wished to relive every moment. Charles was a great comfort to me in both moods.

"Do you ever hear from him?" he asked me once. I did not ask whom he meant.

"No. And I am glad of it," I told him truthfully. It was difficult enough to lay the ghost of his memory without the thorn-prick of letters to disturb my peace. But each night before I slept, I read Baudelaire, until the pages grew thin and worn with handling.

To his credit, Charles never renewed his addresses. "Having met the count, I would not dare," he told me once, with a sort of pointed jollity. I understood his meaning. The count was larger than life; no mere mortal man could ever hope to challenge him on any ground, much less carry the field.

But Charles was a comfortable companion during those long months, and the following year when my book was published, it was Charles who arranged for readings in the most popular salons and stood beside me to fend off an enthusiastic public. The book had been brought out to surprising acclaim—surprising to me, although Charles claimed that he expected nothing less from a thrilling tale of vampires and werewolves and abducted heiresses. I was much in demand, and once or twice found myself addressing rather more exalted company than that to which I was accustomed. The most important of these was a reading Charles had engaged before the Society of Literary Fellowes, a collection of titled gentlemen—founded by a viscount—who dabbled in letters and thought themselves terribly daring for consorting with authors. The society met in the townhouse of the viscount, in a fashionable square in Belgravia, and I dressed myself carefully for the occasion, in new finery of blood-red velvet, befitting an authoress of sensational tales, I thought. I was much sought after that evening, and presented to so many titled heads I could not help but think I was the lone commoner in the room. The elevated company made me rather nervous, and I paused to collect my nerve as I began to read, slowly at first, but then gaining speed and confidence with the excited gasps and sighs of my audience. I finished to warm applause, and for an hour after I was importuned with still more people clamouring for introductions and pressing me with questions about my researches.

"How did you find Transylvania, Miss Lestrange?" asked the viscount himself. "I am told it is a wild and friendless place, full of bandits and bloodthirsty creatures."

I strove for an answer that would be both truthful and just. "I found it unlike anyplace else in the world," I told him at last. "It is a land of myth and legend, and yet the peasants are kindly and generous. It is a curious alchemy of medieval and modern. Manners are free, for a man and woman may walk together without either chaperone or censure, but one must always be alert, for to stir out of doors is to make oneself vulnerable to wolves and other creatures."

As I expected, the ladies shivered in delight, while the gentlemen regarded my answer soberly. "I shall have to organise a holiday," the viscount said. "I should quite enjoy hearing these local legends from the horse's mouth as it were."

"I shouldn't dare," his wife said with a shudder. She was a pretty little thing, with blond curls and half her husband's years, swathed in forget-me-not blue to match her eyes. She turned to me. "I am so pleased the book ended happily. I was desperately afraid the baron would not come for dear Rowena."

I smiled at her. "You have penetrated my secret, my lady. I am a coward. I have not the courage to deny my readers a happy ending."

Her eyes widened. "Oh, you must not say you are a coward, for I am quite devoted to your book and will not hear a word against you, not even from your own lips."

Her seriousness was touching, and I inclined my head. "Very well. Then I will say I am more generous to my characters than I am to myself. I give them the happy ending I have not yet fashioned."

I would have turned then, but she stayed me with a hand to my arm. "One thing more, Miss Lestrange. I was particularly moved that your heroine was able to give the whole of her heart to her beloved guardian, even though she suspected him of being a werewolf. Do you not find it extraordinary that a woman should be so accepting of such a thing?"

I thought of the count then, and the impenetrable mysteries he had constructed for me, the questions he had seeded so carefully in my mind, leaving me to puzzle over, until I had come to understand that some things were never meant to be known.

"I believe in the human heart, and the power of it to love,

even when such love is unwise or even unwanted. It is an enduring thing, love is. It will weather the fiercest storm and stand, bowed but unbroken. And when life is gone, love itself may still live on. That is what I find extraordinary, my lady."

I excused myself then, and turned to find Charles at my elbow.

"There is another gentleman who begs an audience," he said, his colour high and his manner a little stiff.

I followed, and there he was. Charles tactfully melted away and the crowd seemed to have dispersed a little, for we were alone in the corner of the great salon. It was a long moment before I could find my voice, and when I did, it was so low he had to bend to hear me.

"You look well," I told him, for he did. The great slashing scar had faded to a thin, white line that—as I had suspected it would—merely emphasised the elegance of his bones and took nothing from his looks. There was a touch of silver at one temple, and I noticed the black armband of mourning crepe pinned to his sleeve.

"I am well," he said, and the melting honeyed tones were just as I remembered them. He brandished a book, and I saw that it was mine. "I have just concluded it."

I swallowed against the quick dryness of my mouth. "What did you think of it?"

"A compelling tale. It was good to see my country described by one who clearly loves the place."

"I did love it. I love it still," I said, wondering if he noticed that my hands trembled to have him near to me.

He must have, for he took them in his.

"Will you return then? I told you once I had nothing to offer you but a broken and imperfect man in a broken and imperfect place. But I am a better man now than ever I was, and if you will have me, I am yours."

I considered it carefully. "I am not the sort of a woman you would marry, you told me once. And even if that were untrue, I cannot be content breeding sons and ordering servants and sewing your shirts. I know my place in the taxonomy," I added with a small smile. "I cannot be the wife you expect."

"But you are the wife I want," he said firmly. "I was a fool to ever think otherwise. I want a wife to stand with me, to believe in me, to love me for the man that I am and the man I can yet become. I want you." He reached out his hand to my shoulder, the heavy silver ring gleaming in the light, and I saw that it had been set with a great pigeon's blood ruby. "I have put aside my tricks, my stratagems and sophistries, and I am nothing, have nothing, but my heart. And poor and wretched as it is, it is knit to yours and cannot be unbound."

And those simple and honest words mended all that had been broken before. I put my hand in his, feeling his fingers close over mine, warm and strong and possessive, and I gave myself up to my own happy ending.

In the end, the life we fashioned for ourselves was a compromise. I learned to shake hands with domesticity, and he learned to love freely. He found a calm and centered peace in our life in his homeland, and I found infinite inspiration. Curious, I often thought, how two such different people could be happy in the same place, but we found contentment there. There were shadows from time to time, as there must be in such a land, for we walked with ghosts there, and the dead do not always lie quietly in Transylvania. The Popa men continued to take to the mountains when the moon rose full and low over the Carpathians, and in spite of my best efforts, folk in the village still crossed themselves when my husband passed. But they accepted him with a sort of fierce and peculiar loyalty, and whether they believed him a *strigoi* or not, they became devoted to him and called him master with genuine affection.

They accepted me as well, although they found me meddlesome at times, and thought my stories curious and strange. They tolerated my inquisitive prodding into their legends and tales, which provided endless inspiration for my novels through the years, and together we created a prosperous and happy time in the valley.

And as the sun gilded the birch forests on the side of the mountain one afternoon, I scribbled upon my latest effort in the library, rocking my baby's cradle with my foot and pausing occasionally to read a passage aloud to Tycho. As I did so, I thought of that long-ago day when my brother-in-law felt the weight of responsibility for me, and I thought with some satisfaction that I had solved the problem of what to do with Theodora rather well on my own.

★ ★ ★ ★ ★

READERS' GUIDE QUESTIONS

1. Theodora Lestrange is not the typical Victorian heroine. How does she differ from other women of her time?

2. Which of Theodora's two suitors—Charles Beecroft or Count Andrei—is a better match for her? Why?

3. Why does Theodora remain at the castle when events take a dark and frightening turn? Would you?

4. Many of the characters have interests which are reflective of their personalities. Discuss how Cosmina's work with medicinal, Florian's music, and the count's passion for astronomy extend their characters.

5. Are the strange events at the castle supernatural or are there logical explanations for Theodora's experiences?

6. What elements of classic Gothic literature did you find in this novel?

ACKNOWLEDGMENTS

As ever, I am tremendously grateful, not only for the support and many kindnesses I have received, but also for the chance to acknowledge them. Great appreciation and tremendous thanks:

To my family—my daughter for laughter and hugs and cups of tea, my mother for tidying up everything in my life, including my manuscripts, and my father for unfailing support.

To my agent, Pam Hopkins. I ought to have the words to adequately express my appreciation for all that she does, but they do not exist. I can only say that not a day passes that I do not marvel at the gift of her friendship.

To my editor, Valerie Gray, whose attention to detail and quest for excellence are equally inspiring.

To my dear friend Kimberly McArthur Taylor, whose enthusiasm for her work in epidemiology is surpassed only by her generosity of spirit, and without whose contributions this book would be less than it is.

To all of the unsung heroes and heroines of publishing, the many hardworking people through whose hands my books passed to be made better and who work so tirelessly to get my books into the hands of readers: editorial, marketing, sales, public relations and production. Particular thanks to the gifted and attentive Michael Rehder for his beautiful cover.

To the many booksellers who have shared their enthusiasm with their customers and converted them to readers.

To the readers of blog and books who have been so gracious and enthusiastic, who have written and e-mailed and traveled to book signings and who humble me every day with their praise. Thank you.

DEANNA RAYBOURN

"Let the wicked
be ashamed,
and let them be
silent in the grave."

These ominous words are the last threat that the darling of
London society, Sir Edward Grey, receives from his killer.
Before he can show them to Nicholas Brisbane, the private
inquiry agent he has retained for his protection, Sir Edward
is murdered in his home.

Determined to bring her husband's killer to justice,
Julia Grey engages Brisbane to help her investigate Edward's
demise. Together, they press forward, coming ever closer to
a killer who waits expectantly for Julia's arrival.

Silent in the Grave

"[A] perfectly executed debut."
—*Publishers Weekly* (starred review)

Available wherever books are sold.

MIRA®

www.MIRABooks.com

MDR2817TR

The marvelous sequel to
the evocative *Silent in the Grave*

DEANNA RAYBOURN

Fresh from a six-month sojourn in Italy, Lady Julia
returns home to Sussex to find her father's estate
crowded with family and friends—but dark deeds
are afoot at the deconsecrated abbey, and a
murderer roams the ancient cloisters.

When one of the guests is found brutally murdered
in the chapel and a member of Lady Julia's own family
confesses to the crime, Lady Julia resumes her unlikely
and deliciously intriguing partnership with
Nicholas Brisbane, setting out to unravel a tangle
of deceit before the killer can strike again….

SILENT *in the*
SANCTUARY

"Fans of British historical thrillers will welcome
Raybourn's perfectly executed debut."
—*Publishers Weekly* on *Silent in the Grave*

Available wherever trade paperback books are sold!

www.MIRABooks.com

MDR2492TR